The Lost Kingdom

Book Two of the Sevordine Chronicles

by

Shawn P. B. Robinson

BrainSwell Publishing
Ingersoll, Ontario

ISBN 978-1-989296-60-8

Cover design and artwork copyright © Shawn Robinson
Interior Page Dividers designed from images downloaded from Freepick.com.

BrainSwell Publishing
Ingersoll, ON

Dedication and Thanks

To my Beta Readers. You are awesome, I appreciate you, and you help me to see both what the book shouldn't be, but also what the book can be. Thank you.
To that Italian restaurant in Erin that makes deep fried panzerottis and doesn't skimp on the cheese. Not all heroes wear capes. You are loved.

This book is a work of fiction.
I always find it strange that I have to say this. In fact, I'm not even sure that I do have to say it, I just see that most authors do make a statement like this. I think saying that a fiction book is made up and not true is kind of like telling people not to eat the insoles of their shoes. Most people can just roll with the idea of not eating insoles without the extra direction.
But, for those of you who really like the clarity, this book truly is fiction. Not only does the world I write about in this book and series not exist, as far as I am aware, but I'm doubtful anyone has traveled between our world and theirs. So… it seems reasonable to assume that all characters and details in this book are fiction, unless I have some shocking interdimensional or transmultiversal gift that allows me to intuitively know these details. If this is true, then I offer my apology to those of whom I have written.
However, I think that is unlikely.
As such, I believe you will benefit from accepting the idea that this book's story is fiction. This way we can all move on together.

Preface

When the idea for book one hit me, it was just a single book. It was open ended and unfinished (as book one is), but I just didn't have any clue where to go from there, other than a big turn-around attack on the main city to regain control of the kingdom.

But, that didn't seem right.

As I worked with the story, it seemed to grow and, believe it or not, this book made me uncomfortable… because I didn't know how to fix the obvious problems it creates.

But alas. I don't know if everything is fixed, but I am more comfortable, and truly, what else might matter in the eyes of a reader than my personal comfort?

Shawn P. B. Robinson

P. S. To those who cannot roll with a joke… first, reading my books might not be helpful for you. Second, the above was a joke. I am aware that my comfort is not your main concern, although I am unsure as to why that might be.

CHECK OUT THESE BOOKS BY
Shawn P. B. Robinson

Adult Fiction (Sci-fi & Fantasy)

The Ridge Series (3 books)
ADA: An Anthology of Short Stories

YA Fiction (Fantasy)

The Sevordine Chronicles (5 Books)

Books for Younger Readers

Annalynn the Canadian Spy Series (6 Books)
Jerry the Squirrel (4 Books)
Arestana Series (3 Books)
Activity Books (2 Books)

www.shawnpbrobinson.com/books

Table of Contents

1

The Caves

I sit on the edge of my bed. Actually, it's more of a cot. Well, it's a cross between a cot and a bedroll. It's up off the ground, because the cave floor can get a little damp at times—at least that's what they tell me—but it's just barely off the ground, and my cot is lumpy and hard.

I was more comfortable sleeping out in the open in the Talic Region.

Across from me, sit my armor and my sword. I'm supposed to wear both every day as we have to be prepared for battle at all times, but no one has ever had to fight in the caves. Apparently, the Regent knows we're here somewhere, but he's never quite figured out where. Any spies sent to the mountains have all been killed—regardless of where they look—so the Regent hasn't even nailed down a general location.

I stand and stretch, doing my best to avoid knocking the candle. I've knocked the candle over every day since I arrived. My little cave is so small, if I turn too fast, I either burn myself on the open flame or tip it over. The corner of my blanket is singed, and my pillow has burn spots on it.

I pull on my armor and shake my head to try to wake up. We get up early in the caves—at least I think it's early.

There's no way for me to tell time, and most people seem content to only know a rough idea of what hour it is. They tell me I'll get used to it, but I haven't yet. It's only been a week, though.

I do up the last of the straps on my leather armor and secure my belt with my knife and sword. I don't know about the others, but I haven't told anyone about the enchantments. I'm afraid if they learn that my sword can cut through anything and that my armor can protect me from any weapon, I'll lose them both. It's not that our hosts have shown themselves to be untrustworthy—I don't think they're thieves—but I know what they want more than anything is to win this war. A sword and armor like mine could help them win. That is… if it's not in the hands of someone like me.

I prepare myself to be called "Draydon" again. I found out it's my actual name, and I think I remember it somewhat from when I was really young. But I've been called Caric for so many years, I think I prefer my normal name, rather than my real name.

I step out to find my uncle busy pouring over reports. I've never had a family before, at least since the rebellion took my parents, so this is a little strange for me. I'm not sure what to think of this man. He seems genuinely happy to see me and to have me, but… it's very different.

"Draydon!" Uncle Lirnal says. "I hope you slept better last night. I know this is far from life in the castle."

I don't know if that's genuine or a reminder of how easy I've had it so far. I decide to walk carefully. He's given me no reason not to trust him, but I just don't know…

"I slept better last night, thank you. I'll get used to sleeping here. I've slept on the ground for the last couple weeks, so this isn't much different."

"Oh, Draydon," Uncle Lirnal laughs. "This is MUCH different. I've slept on the ground countless times, and I would take any one of those nights over this. There is nothing comfortable about sleeping on the floor of a cave. I would love to agree that you'll get used to it, but after ten years, I still don't sleep right."

"Nothing to look forward to then?" I ask with a forced smile. I think I'm feeling sorry for myself. I just didn't expect a life quite like this.

"On the contrary!" Uncle Lirnal says. He stands and comes over to me. He only has to take a step. Even the top General in the free Sevordine armies doesn't get a large cave to sleep in. "Draydon, listen closely. All this is temporary. What you did in bringing Prince Roran back to us means we have a very different future ahead of us. We can now return to Sevord. We can now reclaim the throne."

I find myself smiling. Something like that picks me up right away. He's right.

A week before, we had arrived with Prince Roran, or Mic, as we thought he was called. We're all kind of heroes, which is pretty great, but the big news is since Prince Roran is now with the rebel armies—I mean the free armies, I have to get used to that—we can return and claim the throne. We can drive out Regent Parthun and… and then I'm not sure what happens after that. But at least the right person will be on the throne. And Ellcia, Marleet, Hemot, Rulf, and I helped to bring this about. We played a big part in it.

The thought of the others raises a question. "Can I see my friends today? I haven't seen any of them since we arrived."

Uncle Lirnal's eyes shift to the side, and he looks troubled. A forced smile shows up on his face, but I can see he's unsure how to answer.

"Well," he begins. "Yes, and no."

I shake my head. That's not much of an answer.

He laughs and then points to the chair opposite his at the table. Once we're both seated, he says, "Some of your friends you can see, while others… maybe not. For instance, I see Prince Roran every day, but you don't have a specific reason to see him, so you're not likely to be granted permission—unless he specifically asks for you. We could probably arrange for it, if necessary, as you are the Prince's cousin, and truthfully, next in line for the throne, but at the same time, we are all a little nervous about the Prince's safety. Despite the fact that you traveled with him across the Sevordine lands, the Nobles will not likely allow you anywhere near him."

I'm not sure how to respond to all that, so I wait for him to continue. I would like to see Roran, or Mic as we knew him, but I was never really close to him. Since he pretended to be barely capable of conversation for our entire journey, we had never spoken much.

Truthfully, I don't actually know Prince Roran at all.

I wouldn't mind seeing Rulf, however. But he's not the one on my mind. I really want to see Ellcia, Hemot, and Marleet.

"Rulfor," Uncle Lirnal says, continuing on, "is a strange one. Well, maybe he isn't, but his parents are. They are two of the greatest fighters we have. They are also a little out of control, as giant folk often are. They don't understand discipline or boundaries or anything. They might just walk in here at any moment and lie down on the floor and take a nap, or we might not see them for a month. If Rulfor is with them, then I have no idea when you'll see him next. When he's not with his parents, he's typically with Prince Roran. The two are close, and the Prince has given him free access to himself at any time of the day or night."

"What about the others?" I ask.

He laughs. "Well, Marleet, that's the small one, right?"

"Yes," I say. Marleet is quite tiny. She's the smallest of all four of us who grew up in the castle.

"You might not know this," he says, "but Marleet's parents are both still alive. They survived the attack and managed to get out of the city. They were loyal to the throne and would have been executed. The only reason they left without their daughter is because they had been told she had been killed."

I'm shocked at this, but then again none of us knew what to expect. I wonder what they're like. I hope Marleet really likes them. I hope they're good to her.

My uncle leans back in his chair and smiles. "Her parents, the Lord Yune and the Lady Aldora, are actually extremely important to the war effort. Marleet's family is quite rich, and they are largely funding the army during this time. If it weren't for their support and the support of a few others, we would not have been able to survive—at least as we are."

"What about Hemot and Ellcia?" I ask.

"Hemot?" he says with a smile. "He's the boy you came in with? Well... he's... tell you what. I'll let him bring you up to speed." He ends with a big laugh.

I'm not sure I like this, but I'm guessing it's not too bad, if my uncle's laughing about it. But Ellcia... she's the one I'm most worried about.

"Now, the girl..." he says, eying me closely. "The pretty one."

I feel my face turn red. It doesn't help that he hasn't taken his eyes off me. He's barely blinking. And that smile... it's not an evil or dangerous smile. It's a smile that says he knows that she's the one I'm thinking about.

"Yes," he continues slowly, his smile growing larger by the second. "The girl... the one you were standing close to the entire time when I met you in the cave. The one you were trying to protect with every move you made, even though she was in no real danger... the one who looks at you in that special way... the one..."

"Yes!" I say with a frown. My face feels like it's on fire. "That one."

He laughs again and says, "Well, it turns out she is the sister of one of my most trusted men. His name is Captain Granel. Rarely is someone promoted so young to the rank of Captain, but he has proven himself time and again. He was injured terribly in the rebellion, but one of the families found him in the streets and got him out of the city. Ellcia has been staying with him."

I shift in my seat. I'm so glad to hear Ellcia is safe, that her brother is alive, and that she is doing well. But there's something else on my mind. "So, Captain Granel… was his family and our family… close?" I don't want to come out and say it, but considering the way I feel about Ellcia, I really don't want to find out that she's a cousin or something.

"Draydon," he says, but pauses.

It's at that moment that I realize I hate the name Draydon. "Can you call me Caric?"

My uncle's eyebrows shoot up. Not much surprises him, so I'm glad that I've been able to do it this one time.

He nods. "I'm disappointed, Caric," he begins. "I would like you to keep the name your parents gave you. It's not only an old, honorable name, but it's a name which has been in our family for generations." He takes a breath and lowers his head. "But I know you have lived with a different name all these years. I will honor your choice."

I smile back at him. For some reason, this is the moment when I decide to trust him. I realize that I do appreciate him, and I think he's a good man. But then again, I had thought the Regent was a good man, and he turned out to be the one who killed the King and my parents.

"But as for your relation to Captain Granel," he begins, and the smile reappears as he examines my face. "You have to keep in mind, Caric, that I'm a general. I've been serving in that capacity for over ten years, and I've been a military man since I was younger than you. I not only see strategies and dangers, but I can often see what's going on in other areas of life. You have a deep interest in this young Ellcia. She is pretty, there's no doubt about that, and the two of you seem close. You are afraid that you are related to her, which would make things… awkward… to say the least."

I find myself smiling, although it's an uncomfortable smile. I just want an answer.

"No, Caric," he says. "You are not related at all. Our families were close; your father and her father were friends from their youth, but there is no blood relation. So, you can rest at ease."

I feel my shoulders relax. That certainly is good news.

"But," he says, rising to his feet, "there is no time for that. We've talked too long. I need to deal with one more matter and then we must leave."

I nod my head and stand. I'm not sure what else we need to talk about.

My heart goes cold as my uncle orders, "Give me your sword."

I stare at him for a moment, but I know I have no choice. If he's the General and recognizes the sword, it's just a matter of time before it's in his hands.

I draw it, and he gasps. The sword is beautiful, there's no doubt about that, but I expect it's not the beauty that shocks him.

He recognizes it.

I hesitate for a moment but give in and hand it over. I don't think I have any choice. I certainly can't attack him.

He takes it carefully, holds it by the grip, and steps close to a lamp. Bringing the sword up to his eyes, he examines it.

I'm still hoping that he doesn't know about the enchantments, but that hope disappears as he takes it to his bed, stretches it out, and uses the blade to slice through a small area of the rock wall sticking out above his bed. Watching the chunk of rock fall to the floor with a satisfied grunt, he mumbles, "I've knocked my head on that rock for the last time."

I want to groan to myself. I'd grown attached to the sword, but I guess it's no longer mine.

He comes back to me and asks, "Do you know much about this weapon?"

I shake my head.

"Do you know that it has magical properties?"

I nod.

"Tell me what it can do," he orders.

My first impulse is to lie and say something other than what it can do, but he obviously knows. "It seems able to cut through anything."

He smiles and turns it over in his hands, examining the blade again. As his eyes roam over the letters and designs in the blade, he says, "That's right, but it does a few other things as well. It was actually your father's sword."

My eyebrows shoot up at that. I think maybe that means I might have a claim to the sword. So even if the General takes it away, I might be able to get it back again.

"We don't have much time, but sit down for a moment, Caric."

He lays the sword on the table, careful to keep the sharp edges from touching anything. He stares at it for a moment, then smiles yet again. When he looks up at me, I'm not prepared for what he tells me.

"This is the King's sword. Actually, it *was* the King's sword. The sword which Prince Roran carries is now the King's sword. When the Prince was in the throne room before you left, he grabbed it as he knew it belongs to the King—he knew it was his sword now."

I'm confused by that explanation. I don't know if my sword is the King's sword or not.

"Your grandfather and the kings before him carried this sword here. It was considered one of the Kingdom's greatest treasures." He takes a deep breath. "But then one day, your grandfather, my father, was enchanted. A spell was placed upon him which caused him to do all sorts of cruel and wicked things. So, the Nobles sought out one of the few loyal Spellcasters of the time, and a new sword was enchanted. That new sword was created to cancel any enchantment."

The look of confusion on my face lets my uncle know that he needs to explain that one a little differently.

"I'm sorry, Caric. I know I'm not making a lot of sense. I'm just surprised to see this sword, your father's sword. The King's sword—the one Prince Roran carries—is special. It's unbreakable and never needs to be sharpened. In some ways, it can work almost like your sword, but the important part is that whenever the wearer draws the sword, it cancels any enchantment that might be placed upon the wearer. There is a law in Sevord that cannot be broken. It allows any officer in the army or any nobleman or noblewoman, regardless of their position, to order the King to draw his sword at any moment of any day. If the King does not, the King is immediately placed under suspicion until he does draw his sword. It prevents the kingdom from falling to such a terrible curse ever again. That is the sword currently known as the King's Sword."

He smiles at me. "So, this sword here—your sword—was then offered to your father as the second-born son of the King, as the new sword would be held by the King. Your father then became the new owner of the sword, and it is now the rightful inheritance of your father's line."

He slides the sword across the small table to me. "It is yours now. Not only because you were given it in the castle, but because it is part of your inheritance. It is a sword with a great history. It is said that your great-grandfather, in his early years, before he became King, fought a Talic Wolf with it, but that is likely just rumor."

I decide not to comment on the part about the Talic Wolf. Instead, I stand up, pick up the sword, and slide it back into its sheath. I can't help but smile—not just that I have the sword back, but from everything I've learned.

My uncle leans forward with a serious expression. "Two warnings, Caric. First, that scabbard is the only scabbard enchanted to hold that sword. It'll slice through any other. Second..." He pauses and adds a stern look. "Do not tell anyone what this sword does or that it was your father's. Most of the men and women among us are honorable, but you may find some who are not. Those without honor will take your sword without a moment's hesitation." He looks down at my sword and smiles. "I had actually thought it was lost. When the kingdom fell, and your father was killed, my understanding was an old soldier stole that sword—a Sergeant by the name of Hob. I assumed he had sold it."

"No," I say, speaking up for the first time in a while. "He guards one of the armories. Hob gave me this sword and called me 'your highness'."

My uncle's eyebrows shoot up again, but then his face softens into a smile. "Well now, that's interesting. So, Hob did take the sword..." he appears deep in thought for a moment, "but not to sell it, but to keep it safe. And then he gave it to the son of the man to whom it belonged." He nods slowly, looking up at the roof of the cave and adds, "It's good to know we might have another ally in the castle."

He shakes his head, and his eyes focus on me. "But, that's all the time we have for conversation. Grab that chunk of bread and that jug of water and come along. It's time to head out. I think you might actually see Ellcia and Hemot today."

I grab the water and guzzle down as much as I can, then snatch up the bread. The thought of seeing at least those two gives me the boost I need, and I run out after my uncle.

The last two days have been busy. I've been put into a training regimen that involves sword-fighting and some basic hand-to-hand combat. What I learned from Rulf was nothing compared to what these people can teach me. I like learning at this level. Unfortunately, these people are less forgiving than Rulf ever was—and Rulf was never forgiving.

I've also been interviewed by a half dozen different people. They ask questions about life in the city, what kind of guard there is in the castle, what the Regent's habits are, and more. It turns out they know very little about what goes on in Sevord City. They get bits of information sent to them from Captain Tilbur and a few others, but much of what they receive is in code and without enough information for them to do much with it.

I haven't quite learned my way around the cave system yet. Most people say it's pretty simple, but to me it just looks like a mess. I never know where I'm going or where I'll end up. Sometimes I head down a tunnel which I'm sure I've been down a dozen times, but then it opens up into a room that I have never seen before. One time I ended up in a large kitchen; another time I ended up in what appeared to be the laundry room; another time I found myself at the edge of a large underground river; and each time I was looking for my own cave with my own bed.

This time, I count the caves. I think I remember that taking the first left, then skipping two caves, then turning right takes me to the training grounds. I pay close attention as we move through and am pleasantly surprised to see that

I was right. I'm not sure I can find my way back okay, but someone always helps me.

My uncle comes to a halt just inside the large cavern. "All right, Caric. This is where I leave you. You'll spend the morning in training, then one final interview, then you'll meet with a couple people to help determine what your role will be in the operation. See you this evening."

I watch my uncle move off through a small cave—not much more than a crack in the wall. He turns sideways to squeeze through.

The people here call the whole "army in the caves" thing the "operation". I guess that makes sense. They don't want to call it the rebellion since technically speaking, what the Regent has done is rebellion.

I sit down on a rock to wait. Typically, I have to wait for someone to pull me into the training. They have a specific plan for me, and I'm not supposed to deviate from it at all.

I think back to a conversation I had with my uncle two nights ago. He explained my—I guess "our"—family situation. I'm actually the cousin to Prince Roran. If he had died, then the throne would have fallen to my father, then to me. Since my dad is dead, the only one who stands between me and the throne is, strangely, Prince Roran himself. I feel a wave of fear pass over me as I once again think about how important it is for me to keep Prince Roran alive.

If he dies, I'll have to be King.

That seems like a bad idea to me. I certainly don't want to end up in that situation. And I doubt that would be good for the kingdom.

The other thought that comes through now and then, when I start feeling suspicious, is that after me, my uncle here in the caves is next in line. Which means that if he has aspirations for the throne, he'll have to kill both Roran and me. I don't think that's realistic, though, because through all the years that Roran had not been found, and I was thought to be dead, my Uncle Lirnal never once made a claim for the throne—not even once. After him, since Lirnal has no children, is the Regent, who happens to be another uncle. So, if Roran, Lirnal, and I die, Regent Parthun is legally the King. After that comes General Corter in the castle—the general who serves the Regent—and then Captain Tilbur, my other uncle, who lives in the castle.

It seems complicated to me, but anything to do with a monarchy always is. I start to go over some more of the information that I've learned about my family, doing my best to commit it to memory, when I hear someone call my name.

I turn around and arms wrap around me. It's Ellcia, and I don't think I've ever been so happy to see anyone in my life. We hold each other for a long time before I feel us pulled apart. Hemot pushes Ellcia away and stands there with a big grin on his face. He shouts, "My turn!" and grabs hold of me, hugging me for an uncomfortably long time.

When he finally lets go, he says, "Where have you been?"

"Me?" I ask. "What about each of you?"

"We've been together for much of the last two days," Ellcia says. "We've only seen Marleet twice, and then only for a few minutes, but a lot of the rest of the time, it's been the two of us."

A wave of jealousy passes over me for a moment before I do my best to push it away. "I'm sorry. My uncle has kept me pretty busy. Tell me about what's going on with you guys!"

We sit down, and they bring me up to speed. My uncle has always taken me to the training grounds early, so I know there's time before they'll start me on drills.

"Well," Ellcia says, starting out on her story. She has a big grin on her face. "It turns out my older brother is still alive! I kind of remember him a bit, but not much. He's a

Captain. I've been staying with him. He tells me that we're part of a noble family, but all that has been lost in the rebellion. He's been really nice to me. He remembers me quite well, even though I can't really remember him. He's told me all about my parents." As she speaks, her grin grows larger. I'm glad to see her so happy.

I turn to Hemot, but he's shaking his head. "I haven't been quite so lucky."

I examine his face for a moment. He seems happy, yet disappointed, yet confused. "What's up?"

"Well…" Hemot frowns. "It turns out my family was all killed, but my nanny survived."

"That's at least some good news, isn't it?" I ask, a little unsure.

"Well, yes," he says, still looking confused. "I remember her, actually. I loved her a lot, and she was always there for me. But… she seems to think that I'm still six years old. She kisses me on the head all the time, licks her finger and washes spots off my face, offers to help me dress in the morning, and calls me Buttercup."

Ellcia and I both laugh. Hemot, however, looks genuinely distressed.

"Not only that, but one of my favorite memories of her is that she used to make me buttertarts. They were so good! I remember pleading with her to make them all the time."

"So, what's the issue?" I ask.

"She won't make them anymore! She tells me that when she lost me, she vowed she would never again make buttertarts. So, obviously, I told her, 'But you have me back now! You can make them again!' and she hollered, 'No! I swore I would not make them again, and I can't break that promise!' I think she then called me Buttercup and gave me another kiss on my head before sending me to bed at somewhere around 5:30 last night. The only nice part is she reads me stories before bed."

I hold in another laugh, and I see Ellcia is doing the same. I decide to change the subject. "And Marleet?"

Both of them shake their heads. Ellcia explains that when she had last seen her, Marleet had given her a quick hug and then had needed to run off.

I tell them what I learned about her. I'm hoping we'll get to see her soon. I'm assuming she's okay.

"On your feet!" a man screams.

We jump to our feet and spin around. A short distance away stands a large man. He's shorter than me, but he's built like an ox. His face is filled with rage, and he looks ready to strangle us. I check his uniform's insignia to see that he holds the rank of Captain.

He grinds his teeth and then barks, "I'm Captain Frindor! I oversee training of new recruits when I'm not doing something important."

The man stares at us for a moment, and I'm left with the impression that I'm supposed to say something in response to that. I have nothing to say, other than, "So, does that mean you just got back from something important?"

He rushes forward and stops once his nose is nearly touching mine. "You think that's funny?"

I open my mouth to answer but close it again. I really have no response that I think will turn out well.

"Get out on the training floor!" he hollers.

I grab Ellcia and Hemot and pull them along, since this is their first day of training. We run to the area they call the armory, which is an area of the training ground with a pile of wooden swords. We leave our real weapons in that area and grab a wooden sword before heading into the center of the large cavern.

We spend the next few hours training. I'm a little ahead of the others. The extra couple days of training and practice has certainly made a difference. I think I also take to the sword better than either Ellcia or Hemot. Some of my teachers, when they're not yelling at me, have actually told me I'm a fast learner.

By the time mid-day comes, and Frindor lets us finish, we're exhausted, smelly, and dripping in sweat. Some people show us the way to a small underground stream where we can clean up, and then we head out to find lunch.

I have to remind myself that though life in the caves is far from what we're used to, it's better than running for our lives.

2

The Attack

I adjust my sword on my belt as we walk, making sure I remain armed, according to the rules.

There isn't much worry about an attack. The rebel army is bigger than the Regent's army and, truthfully, my uncle has more claim to the throne than the Regent does, so the Regent's army might even come over to our side if given the choice, but we need to be prepared.

Someone points the way toward the cave where we eat. They call it the mess hall. I don't think that makes sense, but maybe it has something to do with people having to clean up after. I should probably ask, but I just don't want people to find out how little I know about everything.

When we reach the mess hall, I explain to Ellcia and Hemot how the system works for getting food, but they both know already. They tell me that they've eaten here every meal for the last couple of days. I'm surprised at that because I've never seen them here, but I suspect we've just missed each other.

We grab our food and have a seat. Until today, I haven't sat with anyone during my meals. None of the other people are very friendly with me. I've had a few scowl at me, but nothing too bad—they just don't like me.

It's strange. In the castle, the soldiers didn't mind us. In fact, most ignored us. We were only servants, after all. If anyone pushed us around, however, the soldiers would come to our aid. Here, however, I get the impression that no one wants us around. And if we get into trouble, I don't know who to look to for help.

That seems odd to me. We've found out that Ellcia and Hemot are from Noble families and… well… I'm second in line for the throne—an actual Prince. I would think people would want to be our friends, but they don't seem to. Ellcia and Hemot get the same mean stares that I get. I suspect it's because we all lived in the castle all this time, but I can't be sure.

But aside from mean looks, until today, I haven't faced any direct hostility—it's just been in people's attitudes and looks.

But something's changed.

As we're trying to leave after lunch, four men step in front of us. The looks on their faces let me know that we're in for a world of trouble.

"Where are you going?" the man in the lead asks.

Normally, Ellcia or Hemot are quick to answer in a confrontation, but they can see this is not normal. We aren't as safe as I would like.

I step forward and try to be nice. "We're going to go see my uncle."

I hope I can leave it at that. I'm sure they know who my uncle is.

"You think because the General happens to be your uncle that everyone's going to be nice to you?" All four men laugh at that. The man who spoke then steps forward in a threatening manner and growls, "He's not going to protect you."

I take that as a bad sign and try to move back. I reach out and gently push Hemot and Ellcia away from the men, but I find my friends don't move. I glance back to see two more men behind us. There's nowhere to go.

A quick look around the dining room lets me know we're alone. It's not that there aren't other people around. There are plenty of others—dozens, actually—but most aren't looking, and others watch with grins on their faces. We won't find help from them.

"What do you want with us?" This time, I don't hide any disdain I have. It always disgusts me when I see this kind of thing. Six full-grown adults taking on the three of us! We're in our teens, and we barely know how to use our swords or defend ourselves. They're soldiers in their prime, and not one appears to have anything less than a disproportionate amount of muscle.

The man in front who seems to be in charge smiles at me. I don't like his smile. His teeth are too big, and his eyes are full of threat. "No," he says with a laugh. "We don't actually want anything to do with all three of you. We have no problem with those two. It's you we want."

I turn around at the sound of a struggle and find Hemot and Ellcia are each held tight by the men behind me. I steal a quick look at the other four men. They've circled around.

I pull my knife out and hold it ready. I don't dare pull out my sword. I know that if they get too close, I could easily slice them in half. I don't know what they have in mind, but I'm pretty sure I don't want to kill them. I also don't want anyone to know what my sword can do—yet.

A hand comes around and grabs my wrist and a moment later, my knife is no longer in my hand. I know I'm greatly outmatched, but I hold my fists ready. Unfortunately, I don't even have a chance to defend myself. The first hit comes from behind and slams into my right kidney. I drop to the ground just as a foot drives into my side. I hear Ellcia and Hemot scream for them to stop, but the beating just keeps coming. I think after a while, it should no longer hurt, but every punch and every kick hurts more than the last.

I take one to the head, and the cave spins around me. The blows have stopped for the moment, and it looks like the men who attacked me are flying through the air. I think they must have hit me harder than I thought.

I see another shape. This one is very thin and very tall and has long blond hair. The hair seems to have a life of its own as it flies around. She's screaming. A lot. Not much of what she says is understandable.

I shake my head to clear my vision and try to make sense of what's going on. I see a woman. She's very tall and very angry. Her face is red, her teeth are bared, and her hands are held nearly, but not quite, in fists. It's as if she might either punch or claw someone.

At first, I can't figure out who she is, then it comes to me. She's Rulf's mother. I follow her gaze, and I see four crumpled shapes on the ground. Not one moves. She turns back to the men holding Ellcia and Hemot.

She growls and takes a deep breath. "These are my son's friends. You hurt one of my son's friends, and I see you hold two others. So, now there are only two options for you. Let them go and run away, and you will live. Hold on to them, and you will die."

Both men let go immediately and run for one of the caves leading off the mess. They're in such a rush to get away that they scramble over top of each other as they run. I lose sight of them in a matter of seconds.

Ellcia and Hemot run to my side, and they check me over. Both of them look sick, and Hemot says, "I'm sorry, Caric. We tried to help you, but we couldn't."

"Don't worry about it," I say. "Did you see the hits I got in?"

"I think I might have missed that," Hemot says with a grimace.

"Me too," I say as I try to get up. Everything hurts, and I feel my right eye has already swollen. I can't help but think I'll not be able to see out of it for a bit.

Ellcia helps pull me to my feet and brushes off my shoulder and back. She hasn't said anything, and I can see why. Tears stream down her cheeks, and her lip trembles.

"You take a punch well!" Rulf's mom says. Her voice is low and husky and far too loud. "My name is Nareesa!"

I glance at the four men. "Are they going to be okay, Nareesa?"

Her face fills with confusion. "Are they going to be okay?" she asks, incredulity filling her voice. "What do you mean? They're dead."

I look back in shock, and their crumbled bodies look quite different to me now. She doesn't look like a giant, but she's definitely got giant blood in her. No one could toss four large men like that without some magic or secret power.

"Why did they attack Caric?" Hemot asks.

Ellcia has broken into quiet sobs. My heart goes out to her. I know how I would feel if the same thing happened to her.

"Who's Caric?" Nareesa asks.

"I'm Caric," I say. I lean over and spit out some blood. All my teeth seem to be in place. I'm glad about that.

"I thought your name was Draydon." She looks annoyed.

"It is," I say, shaking my head, "but I go by Caric. It's the name I've used the last ten years or so."

She grunts—just like Rulf. "That's not simple, skinny boy. Are you trying to confuse people?" She eyes me for a moment then asks, "You really don't know why they attacked you?"

I shake my head, and she frowns. I glance over at the other two, but they look just as confused as I feel.

Nareesa takes a deep breath and frowns. When she speaks, she sounds even angrier. "It's because of the rumors about your father."

I'm shocked to hear that. I don't know what my dad has to do with anything. It hurts to think that people hate my dad enough that they'd want to harm me.

After a moment, Nareesa growls and lets out a deep sigh. "About three days before King Hartor was killed, your father was seen meeting with Parthun. No one thought anything about it at the time, of course. But once the castle was stormed, the King killed, and Parthun claimed the throne as the Regent, word spread that your father was in on it."

My mouth drops open as what she's said comes crashing down on me. "They think my dad was a traitor?" I know my voice is carrying over the mess hall, but I'm too shocked to care.

"Yeah!" she says. "There's no proof that he did betray us, but there's no proof that he didn't."

"Do you think he did?" I ask, my voice growing quiet.

"What?" she hollers. "Never!"

If I had worried that my voice carried across the mess hall, it's nothing compared to Nareesa's voice.

"Your father was loyal without question! That's why King Hartor kept him so close. He was an accomplished and skilled General and strategist, and the King insisted on having him nearby all the time. Your father would never have betrayed his brother! He was also a good friend of my husband. We spent a lot of time with your parents over the years." She dropped her gaze to the floor and looked quite sad for a moment, but then smiled and looked back at me. "But, that's not what's important right now! Right now, I need to eat!" She then turns and bounds off toward the line for the food.

Ellcia wipes another tear from her eye and says, "Let's get you to a doctor or someone who can care for these cuts. We need to bandage you up."

I try to tell them I'm okay, but from the looks on each of their faces, I get the impression that I don't look okay. We get some directions from a soldier we find in one of the caves and head toward the infirmary.

When we arrive, the doctor seems more irritated than compassionate, but he's still kind and careful as he bandages me up.

We move on through the rest of the day. I have a few classes that involve some strategy lessons and more. Ellcia and Hemot join me, and we sit with children half our ages as we learn. Everyone is considered to be either a soldier or a soldier in training. Their entire lives revolve around preparing to return to Sevord and claim the throne. Now that the Prince has finally been found, everyone is excited and talks as though they have new purpose and meaning in life.

On the way back to my cave, Ellcia tells me she has to get back. Her brother is expecting her at their cave. She heads off down a passage I've never used before—or at least I don't think I have. She doesn't seem to struggle as much as I do with the labyrinth of caves.

When she's gone, Hemot leads the way. He's memorized the cave system. We walk on together as he tells me where everything is and tries to describe a rough layout of the caves through the mountain. When we're nearly back to my cave, a short round woman comes bounding into view.

"Buttercup!" she exclaims, her voice filled with joy. "I finally found you! I've been looking for you all day!"

Hemot starts to back away, but from the look on his face, I see he thinks running is pointless. He hangs his head in a sign of defeat and steps forward.

The woman comes up to him and pulls his face down to hers, so she can reach it. She licks her thumb and wipes away what I suspect is an invisible speck of dirt on his cheek. He looks disgusted, but she doesn't notice.

"There we go, Buttercup. All better now? Yes? Well, I've been looking for you all day because you left your tie at home." She throws what looks like a noose around his neck, tightens it until his eyes bulge, and then adjusts it to make it perfectly ugly. "Oh, I remember the adorable little ties you used to wear, Buttercup. You were such a little man!" She then grabs the tie, pulls his face down, and gives him a very, very wet kiss in the eye.

A shiver passes over his body. As soon as his nanny looks away, Hemot wipes away a fair amount of saliva. He then points to me and says, "This is my friend, Caric."

The little lady looks at me as if seeing me for the first time. Her face fills with distrust, and initially, I think it's more of the suspicion that we faced in the dining hall, but then it becomes clear it's something else.

"Is he a good friend for you?" she asks Hemot in a too-loud whisper. "He's not a bad influence on you like that Garrel was."

Hemot looks confused for a moment, but then shakes his head. "I assume Garrel's some kid I knew when I was like four years old." He shakes his head again and continues. "I have no idea if Caric is like Garrel. But Caric is a good friend. He's the best."

She looks at me and smiles, but I can see she's unconvinced. She grabs Hemot on the arm and very forcefully pulls him away. I hear her say, "It's getting late. We need to get some food in you and then get you straight to bed. Oooohhh... you really smell, Buttercup. I think we will have to move tomorrow's bath to today."

Hemot looks back at me and mouths the words, "Help me!" They move off together and disappear around a corner.

"Well, that was weird," I say to myself.

I turn around, and for once, I recognize the area and take a cave that I'm sure will lead me to my own cave. I move along and find myself at a point where the cave breaks off in two directions. I don't remember this place at all, but I decide to try the cave on the left.

Within a minute or so, I know it's not the cave I want. The roof and walls are solid stone, and they close in on me more and more the farther I walk. It's not long before I'm squeezing through a small area. I would turn around, but I decided the day before that I would keep going when I got lost in the hopes that I would eventually figure my way around.

I hear voices ahead and come to a halt. Something about their tone lets me know these are not men I want to surprise. They talk like they're involved in some kind of conspiracy. I can't make out everything they say, but I hear one of the men hiss, "We'll take the northwest cave near the lake just before lights out. It turns to the west and comes out through a small area near the Game Road. We can meet with…" at that point, I think he either lowered his voice, or he turned his head. I try to hear more but only hear the occasional word after that, none of which makes any sense to me.

I turn around and move back as quietly as I can, but then I hear quick footsteps. I fear they heard me, so I rush off. When I reach the area where the cave turns off in two directions, I take the other cave, the one on the right. I rush down it and find myself stumbling out into a large cave. I see no close exits, and even at a full run, I'm not sure I can get out of sight before the men reach this area.

I run down the cave about twenty steps, come to a halt, do my best to calm my breathing, turn around, and slowly start walking back toward the cave I just ran out of.

A moment later, three men dressed in regular clothing rush out. They see me, but don't pay any attention to me at first. I'm not running in the direction a fleeing man would run.

Finally, one of the men hollers at me, "Hey! You! Did you see anyone come out of this cave?"

I shake my head. "No, I'm the only one here."

The men look angry at first, but the smallest of the three says, "Maybe I didn't hear anyone. I was pretty sure I heard footsteps, but… maybe not."

The tallest of the men punches the shorter man in the shoulder and says, "Next time, don't say you hear someone unless you really do!"

They disappear back into the cave they came out of, and I continue to move along slowly. My heart eventually calms down, and I begin to recognize the area. Most of the caves look the same, so recognizing a rock wall doesn't always mean anything, but I come around a corner and find two soldiers standing guard. There are always two soldiers there, although they're often different people. This area is where most of the officers' quarters are, and no one is allowed in unless they have been authorized. The two soldiers today are named Harrol and Filk. I've chatted with them before. They're both good guys.

As I'm walking past them, Harrol stops me. "Prince Draydon!" he says, using my real name. "The General left a message…" he stops and looks at me funny. "What happened to you?"

I had kind of forgotten that my face was covered in cuts and bandages. The whole incident with the strange men in the caves seems to be all I can think of. I just want to get to my room and find my uncle. Aside from my friends, he's the only one I think I can tell about what I heard.

"I, uhh…" I begin. "Four guys attacked me in the mess hall."

The two men shift on their feet. I remember my uncle told me that only the most trustworthy of soldiers were placed as sentries to the officers' quarters. Trustworthy soldiers would not take part in what happened in the mess hall.

"Did you report it?" Filk asks.

"Um, no," I say. "Nareesa showed up and…"

"Nareesa!" Harrol groans. "Are the men dead?"

"Yes."

Both men frown before Harrol says, "I think she helps to keep the men in line, but…" He shakes his head and then takes a deep breath before saying, "The General left a message for you. He has had to leave the mountain and does not expect to be back for three or four days."

I stand there in shock for a moment. I guess Generals have to do that kind of thing, but I was just getting to know him. And I need him. I'm not sure who else to tell. The soldiers in front of me are trustworthy, but I really don't have much to go on other than to say that their voices sounded "sneaky".

I ask the men if they know where Hemot or Ellcia are staying, but neither one even knows who they are. I ask about Prince Roran and about Rulf, but from the looks on their faces, that's not a question someone like me is allowed to ask. I try one more. "Where is the northwest cave?"

The soldiers both smile at me, and Filk says with a laugh in his voice, "Which one? There are a lot of caves on the northwest side of the mountain."

"The one near the lake?" I ask. "I really don't know my way around yet."

Filk nods. "That's a little tricky to find. He points down a passage leading away from the officers' quarters, but then stops. "Why don't you go grab a piece of paper? I don't think I can explain it in a way that you'll remember."

I run back to my quarters and see a note there from my uncle. I leave it for the moment and grab a piece of paper. When I get back to the men, Filk writes out a complicated set of instructions for me. I go over it with him, but I'm a little unsure if I can figure it out. I thank them both and run back to my room.

There's a meal left there for me. We have had supper together each evening so far. It's not the same eating by myself in the cave, but I get the food in me while I read through the note left for me. The note doesn't say much, other than to let me know that my uncle has been called away on "business". I think that's an odd way to describe a General's work, but then I realize that he can't leave details of what he's up to, otherwise there are security threats. I remember that he often spoke of his activities as business.

I spend some of the evening reading a book my uncle recommended, and when I think it's about time, I strap on my sword, make sure my armor's in place, and set out. I don't know if this is important, but if I'm part of this "operation", I need to do my part.

I wave to Harold and Filk as I pass by, and they remind me to be back by lights out. I follow the map Filk made for me, and it turns out it's quite helpful after all. The caves are clearly marked out, and as long as I don't try to figure out the whole map all at once but take each turn when I come to it, it's easy to follow.

I arrive at the northwest cave and then realize my problem. I don't know what to do now that I'm here. I had thought maybe I could hide, but there doesn't seem to be any small caves leading off the sides or little cracks or crevices—at least ones big enough for me to fit in.

I start down the cave, hoping to find some place to squeeze into. I feel pretty dumb. I can't believe I'm here to spy on men who might have only been talking about going for a walk.

I continue down the cave for a long time, seeing and hearing no one. The air grows colder the farther I walk, and I get the impression that I'm not only near an exit, but I'm likely farther up the mountain than where we entered. Coming to a halt, I feel my face grow hot with embarrassment. What am I doing? Turning around, I start to make my way back. When I'm nearly at the point where I entered the northwest cave, I hear voices ahead. They sound angry. I spin around, looking for a way out. A small crevice I hadn't seen before catches my eye, and I squeeze myself into it. It's a tight fit, but I just barely get myself in as a group of men come around the corner.

There are five of them, and they're wrestling with a sixth. I can't see who their captive is, but whoever he is doesn't want to go with them. His hands are tied behind his back, and there's a hood over his head.

The captive man wrestles hard against them, and I wonder if I'm supposed to do something. The men are dressed as soldiers, and I recognize three of them as the men who chased me through the caves earlier. I think they're up to no good, but what if this is a prisoner who's supposed to be arrested? Maybe they're transferring him somewhere.

The man in the hood twists around violently, and his hood comes up enough that I can get a glimpse of his face. My heart goes cold as I realize who he is. It's Mic—or Prince Roran, rather. These men are kidnapping the Prince just after he's been returned to them!

There's not a moment to lose! I briefly consider waiting until the men have passed by and then running to find help, but I might be too late. I can't fight off all five, but I can at least try. Mic is a friend, and he's my Prince.

I push myself out of the crevice, but my foot catches on a rock, and I tumble to the ground. By the time I get up, at least one of the men has seen me, but he hasn't called out a warning just yet. I charge forward and crash into him before he can say anything.

"Caric!" Prince Roran hollers out. "Run! Get help!"

I jump to my feet and slam my elbow into the gut of another man before pulling my sword from its sheath. Without a moment's hesitation, I shove it toward one of the men and it slides right into his belly. As he goes down, I pull it back and see Mic is only held now by one man. The other man is coming for me.

I feel a sense of exhilaration knowing I've managed to take down three soldiers in a fight. If I can take down two more, I might be able to rescue Roran.

"Run!" Roran screams again.

I should do as he says. I know he's right, but I hesitate for a second. I can't leave Roran to these men.

The man before me charges. I swing my sword, but he dodges and grabs hold of me. As I fall back, I catch a glimpse of Roran. He's wrestling with his soldier, and he's just about gotten himself away.

I hit the ground hard, and my sword falls out of my hand, clattering across the stone. Another quick glance toward Roran, and I see he's pushed himself away from the soldier, but he loses his balance in the process. With his hands still tied, he hits the stone floor of the cave, and my stomach twists as I hear the sound of his head connecting with solid rock.

Shouts and voices surround us as a dozen soldiers rush around the corner, all with swords drawn. I smile at the man on top of me whose face is filled with fear, but then a smile crosses his face as well.

He stands up quickly and yanks me to my feet. He hollers out, "We caught him!"

"What?" I'm very confused, but then terrified as the soldiers grab me and throw me to the ground. The man I had fought a moment before shouts, "We chased him down this way. I thought there would be more of them, but it was just this young guy, dragging our dear Prince Roran away. I expect he was going to murder him!"

I try to tell them this isn't true, but a gag goes in my mouth as my hands are roughly tied behind my back. I steal a glance at Roran. He's safe, but unconscious. Until he awakes, I'm not only a criminal, I'm the guy they think was trying to assassinate the Prince of Sevord.

3

⎯ ● ⎯

The Cell

The guards are anything but kind.

In fact, they're enraged at me.

All these years, they've been searching for the Prince. They finally have him back, and the guy who returned him into their arms just tried to kill him—or at least that's what they think.

I don't blame most of them. I only blame the kidnappers.

The soldiers gather around me in my cell, spitting at me as another fist slams into my gut. The men responsible for kidnapping Roran are here as well. Their looks of hatred are mixed with looks of pleasure.

The hit nearly knocks me off my stool, but they grab and steady me. I know it's not out of compassion, but to keep their target where they can easily reach him.

I want to tell them who's really responsible. I want to make sure Roran's okay. I want to see my uncle. None of these things, however, are anything I can ask for with a gag in my mouth.

One of the soldiers on my left drives his fist into my temple, and my world spins. As strange as it is, I find myself laughing. They're not holding back, but none of them hit like Rulf. It had never been his intent, but I think the big guy trained me well.

"You think this is funny?" one of the men screams at me. He pulls out a knife and comes at me, but stops the moment an officer walks in.

I haven't seen this man since the day we arrived, but back then I didn't really get a good look at him. Today, up close, but in the dim light of the cell, my first thought is that he's absolutely ugly. His face doesn't make sense to me, but then I see what's really going on. He's terribly scarred. It looks like a combination of scars left from cuts and burns. I don't know what happened to him, but I would think this man would be left with nightmares.

"Is this the boy?" he asks the soldier with the knife. His authoritative voice is calm, but scratchy.

"Yes, Captain!" the man says and steps off to the side as he puts his knife away.

The Captain moves toward me. As he speaks, his eyes never leave my face, and his voice remains calm and passive. I feel like he's looking into my very soul. "I'm assuming responsibility for the security of this young man as we await his trial." He points to three men, none of whom were the men who tried to kidnap Roran. "You three are on duty. One of you will clean him up and see that he gets food and water. The other two will stand guard."

He then addresses me in the same voice. "I am Captain Granel. I will be interrogating you in approximately one hour. I recommend you be honest in every way. Lies and deception will not benefit you. The rest of you," he says, finally turning away from me, "return to your posts or assignments."

The men salute and file out, but another man steps in. It's Captain Frindor—the guy who trained Ellcia, Hemot, and me earlier today. He's not someone I want to see right now. With his arrival, some of the soldiers tense up, while the men who kidnapped Roran relax.

Frindor looks at me with disgust and then announces, "I am assuming responsibility for the security of the traitor. My first order is…"

Captain Granel waves his hand and shakes his head. "I apologize, Sir, but I have already claimed responsibility."

"I'm the senior officer here!" Frindor barks. "You'll hand over responsibility to me."

I find that confusing. I had never understood how two soldiers with the same rank interacted, but it seems that even Captains can be over other Captains.

"I apologize again, Sir," Granel says in a voice filled with respect, but still the same authoritative, yet passive tone. "I am unable to relinquish responsibility except at the order of the base commander. That is currently General Lirnal, so we will have to await his return. At that point, you will be able to assume control."

I am grateful for that. I don't know if anyone else will listen to me, but I think my uncle will.

Captain Frindor growls, and I see him glare at Granel. After a moment, he nods. I can only guess, but I suspect this is a matter of policy that can't be overruled. I think I'd rather be under Granel's watch anyway, especially after seeing the way the kidnappers responded to Frindor.

"Then, Captain," Frindor says, his voice filled with malice, "I will recommend three men for you. I strongly encourage you to make them part of your guard." He points out three men, and my heart races as I see they're the kidnappers.

"Thank you, Sir," Granel says. He then turns to the soldiers and orders, "The three of you will report to me within the hour for your scheduled rotation."

I groan inside. I thought maybe Granel might be an ally, but there's no chance of that.

Before they can leave, three more people walk in. From their attire, they're Nobles. The cell is not large, by any means, and it's getting cramped. Fortunately, all the soldiers file out after bowing to the three new arrivals. Only the two Captains remain as the Nobles examine me.

I recognize two of them, a man and a woman, although I don't know their names. They were each in the cave where my uncle met us when we first entered the mountain. The third one, a man, is tall and quite slim. He has a thin face and a small mouth. His eyes appear tired, yet cheerful. His most standout-ish feature, however, is his nose. It's… not small.

I can't quite put my finger on what it is about him, but I can see some kind of resemblance to Marleet— although she is quite pretty, and this man is… not.

Out of the three, he's the only one to speak. The others remain silent and stand back near the door to my cell. "I belieeeeve this is one of the young mennnn who helped bring my Marleeeeteeee home to meeee." His voice is slow, drawn out, and carries with it a sound of generational nobility. It's also quite a boring voice, but, for reasons I don't understand, I immediately like the man. There's something about him…

Captain Frindor shakes his head. "That doesn't matter, my Lord."

Marleet's dad turns to the Captain. His eyebrows slowly raise, and he frowns. The resulting expression is quite comical, and I might have found myself laughing, were I in different circumstances. "And why noooot, Captainnnn?"

"My Lord, first, he was caught trying to kidnap the Prince. It's obvious he had nefarious intent. Second, he didn't know you were here, nor did he know Prince Roran was actually the Prince when he returned our Prince to us. He was not acting out of virtue. He was merely protecting himself. Once he found out who Prince Roran actually was, he obviously set out to kidnap him and either kill him, ransom him, or return him to the Regent. Don't forget that this one was particularly close to Parthun. On top of this, he was involved in an altercation with some of our soldiers in the mess hall today, and four of them are dead."

Marleet's dad, after holding his frown and raised eyebrows the entire time, manages to add a smile to the mix without hindering the continued effect of the frown. I blink a few times to try to make sense of what I'm seeing, but in the end, I just have to accept that what I see is what I see.

"Captainnnn," the Noble says, "did you say allll that for no other reasonnnn than to find an excusssse to use a worrrrd like 'nefarioussss'?"

At that, I cannot control my response. I laugh quite loud despite the gag in my mouth.

The laugh earns me a fist to the side of the head from Frindor. When my head stops spinning, Marleet's dad has an expression on his face that I find I simply cannot comprehend. The overall effect is disappointment, mixed with anger, mixed with joy, mixed with a few other things.

"Captainnnn," the Noble says in his slow voice, "I am goingggg to have to ask you to leeeeave. You may stand outsiiiide the door and listennnn, if it pleases youuuu, but I think I cannot trust youuuu to control yourseeeelf."

The Captain clenches his fists and grinds his teeth, but immediately bows respectfully and obeys. Obviously, Marleet's dad has a lot of influence. The Captain walks to the door, and I hear his footsteps continue down the hall.

"Now young mannnn, perhapssss we can take out your gaaaag," the Noble says, reaching for me.

"I'm sorry, Lord Yune," Captain Granel says. "I cannot allow you to ungag him before his interrogation. Any interaction with him in this situation could be used to implicate you in his crimes."

"But we don't knoooow if he has committed anyyyy crimmmmes," the man says, his voice both soothing and irritating.

"I'm sorry, My Lord," Granel says with a bow. "This is not a matter on which I can compromise."

"I understannnnd, Captainnnn," the man says.

He leans down until his face is level with mine. I feel like I should stand up since he's a man of such high status, but then I remember that I'm a prisoner. I'm also a cousin to the rightful heir to the throne and second in line for the throne. I feel like a prisoner doesn't stand in the presence of nobility. I also suspect that, as a Prince, I am of a higher position than this man.

I feel confused.

He examines my face for a long time. Finally, he pulls out what I hope is a clean handkerchief and begins to wipe away the blood from my face. When he's satisfied, he says in his slow deep voice, "There, you goooo, young mannnn. I wissssh you the besssst." He then stands up straight, nods to me, then the Captain, then leaves with the other two Nobles.

I look at the Captain, and the expression on his face tells me that this is normal behavior for Marleet's dad. He then glances at me and says, "I will return shortly for your interrogation. Do not speak to anyone else—even if your life is on the line. Do you understand?"

I nod my head. There's not much else I can do.

The next hour passes slowly. I wish I had used the toilet before I rushed down to the northwest cave. I'm not sure how tied up prisoners are supposed to address that problem. I've read a lot of books over the years, but none of the stories ever explained this part of what it's like to be a captive. When the Captain does return, I'm nearly squirming on my seat.

Granel brings in his own stool and sets it before me. Judging from the speed at which he moves, he's not in a rush. I wish I could speed him up, but I'm afraid that anything I do will slow him down more.

Two other soldiers come in along with a man with a stack of papers. I see the pages are blank. I gather they expect a confession.

Granel sits down on his stool and faces me for a moment before he says, "All right, Draydon, or Caric, as others call you. I expect your uncle will want to speak with you when he returns, although I do not carry the authority to decide what will happen to you over the next few days, only to guard you in the meantime. I am going to ask you some questions, and you will answer them. If you do not answer directly, it will be noted and considered as a form of resistance. Resistance suggests guilt. As such, I would recommend a quick and honest answer to every question I ask. Is this understood?"

I nod my head. I really can't hold it much longer.

He slowly unties my gag. I hadn't realized how uncomfortable it was until it comes out, and I cough twice.

I want to ask about the toilet, but there's something more important. "Is Prince Roran okay?"

The Captain smiles at me, at least I think it's a smile. His face is so twisted that it's difficult to make out all that's happening. "Yes, Caric. He is still unconscious, but he is well guarded and is expected to awake soon."

I smile, despite my circumstances. I notice the man with the paper is writing notes. "Please, Captain," I say, "I have to use the toilet."

He looks at me with a bit of confusion for a moment. He then slowly says, "Part of being a prisoner, Caric, is that you have to suffer the indignity of your situation. Typically, prisoners are expected to soil themselves. It is simply one more way the cell becomes something to avoid."

I nod. That makes sense. "However," I say, "I am not guilty. As soon as Prince Roran awakes, he will confirm that."

The Captain slowly nods. I wish he would move faster. Finally, he stands and motions to the soldiers. They come to me and cut the ropes holding my hands behind my back, and I rush to a corner of my cell. I think having to be in such a situation with four men watching me is enough indignity.

When I return, I sit down and face the Captain. He seems amused… or maybe angry. The scars make his expressions unreadable. I decide I'm no longer interested in trying to figure out his face.

"All right, Caric." His voice is both authoritative and unemotional. "Tell me exactly what happened. Tell me everything you can think of. I won't interrupt unless I have a question."

I lay it all out for Granel. He doesn't react in any way that I can see, other than to nod at odd times. The soldiers behind him stand perfectly still. Their eyes remain on me the entire time. The man off to the side taking notes scribbles furiously. At no point does he stop even for a second, except to dip his quill in the inkwell or drop a page on the floor so he can start a new one.

When I'm finished, Granel remains quiet for a long time. Finally, he nods and confirms, "The three soldiers who Captain Frindor insisted I insert in the rotation… they were three of the men who kidnapped the Prince?"

I'm surprised by that question. It sounds to me like he believes my story. "Yes, Sir."

He nods again and then waves at the man taking notes who scribbles a few more words, then stops. Granel then glances back at one of the soldiers behind him. The man steps out into the hall for a few seconds, then comes back in. "It's only us, Sir."

Captain Granel turns back to me and says, "I had suspected much of what you have told me. You will remain here in this cell for the time being. I cannot confirm your story until Prince Roran awakes."

He remains seated with his gaze focused on me. I get the impression he's working through a lot of information. Finally, he says, "Listen closely, Caric. You are to speak to no one about any of this. If you are questioned, you must remain silent on the matter. Do not say a thing to anyone. Do you understand?"

I nod.

"Good. We expect Prince Roran will awake soon. Unfortunately, that is not good for you."

"Why not?" I ask, feeling frustrated. There is always so much in this world that I don't understand.

Granel lowers his head, eyes focused on the floor as though he's deciding something. After a moment, he looks back up at me. "I believe he will corroborate your version of events. Assuming this is so, if there is someone who wants you blamed, it means you might not survive long enough for the Prince to awake. My soldiers will remain outside, but we will need to move you before the soldiers you identified are put into the rotation." He puts a hand on my shoulder and leans in. "I will provide food and water for you. You must eat everything that is brought to you, and you must move around a lot. Your muscles need to be warm, so when it comes time to leave your cell, you are ready to run. Is this clear?"

I nod again. My heart is racing. I see now that not everything is quite as simple here among the free armies as I would have hoped. "What about my uncle? He won't allow me to be harmed."

"No, he won't," Granel says. "But he is not scheduled to arrive back for another two days. I expect Captain Frindor will insist on holding your trial first thing tomorrow morning."

I'm reminded that it must be the middle of the night. I had reached the northwest cave just before lights out. "I'll be ready, Sir."

He nods and then stands. Before he can leave, a soldier rushes in. "Someone's coming, Sir."

A moment later, Captain Frindor enters. He looks around and sees the man with the notes. "You did the interrogation already?"

"I did, Sir," Captain Granel says. "I hope that is acceptable. It is finished, and I will do the customary review of the notes before I submit them to you. I hope to have them to you by mid-morning."

"Why so long, Captain?" Frindor asks. It's clear he's not only angry, but he also despises Granel.

"Well, it is late, Sir," Granel says. "My men and the clerk will need a bit of sleep so we can be sharp when we present the report to you."

"I don't care if you're sharp!" Frindor hisses. "I want the report within the hour."

"Yes, Sir," Granel says. "I can have it for you by six AM, if that is acceptable. That will give us time to ensure that all the protocols are followed. Otherwise, the defense will be able to demand the case be thrown out. We wouldn't want that, would we, Sir?"

Frindor growls in response and says, "By six AM! No later! We will begin the trial at seven!"

"But Sir," Granel says. "Should we not wait for the General to..."

Frindor's expression makes it clear that Granel should stop, and he does. "The trial is at seven!" Frindor turns to me, spits, and then storms out.

Once he's gone, a soldier steps in and signals to Granel. The Captain turns back to me and says, "It is an hour past midnight. That means I have five hours until the report is due, and you have six hours until you are condemned to death. We have lots to do, so that does not happen."

He moves out of the room, followed by the clerk. Before the two soldiers leave, they give me a look of pity. I'm quite confused with all that's going on, but I find myself overcome with exhaustion. I lay down on the cot in the corner of the room and, once the door closes, fall asleep in seconds.

When I awake, it's to the sound of the door opening. I jump up and instinctively go for my sword, but my hand grasps nothing, and it takes me a moment to recognize the soldier as one of Granel's men. He sets a tray of food down, along with a jug of water. It's far more food than I would have expected, but I set about eating it, then walking around my tiny cell.

I don't know what all's going to happen, but I'll be ready.

I don't know how much time has passed since the food came, but I'm about to lie down again and sleep when I hear whispered voices out in the hallway. I wait for a few seconds, but the whispering only continues, so I move to the door to listen. I can't make out any words, nor can I recognize who's speaking. Whoever it is, doesn't sound pleased.

Finally, I hear a couple quiet thumps, followed by angry voices, then loud thumps mixed with grunts. The whispering continues, but now the voices are really, really angry.

I hear the jingle of keys and then a key in the lock on the other side of the door. Whoever's working it doesn't seem to know which key to use. Finally, I hear a frustrated whisper, and I make out the words, "Just give it to me!"

A moment later, the door unlocks, and I step back. The door opens outward and before me stands a thin person with a thick cloak wrapped all around and a hood over the face. Behind that person stands one of the Granel's soldiers. He looks angry and has a stream of blood flowing down the side of his head. The other soldier is on the ground but propped up on one elbow. He also has a gash on the side of his head and looks just as angry as the first man.

The person in the cloak pulls back the hood, and I nearly cheer. It's Ellcia. She's smiling, but I can tell from the urgent expression on her face that we have to move quickly.

The soldier on his feet shakes his head and lies down on the ground. A moment later, he's quite still, and the other soldier has stretched out on the floor as well. With the gashes on their heads, they now look like they've been knocked out.

"Come on!" Ellcia says. "We don't have much time."

I get out of the cell and find Hemot and Marleet waiting for me. They look both thrilled and terrified.

We start down the tunnel but almost immediately stop at the sound of an urgent whisper. "No." one of the soldiers says. "The other way!"

We turn around and rush in the opposite direction. As I pass by the two soldiers pretending to be unconscious, I hear the one say to the other, "It's like they didn't even plan this out!"

We move down the passageway for a short distance before Ellcia and Hemot pull me into a side cave. In that cave, I find my traveling pack, a thick cloak, my armor, and my sword and knife. I strap on my weapons and armor and put on my cloak and pack without a word. When I'm finished, Ellcia has her finger on her lips.

I hear the sound of a group of men as they move through the cave. None of them look in our direction. There is just enough light that they might see us if they do, so I'm grateful their attention is elsewhere. I count eight men, and they move in the direction of my cell. I figure at the speed they're walking, we have about two minutes before they find I've escaped.

Once they're past, Ellcia waves us out. We rush along the cave, away from the men, and down passageway after passageway. Hemot whispers the turns that we need to take, but Ellcia leads the way. I notice the caves slowly move upward as we go. I have no idea where I am, so I don't know if this will bring us up to ground level or way up high into the mountain.

As we make another turn, Hemot whispers, "Not far now."

We move as fast as we can in the dim light. At times, we're nearly at a run. I find myself enjoying the movement again. I have a lot more endurance than I did when we first set out from Sevord City.

We round another corner and come to a grinding halt. Before us stand three people: Captain Granel, Lord Yune, and a woman whom I suspect is Marleet's mom. Before I can say anything, I find myself nearly knocked over as Marleet slams into me, wrapping her arms around me. Now that we're away from the cell and the soldiers, she seems to need to hug me.

"Are you okay, Caric?" Marleet asks as she examines my face. She's upset, and I'm reminded yet again of how messed up I must look. I've taken two serious beatings in the last day. She runs her hands over the cuts on my face in her typical motherly-Marleet fashion. A few seconds later, she has some ointment in her hands and is dabbing it in spots on my forehead.

"I'm fine," I say.

Ellcia comes over and pulls her away. "We don't have time to do this now. We have to leave."

The woman whom I think must be Marleet's mother, looks quite distressed, and her father looks… hmm… I realize what it is. I can see it now. He looks like a turtle. I see enough family resemblance there to know for sure that he and Marleet are related, but Marleet obviously got her looks from her mother.

"Marleeeeteeee," her dad says in his slow, deep voice as he pulls her into an embrace. "Youuuu take good care of these threeeee. Remember where to find my friendssss. Be couraaaageous and be confidennnnt in your blade."

Marleet's mom then comes in and hugs her tight, covering her with kisses. Marleet seems very content in the embrace of each of her parents. I feel a stab of envy, but I also feel so happy for her.

Captain Granel wraps his arms around Ellcia, and I finally put it together, remembering what my uncle told me. He's her older brother. He only whispers, "Come back safe to me."

I hear her whisper back, "I will." When she lets go, she asks, "What if you're caught?"

"What?" he says with a laugh. "Caught? Do you think it'll be a problem to be found walking the caves with Lord Yune and Lady Aldora? If anything, I might be up for another promotion!" He gives what I think might be a smile, and Ellcia hugs him again before grabbing me and leading me down a small passageway.

At some point, I'm hoping one of my friends will stop long enough to tell me the plan, but for the moment, I can figure out we're obviously leaving. That's enough for the time being.

But the thing that surprises me the most is that Marleet is with us. I know Hemot would go for the adventure. I know Ellcia would go because… she's Ellcia. But Marleet looks like she has everything she's ever wanted here in the caves… except Hemot. But I don't think she's going because of him. But… maybe.

The cave starts to get a little smaller and then branches off in two directions. When this happens, Hemot moves up to the front and guides us through. I have no idea how he figures out where to go, but we're definitely getting closer to the outside. The temperature is dropping. It must be a cold day.

We come around a corner, and I stop in my tracks. It's not just a cold day, it's winter! For a moment I wonder if we've been in the mountain for months, but then I discard that thought. It's only been about a week.

My cloak has some clasps on the front, and I secure them together. Ellcia hands me some mittens along with a scarf, and once I've put them on, we set out into the cold.

The moment we step out into the morning, we shield our eyes. I'm grateful the sun is still behind the mountain, leaving us in shadow, but after being in such a dark place for so long, the daylight with the white snow makes my eyes hurt. None of us move for a few moments while we try to adjust.

What makes it all worse is the wind. It just cuts through my cloak and finds ways through my armor. It's so bitter I feel the chill through to my bones. When I look in the direction of the wind, blowing flakes of snow bite into my eyes, cheeks, and lips.

"Which way?" Hemot hollers above the wind. "I only know how to get us to this point. I haven't gone beyond the cave entrance."

I'm amazed that he's come up here. As I think about it, he might like to explore. We've been friends for most of our lives, but I always assumed his desire to search out new rooms and areas of the castle was an attempt to find new places to hide from work. Maybe it's not laziness. Maybe he does just like to find what's out there.

Ellcia calls out, "Granel said we head north for a short distance until we come to a cliff, then follow it around till we get to a frozen waterfall and head down the mountain from there. We just have to make sure we avoid any patrols or hunting parties. The patrols will arrest us, and the hunting parties will report us."

It's early in the day, so the shadows from the mountains give a clear idea of which way is north. In that direction, there doesn't seem to be much of a path or any simple way through, but it does appear relatively level and wide enough for us to walk safely.

Without another word, we move north. It's clear no one has come through this way for a while. The snow sits smooth and undisturbed. The path, if we can call it that, moves along with a steep incline on the right and an even steeper decline on the left.

The snow is only as deep as my ankles in some places. In those areas, it's easy to walk, and we make good time. In other areas, unfortunately, the snow has built up more and comes up to our knees. I feel it slowly moving past my greaves and through my trousers. It's not a nice feeling, and it only adds to the cold.

Ellcia leads us along. I walk second, then Marleet, with Hemot bringing up the rear. A quick glance is enough to let me know that Ellcia is focused, Marleet's troubled, and Hemot's thrilled with every step he takes.

By the time the sun is just high enough to crest the top of the mountain, I suspect it's somewhere around the eleventh hour of the day. We see part of the mountain jut out across the path ahead of us. It takes us another half hour or so to reach that point, but when we do, we're all exhausted. My face hurts, even though I keep trying to pull my hood farther down over my cheeks.

When we finally reach the cliff, the wind has picked up to the point where we can barely see through the blowing snow. None of us have said a word for at least an hour. It's as if we all understand that our only goal right now is to get through this. I feel a stab of guilt as I remember that they're all out here because of me.

They've had to give up everything. Again. At least the first time was for adventure and something noble. But this time, they're losing everything because I got myself captured.

I feel terrible.

The cliff offers a bit of a reprieve from the wind as there's a section of it that goes somewhat into the mountain. It's not enough to call it a proper cave, but it's enough for a break. We crawl inside and huddle together for a few minutes before Hemot announces he's going to take a quick look ahead.

He follows the cliff around and disappears out of sight. Neither Ellcia nor Marleet speak, so I hold my questions. When Hemot returns, about ten minutes later, he has a grin on his face.

"We should move right away!" he says. "The path runs under the shelter of an overhang for a little way, and there's no snow or wind in that area."

We get up and follow him. It takes us a while to get around the cliff, and there's an area where the wind is blowing far harder than any other area so far, but when we come to the area Hemot mentioned, we find the way is easy. By the time mid-afternoon has set in, we're in the sun. It makes it hard to see with the reflection off the snow across the mountain, but it's a lot warmer.

When we finally catch sight of the frozen waterfall, I nearly shout for joy. I can't wait to get off the mountain. I look out over the Talic Region to the west, and though I know it's a dangerous area, all I can think of is the warm weather of the plains. I'd only consider staying on the mountain for the night if we could build a fire. The lack of trees, unfortunately, makes that unrealistic.

At the waterfall, we find a steep, yet passable way down the side of the mountain. I expect it continues the entire way, but we can only see a short distance ahead.

Ellcia is about to start when I grab her and pull her back. "Get down!" I hiss.

Just moving into sight is a patrol. From their armor, they're soldiers, rather than a hunting party. For the first time, I realize that if I'm caught, I'll have no chance at my trial. They'll insist that by running, I've declared myself guilty. My friends will be seen as accomplices, and I fear they'll share my fate.

We scramble up the side of the mountain, looking for a place to hide. The soldiers are far from us, so unless they look in our direction, they won't see us.

I see what looks like a small cave, and I point at it. I feel like my voice will carry over the mountain, so I keep as quiet as I can.

When we get to the cave, Hemot climbs inside, followed by Marleet, then Ellcia. Just before I climb in, I glance back, and to my horror, one of the soldiers is pointing at me.

We've been seen.

I glance around and see a way up the side of the mountain. "We've been spotted. We have to keep moving. We don't want to be trapped in here."

They scramble back out of the cave, and we climb. It's slow going, and I know we're leaving a trail, but I can't see any other choice. I'm hoping that we'll find another way down the mountain, but at this rate, we'll be up here when it's dark. I fear we'll freeze to death overnight.

We climb as fast as we can. After a few minutes, we're all gasping for air. My lungs hurt and my legs shake, but we keep going. The way leads between two small hills and once we pass by, I look back to see the soldiers have nearly caught up to us. I'm shocked at their speed, but then remember that they likely climb all over this mountain all the time. They'll have far more endurance than I'll likely ever have.

We have no other option than to continue up the side of the mountain. The steep inclines on each side prevent us from breaking off to the left or right. Ahead is a large cave, big enough I hope we can hide inside without boxing ourselves in. We run in, Marleet in the lead. I wonder if we can somehow slip past the soldiers when they enter.

We move into the darkness, doing our best not to trip. The cave is large enough for all four of us to walk side-by-side, but we continue in single file. I find myself in the lead, doing my best to feel my way along, hoping for solid ground with every step. The only thing I can see is directly behind us where the light comes in. When I glance back, the soldiers are at the entrance with swords drawn.

Just before they step into the cave, I hear a rumble, and the ground feels like it's shaking. The soldiers scramble forward, but it's too late. Snow piles down on them, and in the fading light I see their shapes struggle under the falling snow.

When the avalanche stops, there's nothing but silence and darkness.

4

The Exit

I stand there in the dark and wait for my eyes to adjust. There's very little light coming through the opening of the cave, now that the snow has come down. I can't hear any noise from outside, but I can see just a little in certain spots around where the entrance had been.

Someone grabs my arm, and I put my hand out. I feel their arm and, from the height, guess that it's Ellcia. Someone comes up behind me and wraps his hand around my face. I don't have to ask. It's Hemot.

"Ew!" he hisses. "Why is your face all wet?"

"Why is your hand on my nose?" I reply and push him away.

"We have to find our way out of here," Ellcia whispers.

"I don't like this," Marleet adds in. It sounds like she's on the other side of Ellcia.

"Why are we whispering?" Hemot asks. I feel his hand run down my arm as he wipes it clean.

"It's just melted snow," I say awkwardly, and then change the subject. "We either need to dig our way out through the snow or find a light so we can make our way through this cave. Maybe there's another way out."

I hear someone scramble up the wall of snow at the cave entrance, and I see the shape of Hemot's head against the blue light coming in. He pushes and digs for a moment before scrambling back down.

"Can't go that way," he whispers to the rest of us.

"Why not?" Ellcia asks, keeping her voice down. "And do we need to whisper?"

"Yes," Hemot says. "We have to keep whispering."

I wait for more but realize Hemot's doing one of his annoying things. I wait a bit more and then say, "Please continue."

"Oh, right," he says. "We can't go back through the snow because it'll take too long to dig through it all. There's a lot of snow there. We also can't go back that way because I can hear the voices of the soldiers. If we dig through, they'll catch us. Also, we have to whisper because if I can hear them, they might hear us."

"We can't see in here," Ellcia says, "so there's no way we can just wander through the darkness. There could be a pit just a few steps away, and we wouldn't know until we fell down it."

"No problem," Hemot says enthusiastically. "I brought what we need."

I hear Hemot take a few steps away. If I concentrate, I can make out a bit of movement in his direction. Ellcia's hands are still on my arm.

"What are you doing, Hemot?"

"I brought a tinderbox, and I have some rags soaked in oil. Rulf taught me a lot about how to survive in the wild. I'm all prepared."

"You're so smart, Hemot," I hear Marleet say. There's a lot of affection in her voice.

At first, I want to growl at him. I'm still irritated that he touched my face. I'm not sure why it irritates me so much, but it does. However, Marleet is right. Hemot might be the most prepared out of the bunch of us.

"I brought what we need to start a fire, set traps in the wild, cook food over a spit, and more. I also brought lots of food in case we don't catch anything."

"How did you fit all of that in your pack?" I ask.

"I decided to leave out clothes. I figured I only need what I'm wearing."

I groan to myself, and I hear Marleet whisper, "Oh my!" under her breath, but I let it go. Hemot has to find his own way in life. This might be good for him in the long run.

I nearly jump when I see the sparks, and it's not long before we have a bit of a flame. As it takes, and the light spreads around the cave, I see that he has the rag tied to a stick that he can use as a torch.

I'm impressed. Aside from Hemot leaving any changes of clothes out of his pack, I'm sure he'll be a big help to the rest of us with all his preparations.

As the torch grows brighter, and we see more of the cave, I notice that there's a high enough ceiling that we won't have to worry about banging our heads. I don't see any bones on the floor, so I'm guessing that means a predator doesn't live in here. That gives me a certain amount of comfort.

Hemot looks at me and waits. I realize he's waiting for a signal that we can move on. It seems I'm back to being the leader of the group.

In the dim light of the torch, I check on Ellcia and Marleet. They're okay, so I signal for us to move forward. The cave is wide enough in some spots that we can walk side-by-side, but in other spots, the cave walls come together enough that we walk single-file.

After a while, I realize two things. First, it's getting warmer. That's not a bad thing, and it's not unexpected. The caves are not as cold as the outside of the mountain. They seem to maintain a cool, damp feel all the time.

The second thing I realize is that we could easily be back in the same cave system as the rest of the rebels. That's a problem. If we are, we could bump into Captain Frindor or some soldier who thinks that I should be in a cell... or worse.

We move deeper into the cave, and I catch the smell of something. The smell is sweet and very appealing. Even though I ate a solid meal in my cell, the aroma makes me hungry.

I look at the others and whisper, "There's obviously some people ahead. We need to be careful."

Ellcia nods, but I can see she disagrees. I'm not sure about what. She doesn't seem worried at all.

We walk on a little farther, and I can smell it more. It's definitely something cooking, which means we're near people. The people in this mountain are not going to take kindly to us.

I'm about to tell everyone we need to turn around and take our chances with the soldiers and with the snow blocking the cave, when Hemot announces in a loud voice, "Wow! That smells great!"

"Shhh!!!" I say and give him a punch in the arm for good measure. "We're on the run, remember? We need to be careful."

"I don't think it's a problem," Marleet says in a normal voice and places her hand gently on my arm. "I know you mean well, Caric, but I'm pretty sure we're safe."

"No," I reply in a whisper, "we're not! That could be a group of soldiers ahead. If we're not careful, we'll be captured."

I turn to Ellcia, hoping for some support, but she has an awkward look on her face. She glances at Hemot and then Marleet before saying, also in a normal voice, "Caric, Marleet's right. We're safe. There's nothing to worry about."

"How do you know?" I ask, still speaking in a whisper.

"Maybe I just know some things you don't," she says loudly and with a sweet smile.

I pause for a moment and turn to Marleet, then Hemot. Their smiles suggest they know something I don't. I can't imagine what it might be, but when I turn back to Ellcia, her smile grows larger, and I decide to trust her. They had a plan to rescue me. I can trust this part as well.

I just wish they'd told me what they were up to.

"Okay," I say, still keeping my voice down. "Let's move on."

Ellcia comes in and wraps her arm around me tightly, and she holds me in an embrace as we move forward. She's never actually been this affectionate to me before. I guess whatever she's planned out must be pretty great.

We move on through the cave, and in a little while, I see a torch on the wall. It's not lit, but it sits in a sconce securely attached to the stone. Although it's not burning right now, it's been lit in the past.

With each step, the aroma grows in intensity. It does smell pretty great, and my stomach rumbles. The closer we get to it, the happier the others get. I'm still a little suspicious, but then Ellcia nestles in even closer next to me, and I find the suspicion falls away.

I notice Marleet and Hemot are also walking quite close together. She has her arm around his waist, and he has his around her shoulders.

There's light up ahead, and when we round a corner, I see another torch in a sconce on the wall. This one, however, is lit. Beyond that, the cave opens into a room, and light shines out.

We step into the entrance of the large room, and I nearly gasp. The room is well lit—in fact, it's better lit than any room I've been in while in the caves. It's also well decorated with fancy rugs on the floor, tapestries on the wall, statues and busts of people I don't recognize, and shelves upon shelves filled with books and bottles of what appear to be spices.

On the far side of the room is a large pot over a small fire. Whatever's inside is bubbling, and I expect that's where the delicious smell is coming from.

Standing over the pot, stirring away and humming to himself, is a man dressed in a strange cloak. The color is dark—I think maybe purple, or blue, or green. Actually, I can't really tell what color it is. It just seems to be a bunch of different colors, yet at the same time it appears to be one solid color.

The man has his back to us. His head is uncovered to reveal a distinct lack of hair on top, but his beard hangs down far enough that the end of it sits in the pot. All interest in having a taste of the meal disappears with that sight.

I nearly jolt with shock as I realize what I'm looking at.

Spellcasters are rare. In fact, many think that there are none living at this time. In most of the stories about them, they're evil. They're also very hard to kill.

The man doesn't appear to have noticed us yet, so I say in a whisper, "I think he might be a Spellcaster." I pause for a second and then glance around the room. To the left, still behind the wizard, is a small cave leading back in the direction we came. I'm hoping that's a way out. I point toward it and hiss, "We should head down there and get out of here before he sees us."

Ellcia wraps her other arm around me and gives me a big hug. After a few moments, she looks up at me with the sweetest smile I've ever seen. My heart skips a beat, and I almost forget about the danger. In a dreamy voice, she says "Caric, just relax. This man's a friend."

I look back at the man. He hasn't reacted at all to Ellcia's voice. I wonder if he's deaf.

"You've met him before?" I ask, still keeping my voice down.

She shakes her head and nestles her face into my chest. I can't imagine that could be comfortable with my leather armor, but she seems happier than I've ever seen her.

"He's okay, Caric," Hemot says. "He's a friend."

I look over at Hemot, and he and Marleet have their arms wrapped around each other, just like Ellcia holding me. The look on their faces is also just like Ellcia's, and it no longer looks natural. My heart races. Something is seriously wrong here.

"Welcome!" a voice bellows out. The man is speaking loud enough that I'd think he was yelling, but it sounds just like normal speech. "Welcome to my cave, Marleet and friends."

Marleet giggles over by Hemot, and Ellcia wraps her arms around me even tighter. She lets out a contented sigh.

"Who are you?" I ask.

At the question, the man's head jerks up as if he's surprised. He turns around and scans our faces, stopping on mine. I can almost feel his gaze on me as he studies my face.

"And how do we get out of here?" I ask.

The man slowly shakes his head, and confusion fills his eyes.

I'm not sure if he's confused because he didn't understand me, or if he doesn't know where the exit is. As I consider it, I begin to think that he's surprised that I'm asking.

Without giving an answer, he turns to one of his many shelves, walks over to it, grabs two jars, and returns to the fire. When he reaches it, he opens each of the jars and drops both of them—jar and all—into the pot.

The smell in the room instantly grows stronger, and it's making me feel ill. I quickly catch Ellcia as she starts to droop. Her eyes are half-closed. I pull her to her feet and make her stand on her own. She looks at me with great affection, but then unbuckles her sword, drops it to the ground along with her knife, takes off her pack, dropping it as well, and then drops her cloak. When she's done, she turns to the wizard and smiles.

I hear thuds behind me and turn to see Hemot and Marleet's swords, packs, knives, and cloaks now sit on the floor.

My friends are under a spell, and I'm the only one who knows what's going on.

A wave of panic washes over me, then a wave of doubt. I might only think I'm not under a spell! My pack might actually be on the ground right now, along with my sword!

I glance down to see my sword is where it used to be, and I feel the weight of the pack. I figure I'm going to have to assume I'm not under the spell—because I can't do anything if I think I'm enchanted. I have to get my friends out of here. Maybe there's some reason the spell doesn't work on me.

"Now, Marleet," the Spellcaster says.

"Yes," Marleet says in a sweet, affectionate way. "What do you need from me?"

"I need you to come here," the Spellcaster says.

I quickly rush to Marleet's side and wrap my arm around her. She's thin and tiny, so I have little trouble holding her in place. She doesn't look angry at me for holding her back, just frustrated.

"Now this is interesting," the Spellcaster says, his eyes on me. "For some reason, my magic does not work on you."

I examine his face. He looks quite intrigued, but irritated at the same time. I try to think through what I need to do. I need to get all three of my friends out of the cave, but there's no way I can do that while holding Marleet back. I also won't be able to get their cloaks and packs and weapons. I'd consider leaving that stuff, but we need our packs to survive on our journey, and they need their cloaks to keep them warm on the mountainside.

"I would just increase the strength of the potion," the Spellcaster continues, "but doing that already has had no effect. Which means," he says with a smile, "that you are wearing something that protects you from my enchantments."

He studies me from head to toe as I hold on to a squirming Marleet. Eventually, he says, "Ah, yes. I recognize your leather armor. I think my great-grandfather enchanted it. If you're wearing it, you are either a thief, or you are of the royal line. You are not Prince Roran, nor are you Lirnal, Parthun, Corter, or Tilbur… so… I expect you are likely Prince Draydon, am I correct?"

I don't think confirming my name with the Spellcaster is a good idea, so I merely frown at the man. I wonder if maybe I can get Marleet far enough away that I can come back for the others, but I have no idea what the Spellcaster might do to Ellcia or Hemot while I'm gone. I'm also not sure I can drag Hemot out. He's thin, but big enough that if he struggles, I don't think I can overpower him.

"No need to answer," the Spellcaster says with a smile. "But I can tell you this: I will have Marleet for my purposes."

"What are your purposes?" I don't want to talk to the man, but I'm hoping if I stall, I'll figure out what to do.

"Oh, Prince Draydon," the Spellcaster laughs, "I can't tell you that. It is, however, unfortunate that you are wearing that armor. If I had you in my grasp, and you were not wearing such protection, I would certainly kill you."

"It's a good thing I'm wearing it, then."

"I can see how you would think that. For me, it is an inconvenience, but that is all."

"So, what do we do now?" I ask with a growl.

"Now, you will release Marleet for me, and I will go on with my plans. I have been hired to do something absolutely splendid, and even a princeling with enchanted armor can't stop me."

"But I can hold Marleet. To keep her from you, I'll hold her forever."

"Oh," the Spellcaster says with another one of his obnoxious laughs. "That sounds almost romantic, but I can see she has no feelings for you—at least those kinds of feelings. Besides, you won't hold her forever. You'll be letting go of her in a matter of seconds. Did you forget that the young girl over there clung to you when you first came in? If she clings to you so tightly while under this spell, that means she loves you more than life itself."

I'm not sure how to respond to that, but my heart warms at the thought. I also feel a dread creep over me. I'm scared of what he's going to do. Marleet struggles a little harder, and I firm up my grip around her waist.

"Now," he continues, "I can't be sure of what your feelings are toward her because you are not reacting the way I want you to, but I can take a guess that you won't want her harmed."

The Spellcaster then turns to Hemot and says, "Young man, what is your name?"

"Don't tell him, Hemot!" I say, but then shake my head. Sometimes I'm such an idiot.

"Oh, I don't mind if he knows my name, Caric," Hemot says. He then turns to the Spellcaster and says, "My name is Hemot."

"Wonderful!" The man then points at Ellcia. "And what is that girl's name?"

"Her name is Ellcia," Hemot says. "And you're right. Caric loves her. He's never said it, but everyone knows. He would do anything for her."

I want to punch Hemot, but I know he's enchanted. It's not his fault. I just wish I knew how to stop it all.

"Perfect," the Spellcaster says. "That will make this easier. Hemot, my friend?"

"Yes, Sir," Hemot says with a big smile.

"Kill Ellcia."

My heart goes cold as I turn back to Hemot. With a big grin on his face, he reaches down to grab his knife from the floor of the cave. I quickly turn to look at Ellcia, and she's pulling off her scarf. When she's done, she leans back her head to expose her neck.

"NO!" I scream at Hemot.

He smiles at me and says, "It'll be okay, Caric. I just have to kill Ellcia, and then we can find out what else our friend wants us to do."

I keep my left arm around Marleet and grab Hemot's arm with my right. He smiles at me, and then easily pulls his arm out of my grasp. To the sound of the Spellcaster's laughter, I drag Marleet toward Hemot and place each of us between him and Ellcia, wrapping my free arm around Hemot and doing my best to hold him in place.

I've never been a strong boy, but at that moment, I find I'm strong enough to hold both my friends. I know I can't do it for long, but for now, they're safe.

"Marleet, dear," the Spellcaster says.

"Yes, friend?" Marleet replies.

"I need you to fight with everything you've got to get away from Prince Draydon, or Caric, as Hemot calls him, and come to me."

"Yes, my friend," Marleet says.

She then turns to me and, with the sweetest smile on her face, runs her fist into my right eye. As I'm recovering, she pulls and twists and fights. Even though she's fighting so hard, I know I'd be able to hold her, if I didn't need to hold Hemot as well.

I still have my left arm around Marleet, but Hemot begins to pull harder. My arms start to weaken, and I can see that it's just a matter of time before I lose my grip on one or both.

I look over my shoulder at Ellcia. She has a large smile on her face as she holds her head back. I stare in horror as Hemot has his hand stretched out with the blade only inches from Ellcia's exposed neck. Every few seconds he lurches toward her, and his knife comes within a hair of slicing her open.

I make my decision. I'm not sure Marleet will be killed if I let her go, but I know Ellcia will be if I don't. Maybe I can rescue Marleet later.

I cry out in agony as I let go of Marleet and put my full weight into holding Hemot back. Even though I'm already exhausted, I'm quickly able to push Hemot a few steps away from Ellcia.

When I turn to Marleet, she's standing before the Spellcaster. He has his hand on her forehead, his eyes are closed, and he's mouthing words. I'm sure she's being put under a spell, and I want to scream in rage, but at that moment Hemot lunges toward Ellcia again, and I have to put my full energy into holding him back.

The Spellcaster picks up a tiny wooden statue and waves it toward the rock wall. An area of the rock before

Marleet shimmers. She turns without another word and walks toward it, disappearing through the shimmering section as if it were a doorway.

"Where did you send her?" I scream at the man.

The Spellcaster laughs. "Oh, I won't tell you that. It could, however, be anywhere in the world. She has a mission that she's been specifically selected for. When she's finished, if she can, she may come and find you. Otherwise, that may be the last time you see her." He laughs again and then waves his statue at another area of the rock, creating a new shimmering spot. He then walks through it, disappearing from sight. Once he disappears, both walls return to normal, and I'm pretty sure the doorways are sealed back up again.

Hemot stops fighting immediately and remains still. His face continues to sport the large grin, but he isn't fighting to get to Ellcia. I turn to her, and she's dropped her head back down and is tying her scarf back in place.

I leave Hemot and rush to Ellcia, grabbing her shoulders. "Ellcia! Are you okay?"

She smiles sweetly at me and says, "I love you, Caric."

My heart skips a beat, but I push it aside. I don't know how much the spell or potion or whatever it is might be affecting her.

I turn back to Hemot. He's dropped his knife again, but I say, "Ellcia, Hemot, I need the two of you to pick up your knives and swords and put on your cloaks and packs again.

Hemot smiles at me and says, "No need, Caric. I don't think I'll ever need a weapon again. Everyone just loves everyone else."

"Yeah, Caric," Ellcia adds. "I think you could probably drop yours as well. You don't need them. Will you get rid of your sword and knife for me?"

I growl to myself. "Will you at least pick up your cloaks and packs?"

"Of course, Caric," Ellcia says, and gives me another hug. "Are we going somewhere?"

"Yes. Please put your cloak on, then your pack over top."

They both bend down and pick up their cloaks, putting them on, followed by their packs. I feel sick to my stomach thinking about Marleet. I can't imagine what the man wanted her for. Out of anyone in our group, I'm not sure she'll be able to find her way back to us. And I don't know where to begin looking for her.

I scoop up Ellcia, Hemot, and Marleet's swords and knives and strap them to the side of my pack. I ask Hemot to carry Marleet's pack and cloak, and he picks them both up. I'm not sure what we're going to do with everything she has packed, but if we find her soon, she's going to need it.

"Let's go this way," I say, pointing in the direction of the second cave—the one which we didn't enter through. I give each of them a push to let them know it's time to move. They step forward with glazed-over looks in their eyes, and large smiles on their faces.

I grab one of the torches off the wall. It's larger and brighter than the one Hemot had. I'm hoping we won't need it for long.

Every few steps, Ellcia comes and gives me a hug, and now and then, Hemot pats me on the head. By the time we reach the cave, Hemot has kissed me on the cheek three times. I'm not impressed with him, but at least he whispers, "Just as a friend," after each kiss.

We step into the cave, and immediately the air feels cooler and less heavy. Ellcia giggles and comes in for another hug, tells me she loves me again, then stumbles a little. I grab her and help her back to her feet, and she wraps an arm around me, leaning her head against my side. We walk on in this way through the cave. The torch offers plenty of light, as the cave itself is only wide enough for two people to walk side by side. Unfortunately, both Hemot and Ellcia feel we can all walk in what Hemot calls a "Hug Clump".

After about five minutes, I feel Ellcia pull away just a little, and Hemot walks a little straighter. A few moments later, Ellcia steps away from me, and Hemot stops.

"Where are we going?" Hemot asks.

"We're going this way." From the look in each of their eyes, they're not yet free from whatever the Spellcaster had been up to, but they're certainly better than they were a few minutes ago.

"Okay," he says. "You're the leader."

I start up again, but Ellcia doesn't move. Her eyes are focused back in the direction of the Spellcaster's cave, so I take her hand and pull her along.

I feel a little cold air. We're getting close to an opening. I don't know if we'll be able to get out onto the mountainside from here, but maybe the fresh air will clear their heads.

Our cave appears to meet a larger cave ahead. The new cave heads to the left and the right, but I see natural light coming from the left. When we reach the larger cave, a gust of air blows past us, extinguishing my torch.

"Whoa!" Ellcia says. "I don't remember getting here. Is that the entrance? Did we clear the snow?"

"We must have," Hemot says. "Um, my head feels funny."

Sure enough, in the direction of the natural light is an entrance, just a short distance away—although a much different one than we had used to enter the Spellcaster's cave. Through the opening, all I see is snow and sky. We're still far up on the mountain.

I pull off my pack and hand Ellcia and Hemot their weapons. "Strap these on."

They take their weapons. Both still seem a little confused and are very obedient. I don't know if that's normal after something like this.

As Ellcia straps on her sword belt, she asks in a slow voice, "When did I take my sword off?"

"Just a little while ago," I say. "I'm going to go check out our path ahead. Just don't go anywhere."

"Okay," Ellcia says and gives me a tight hug. She returns to strapping on her sword belt. She looks like she doesn't remember how to do it.

I move quickly to the cave entrance. At first, I can't see much of anything as I have to adjust to the blinding white light of a snow-covered mountain, but as I shield my eyes, I begin to make out a path heading down. I don't recognize the area at all, but I'm hoping the way continues to the bottom.

I return to the others and find Hemot has pulled off his pack and thrown down his bedroll. As I approach, he's in the process of crawling under the blankets.

"No!" I order. "This isn't the time to sleep. We have to get down the mountainside."

I turn to Ellcia to find she's leaning against the wall. Although she's on her feet, I hear the faintest snore.

"Hemot!" I shout. "Get your bedroll put away, your sword back on, your pack on your back, and let's go! Oh," I add, a bit selfishly, "you're carrying Marleet's pack."

He smiles at me and nods as he sets about to get everything in place. I check Ellcia's sword and pack. They're both tied on securely. I decide to let Ellcia sleep for another moment while Hemot gets himself ready.

When Hemot finishes, I shake Ellcia, and we move toward the entrance. With each step, their heads clear a little more.

When we step out onto the mountainside, I wait again while our eyes adjust to the light, then start down what looks like a path covered in a foot or so of snow. It's not long before I realize that, despite the snow covering, it's quite a decent path.

"Where's Marleet," Hemot asks.

His voice is still a little dopey, and I'm too upset. "I'll explain that later, Hemot."

I've been trying not to think about Marleet. There's nothing I can do about her situation. Right now, the priority is to get Ellcia and Hemot away from whatever's controlling them.

We continue down the path for an hour or so. As we descend, the wind slowly dies, and the snow becomes less of an issue.

I keep a close eye on Ellcia and Hemot. They're doing fine, but their expressions let me know that they're still confused. They also aren't as steady on their feet as I'd like them to be on a mountain path.

By the time we reach a point where there's little to no snow, they seem to have much clearer heads. The sun is low in the sky, so I look for a small cave or overhang to get out of the weather. It's nearly dark by the time I find one, and I'm pleased there's a copse of trees nearby. We gather some wood and climb into the cave.

In a short while, Hemot has a fire going, and we start to pull out food. I know it's just a matter of time before the conversation of Marleet comes up. I'm dreading it. I'm also doubting everything I did. I can't help but think I could have saved both Marleet and Ellcia. I don't know how, but I should have found a way. I'm sure I blew it.

Hemot's going to be really mad, and I don't think I'll blame him. I'm afraid Ellcia will never speak to me again.

I look over at her as she stares into the fire. I nearly tear up. I've probably lost her. I've saved her life, and I'm happy about that, but I think I've lost her forever. She'll hate me from now on.

Hemot's staring at Marleet's pack. I think his head is still foggy, but he might be trying to work through it all. I don't know if they remember anything.

"I'm going to bed," Hemot announces.

"Me too," Ellcia says.

I nearly breathe out a sigh of relief. We'll have to talk tomorrow, but at least tonight they don't hate me like I now hate myself.

5

The Journey Down

A scream wakes me, and I scramble out of my bedroll and onto my feet. I spin around, confused and terrified. I grab for my sword at my belt. but it's not there. I duck and move back, turn around and slam face first into Ellcia.

We both tumble to the ground, and she screams out, "Where's the danger, Caric?"

"I don't know!" I say, searching the floor for my sword.

I remember settling down in the cave last night. I probably put my sword right next to me—that's where I always put it—but in the panic, I've turned everything into a tangled mess on the ground.

I grab Ellcia and wrap my one arm around her. I'm not sure why I'm doing this, but I think it seems like the right thing to do. I feel her shoulders shake and look down. She's caught between tears and laughter. We stand there together for a moment, trying to figure out what happened, wondering if we just scrambled around in terror for no reason.

"Where's Hemot?" I ask.

Before Ellcia can answer, Hemot races back into the cave. He runs up to us and screams, "Marleet's gone! Something's happened to her! She's been taken by an animal, or she wandered off in the night, or a Shaloomd got her. We have to find her. Grab your shoes. No time for talk. Let's go!"

Hemot races for the entrance to the cave, but I holler out, "Wait!"

"We don't have time for this!" Hemot barks.

Ellcia's left my side and is pulling on her boots. "Move, Caric!"

"NO!" I holler back. "STOP!"

They both stare at me, anger filling their eyes. "Make it quick, Caric!" Hemot growls.

Neither of them are acting quite normal. They seem to have their wits back, but they're extremely emotional.

"Marleet didn't wander off," I say calmly.

Hemot frowns. "Where is she?"

"I don't know. I can explain. Please sit and calm down a bit."

"No!" Ellcia says, coming up to me and roughly grabbing my arm hard enough that it actually hurts. "You tell us right now! There will be no calming down until we know everything! What did you do with her?"

"What did I… wait… no, I didn't do anything with her! This isn't my fault." I actually don't believe that. I feel absolutely sick with guilt. Because I couldn't hold her back, she's gone.

"Enough!" I yell. I think I'm about to do something foolish, but I do it anyway. "I'm the leader here. I know what happened, and I can tell you, but I won't until you sit and calm down."

They both stare at me for a few moments longer. Ellcia's grip on my arm hurts. She's using her nails. I don't think she realizes how tight she's holding me. I wouldn't be surprised if she's drawn blood.

"Fine!" Hemot says and plops down on the ground. "Talk!"

"No," I say calmly. "I told you that you also need to calm down. And I need Ellcia to let go of my arm." Turning to her, I add, "You're hurting me."

She looks surprised and lets go. I check my arm, and while there is no blood, she nearly broke the skin.

She sits down, and I take a moment and get them some food and water. They eat like they're starving and gulp down the water. I try to put some thoughts together, but in the end, I just decide to figure it out as I go.

When I decide it's time to speak, I come to grips with the fact that figuring it out as I go is a foolish way to approach it. They finish their food, wipe their mouths, and look at me expectantly.

"Okay," I begin. "First of all, you're probably not going to believe me, but neither of you are acting normal. So… um… try to control your reactions. You're both acting strange."

Hemot nods slowly at me as if he's really taking it in. Ellcia looks at me with suspicion but doesn't say anything.

I continue. "Yesterday, when we went into the cave to get away from those soldiers, we came across a Spellcaster."

They both look at me like I'm crazy. I have to admit, saying it out loud sounds crazy to me. Spellcasters are kind of the stuff of stories and legends. I had, until yesterday, believed there weren't any living Spellcasters anymore.

"He put the three of you, including Ma-leet, under a spell of some kind," I explain.

Ellcia turns her head just slightly and asks, "And why didn't he put you under a spell?"

I can hear the doubt in her voice. She doesn't really believe me. I feel irritated by that. I've never lied to Ellcia. If the Spellcaster was right and if Ellcia spoke the truth, she loves me. If she loves me, shouldn't she believe me?

"My armor. My armor seemed to protect me from the spell, or enchantment, or whatever it was. But you guys... it made the three of you all weird and happy, and you all took off your packs, cloaks, and weapons."

I see Hemot's eyes shift briefly over to Marleet's pack, cloak, and weapons, laying on the floor of the cave. He doesn't say anything about Marleet's possessions, but he does ask, "Is that all we took off?"

I roll my eyes. "Yes, Hemot, you all remained fully clothed."

I see both Hemot and Ellcia relax a little.

"He wanted Marleet. He seemed to know she was coming, and he had a plan for her. He didn't know the rest of us. In fact, he had to ask my name."

"You didn't tell him, did you?" Ellcia asks with panic in her voice. "You never know what he can do with your name!"

"No. I didn't tell him, but he figured out my name was Draydon. I didn't tell him the name I go by, but..." I glance over at Hemot for a moment and then add, "It's not anyone's fault. You were both under the spell... Hemot just told him my name."

Ellcia's eyes flash with anger at Hemot for a moment, but then she calms down and appears to understand. She turns back to me and asks, "And what of Marleet?"

"He made her come to him, then put his hand on her forehead. I think he put some other spell on her, then she walked through the wall."

"You didn't try to stop her?" Hemot hisses. "Why did you just let her go?"

I feel anger rush over me, and I holler back, "What makes you think I just let her go?"

Hemot jumps to his feet and screams back, "Well, I wouldn't think she could just walk away if you stood in her way. You're the biggest of the four of us, Caric! You'd be able to hold her with one arm! There's no way she could have gotten away from you!"

I feel my eyes well up with tears, and I drop my head forward. I choke out the words, "I tried," but I don't think it was understood.

"You what?" Hemot yells. I've never seen him angry like this before.

"I…" Through the tears I say, "I'm sorry, Hemot. I'm sorry Ellcia. I tried. I tried with everything I had. But the Spellcaster made me let her go."

I break into heavy sobs, and Ellcia comes and sits next to me. She's crying as well.

Hemot's voice comes through quietly, but filled with rage and hatred. "You should have tried harder, Caric. I don't see how she could have gotten away from you. She can barely hold her sword. She doesn't have enough strength to overpower you!"

I shake my head. "No, she didn't overpower me."

"You said the enchantments didn't work on you," Hemot growls. "How did the Spellcaster make you let her go?"

I raise my head and meet his eyes. When he sees my face and the tears, his expression softens somewhat, but not completely. "I said his enchantments didn't work on me. I didn't say that they didn't work on you and Ellcia."

"We overpowered you?" he asks.

"No," I say, shaking my head. Looking right at Hemot, I explain, "He commanded you to kill Ellcia!" When I say that, I feel Ellcia tense up next to me. "You went for her, and I had to hold you back. I didn't have the strength to hold both you and Marleet. With every lunge, you got closer and closer to Ellcia's neck with your knife—and she just stood there, waiting for it. I had to make a choice. It was either hold on to Marleet, and watch you kill Ellcia, or stop you and hope we could save Marleet later."

Hemot stands there, mouth open, staring at me. He looks like he's about to say something, then he stops. He tries again, but then stops again. I can see him working through it all. He's still angry, but he knows I had no choice.

"There was no other way?" he asks in a quiet voice. "I was really trying to kill Ellcia, and there was no other way to stop me?"

I shake my head. "I held you back as long as I could, but you kept lunging for her. Your knife… it… you almost got her. A few more seconds, and she'd be dead. I couldn't let you go until after the Spellcaster had sent Marleet away and then left himself."

Hemot sits down and stares at the smoldering fire. He picks up a stick and pokes it a couple times, his face unreadable in the dim light of the cave.

I glance over at Ellcia. She's pulled away from me and has her arms wrapped around herself. She looks traumatized. I try to put my hand on her shoulder, and she pulls away.

Her pulling away makes me angry. I don't think she has any right to be mad at me. I didn't do anything wrong. I feel like I blew it, and I feel like it's all my fault… and I really do think I hate myself now… but I actually think I did the right thing. Even though I feel so guilty.

I'm about to tell her all that when I realize something. She might not be mad at me. Maybe she's upset because I had to save her. Maybe she feels guilty, like it's her fault.

I open my mouth to try to help her feel better, but then I close it again. I have no idea what to say.

Breaking the silence, Hemot asks, "Do you know where he sent her?"

I shake my head again. "No. He just told me that he had something for her to do. He said when she was done, she might come find us." I take a deep breath and add, "He said she could be anywhere in the world."

In a quiet voice, Hemot asks, "You think she'll come find us?"

I nod. "I don't know for sure, but I think Marleet will do everything she can to reach us as soon as she's able. Maybe we'll even find her."

Hemot smiles at that. It seems to give him hope.

"And…" I begin, but stop.

"And what?" he asks.

"When we were there with the Spellcaster, he said he could tell that Marleet loved you."

Hemot just stares at me. He looks awkward, then laughs, then frowns, then looks awkward again.

"How could he tell what she felt?"

"He said he could tell from the way she was acting that she loved you. And he could tell how you feel about her."

Hemot stares at the floor, and his face breaks out in a grin. In a quiet voice, he says, "I always liked her. I just didn't think someone like her would ever like me." He then smiles at me and asks, "How could he tell?"

"From the way she held onto you. And he could tell how you feel from the way you held her."

Hemot's smile grows even bigger, and he stands up. "Then we know what we need to do. We need to find Marleet!" He moves for his pack, but then stops. "Wait. What were you and Ellcia doing in the Spellcaster's cave? Were you guys holding each other?"

I look at Ellcia, and she looks absolutely horrified. "Well—" I pause, trying to come up with something witty to say to avoid the awkward truth. "I think that's something I'd only tell if Ellcia asked me."

Ellcia looks relieved and smiles weakly at me. I spend a lot of time in life feeling awkward. At least this response makes me feel less awkward.

Hemot smiles and then grabs his pack. "When do we leave?"

I clear my head for a moment. We've just been through a lot, and I'm still worried about Ellcia. I think she might feel guilty about what I had to do. But at the moment, we need to focus.

"We're going to have to be careful. There are likely scouts all over this mountain. If they catch us, they'll take us right back to Frindor. We also need to figure out for sure where we're going."

Hemot plops down. "Well, we need to go wherever Marleet has been sent!"

I nod, but I don't respond to his comment. We have no idea where she is. "Here are our options. We can just try to make it in the wild. That doesn't sound like fun to me. And I would rather do that with Rulf around."

"I learned a lot from him," Hemot says. "But I still don't know enough to keep us alive."

"We could also go to the cities," I say, but then something about that jogs my memory. "Wait, didn't Marleet's dad say we were supposed to find his friends?"

Ellcia nods. "He did. Unfortunately, only Marleet knew where they are. We hadn't gotten far enough through our escape plan for Marleet to tell us where we were going."

"Okay." I stare at the smoldering remains of the fire. "So, there are the four cities. There's Rainer, but I think it's called the City of Thieves for a reason. We might not want to end up there." Ellcia shakes her head. I'm guessing she thinks Rainer is a bad idea too. "There's also Leito, but I would think the Rebels will be heavily involved in that city since it's the closest to the mountain hideout. If we go there, I don't think it'll be long before we're caught. We could go to Morgin City, but that's where we were supposed to go originally. It's always possible the Regent might have sent men there to look for us."

"So, for cities, that leaves Haner," Hemot says.

I nod. "We could also head back toward Sevord."

Both of them shake their heads. I agree with them, so I announce, "Then, we head to Haner."

"Let's go get Marleet!" Hemot says, and Ellcia nods.

"Wait." I want them both to have hope. But there's absolutely no reason to think she's in Haner as opposed to anywhere else. "I don't know…" I begin to say, but Ellcia cuts me off.

"We're going to Haner to get Marleet!" she says with an air of finality to her voice.

I nod my head slowly. "Okay, so we're going to need to split up Marleet's stuff."

"Wait!" Hemot yells. "She's going to need it when we find her. We can't just split up everything and take it as our own!"

"No," I say, putting my hands up. "I mean, we're going to have to split it up, so we can carry it. And the food she has is not likely something we should save until we find her. It might take us a bit to track her down, and the food might go bad. We need to eat it and any of the other really perishable food. But, Hemot! There's no way we're just taking her stuff!"

I don't think I want to spend every moment dancing around the topic of Marleet with Hemot, but at least for now, he seems somewhat satisfied.

We pack up everything and split Marleet's supplies among us. I'm surprised to find a lot of coins in amongst her supplies, but then I gather that her parents wouldn't send her away without money to buy food and more. Hemot insists on taking her empty pack, her sword, her knife, and her cloak. He stuffs what he can inside his already bulging pack and then straps the rest to the outside. I'm sure he's going to struggle with all the extra weight, but he refuses to spread those specific things around.

When we're finished, we go to the cave opening. We can't see any movement anywhere around, so we set out. My plan is to head west until we find the small path that goes north and south, connecting the mining villages. We'll then head north until we reach the road to Haner and then head west again.

It was a full six-day journey from the city to the mining village when we came this way before. I don't think we have quite as far to go since we've come out of the mountains a little to the north of where we had entered, but I doubt we've saved much time. We also have the problem of not having Rulf with us. He pushed us to keep moving all the time. If I can't keep Hemot moving, it might take us weeks.

As we set out, I see Hemot is not going to be a problem. He seems driven to get to Haner as quickly as possible.

"We can't move that fast," Ellcia hollers.

"But we have to get there right away!" Hemot yells back.

Hemot and Ellcia argue back and forth for a few minutes as the three of us continue to jog along, but I just ignore it. Those two have never really gotten along.

At the moment, I have other things on my mind. I've never done much actual "leading". I think I was officially the leader of our group of three in the castle in our work as servants, but Hemot never really listened to me, and I was always too uncomfortable to order Ellcia around. I never seriously tried for fear that it would turn out poorly.

But regardless of all that, I'm now trying to lead these two to Haner. I don't know what I should be thinking about or planning. I expect there are details I should already have worked out. I can't really base it on what Rulf told me. He never really communicated with us at all. He just did stuff.

I think about what Rulf did for a moment. He pointed the way to go. So, I decide that what I need to do is to at least know the way. I think I have that figured out already—just find the path and head north, then west.

Rulf also took care of food for us. He caught meat for us every night. That's not something I can do, since I don't know how. Hemot, however, learned a lot from Rulf. That'll also take his mind off stuff. I decide that I'll put him in charge of catching, cleaning, and cooking food for us. As I think about it, I realize that he should probably teach us as well.

It hits me that Rulf also paid attention to our surroundings and kept an eye out for danger. I'll have to make sure I do that, or maybe I could make Ellcia the lookout. I shake my head at that thought. It would be best if we were all looking out for danger. One of us might spot something the others don't.

For the moment, I'll start watching. Hemot and Ellcia are still arguing, and I think they're enjoying themselves, so I leave them to it.

I turn and look around. We're off the actual mountain, which is a big relief, but we haven't come across the path just yet. I think we should be there soon, but it's really hard to tell.

The area is certainly beautiful. If I had time, I'd love to just sit down on a rock and take it all in.

Back toward the mining village, I catch sight of the tri-peak mountain. It's one of the more impressive mountains in the area. It's taller than most, and the three peaks make it stand out.

As I turn back to continue on my way, I catch a glimpse of something that doesn't look right. I'm not sure, but I think I see the movement of a shadow. It's late-morning, which means the sun is just peaking past the mountains. There wouldn't be reflection off armor from this angle, but I can see shadows.

Ellcia and Hemot are still moving quite fast, but I walk backwards for a bit. I know that means I'll fall behind, but I need to see. At first… nothing. I'm not really sure where on the mountain I saw it, but then I catch it again. Out from behind a large outcropping of rocks, I see a series of soldiers stream by. Only a few are visible at a time, but there are a lot of them. They're streaming down the mountain, and I can only assume they're after us.

I turn back around and pick up speed. Although Ellcia and Hemot are moving quickly, they're still only moving at a fast hike. I run as hard as I can and catch up. "Time to move! I see soldiers back there!"

They immediately drop their argument and race forward. We weave our way through the boulders and down into dips in the ground and out again as we continue our way west.

"Have they seen us yet?" Ellcia calls out.

"I don't know. I just saw them streaming down the mountain. There are a lot of them. Let's try to stay out of sight, if we can."

We run along, doing our best to keep behind rocks and not run across open areas. When we had started out on our journey from Sevord, we had spent much of our time running. It had been a grueling experience, but it helped to build some endurance. Now, after spending days in the caves, I feel like we still have our endurance, but we're also well rested.

The soldiers may have trained a lot in the caves, but they didn't go very far. A wave of excitement passes through me as I realize that even if they do spot us, they'll never keep up with us on foot.

We run on throughout the rest of the morning. By the time we even think about taking a break, the sun has moved along past us.

I figure it's somewhere around two in the afternoon when I call a halt, and we hide behind a large rock. We peer out and scan the side of the mountain. At first, we don't see anything, but after a bit I catch a glimpse of some movement.

I point to the southeast. "Over there."

Ellcia and Hemot stare off in that direction for a bit until the soldiers come into sight again. "Are they closer than when you saw them earlier?" Ellcia asks.

I shake my head. "No, they seem to have fallen behind. I don't think they know we're here. I think they're just scouting out the area."

"Then we don't have to run," Hemot says.

I consider that for a second. "We still need to move fast. We want to get far away from them. Hopefully, we can get out of the area before they see us."

We push on, but not as hard as before. I feel like we have the energy to keep moving fast, but we might as well save our strength for when we need it.

The ground ahead slopes off quite steeply, for which I'm happy. As we start down, I glance back, and I can't see the soldiers at all. Maybe we'll be out of sight for a while.

"Why haven't we found the path yet?" Ellcia asks.

"I think we'll come to it soon," I say. I think the path veered toward the mountain a bit before we found the mining town. It's just farther from the mountains at this point.

We reach the bottom of the decline, and the ground ahead rises quite steeply. The ground on the incline is rocky enough that I'm afraid we won't be able to keep our footing. I'm also concerned that if we climb that hill, we'll be visible again to the soldiers.

"Let's head north," I say, and point to the right. "We'll move along the bottom of the valley as long as we can, then head west again."

Ellcia nods. "Good thinking. That'll keep us out of sight."

I feel pretty happy to find Ellcia's pleased with my decision and thinking the same thing as me. The thought of being pushed into leading our little group annoyed me at first back at the castle, but I've grown to like the idea. I'm hoping I can learn to be good at it.

It also makes me think that maybe she's not too mad at me for what I had to do with Marleet. The now familiar shame and disgust at myself washes over me, but I shake my head to clear the thoughts. That's not the way forward—not at all. I can't live my life trying to make the right decisions, then hating myself for what I can't control.

I grit my teeth and decide not to let those thoughts destroy me. Before they can take root in my heart, I reject them. What I did, I did because I love Ellcia, and I love Marleet. I was about to lose both, one to death, and the other to the Spellcaster. Instead, the decision I made was to protect the one and save the other, although at a later time.

And I will find a way to save her, if I can. All of us will.

We continue north through our little valley for nearly an hour before we come across a gentle slope leading up and to the west.

We follow the slope. Even though it's not steep, it's not the easiest route, as the ground is covered in shale and loose stones. We find it exhausting to try to keep our footing, but we manage to get to the top.

"Wow!" Hemot gasps. "I think that was more exhausting than anything since we entered the Talic Region."

I nod in reply as I struggle to catch my breath. I turn around and scan the hills behind us while Ellcia sits down on a large boulder nearby and looks back behind us.

"I don't see anyone following us," she says.

I look over the hills once again and agree with her. We might have beaten the patrols.

Once we catch our breath, we continue west. It's not long before we come across the path and head north. Now and then, Hemot points out landmarks that he remembers from the journey through the area. None of it looks familiar to me, but Ellcia seems to remember a few spots.

We find a small grove of trees near the end of the day, and once we have our campsite, Hemot takes us both with him to learn how to set traps. I wish I was a faster learner with that kind of thing. Ellcia picks it up okay, but Hemot tells us that it took him a while to learn it.

We head back to our little campsite and start a small fire. It's cool enough that we need the fire to keep us warm until we climb into our blankets. Despite all that's happened, I'm grateful to be outside, sleeping in a forest again.

It's not long before we're all asleep.

6

The Journey to Haner

When we come across the body of the giant, I'm surprised to see nothing has changed. I still don't know much of what goes on in the countryside as I've spent most of my life in the city, but I thought vultures came down and ate dead things. The giant's body, however, looks untouched.

The skin is a little more gray than it had been when she'd been alive, but aside from that, she looks as if we... or I... just killed her. The sight brings back all the old feelings of guilt and remorse mixed with pride that I took down a giant.

I don't like that combination of feelings.

I turn my head away, and we move on. Aside from a quiet, "There she is..." from Ellcia, neither of the others say anything.

We disappear quickly over the other side of the rise and down into the small valley, and then up the other side. The way is slow going. Hemot's earlier speed is gone today, but he's still moving fast—faster than we had typically moved with Rulf. At this rate, we'll either get to Haner in less than six days, or we'll collapse from exhaustion.

We continue for the rest of the day and into the next. When we eventually reach the path heading west to Haner, it's late in the day. We have trouble finding a decent place to sleep, so we continue on until well after dark. In the light of the moon, we find a cave, do our best to make sure it's unoccupied, and settle in for the night.

The next morning, we realize our mistake. Hemot didn't set any traps, so we don't have a fresh supply of food. If we do that too often, we'll go through more of our supplies than expected. I just hope we reach Haner before we run out.

We set out on our journey, and in time we leave the foothills and enter the plains. The way is much easier once we're away from the mountains. The scenery is far more boring out in the plains of the Talic Region, but since it's all relatively flat and the road is decent, the traveling is good.

We make good time, staying in little forests at night and walking close together in case the Shaloomd find us. They can swoop down, pick up someone, and carry them away, but they don't approach unless someone small walks alone. At the moment, Ellcia is the smallest among us, and Hemot and I keep her between us.

The Shaloomd rarely come this far east, but that doesn't mean they can't. Because of the danger, we stick to the forests at night and keep close together with our eyes on the skies during the day.

By late morning on the ninth day since escaping from the mountain, we reach Haner. We caught sight of it the evening before, but it was still many hours away.

When we approach the gate, it's open. We walk through under the inattentive gaze of six or seven guards.

Back in Sevord, you could not enter or leave the city without special papers. Here, it just seems that anyone can walk in and out. That's just as well with me. I've never been that happy around soldiers—even when they're nice to me.

I think we're going to make it through without a problem, when one of the guards seems to wake up and recognizes me.

"Oy!" he calls out.

I turn to him, unsure on what the proper response to that might be. I nod and give a polite, "Oy," back.

He looks confused for a moment but manages to recover. "You were the guy who saw the Talic Wolf a few weeks back, right? I remember you."

I nod, my shoulders and back have tensed. I don't know what to expect from these guards. The castle guards back in Sevord were always good to me and my friends because we were servants in the castle, but I knew that they could be quite cruel to other people. The way I got through the gates in Haner the last time was to feed the man's desire for gossip.

"That was me!" I say with confidence. "What happened to it? The last I saw, the soldiers were trying to take it down."

"Ah," the guard says, relaxing a little. Gossip was what soldiers looked for most. "Those beasts are difficult to kill. I never saw it myself—on duty all day, you know?—but it took the guys until dark to drive it away. My cousin was one of them. He got bit somethin' fierce. It's only healin' now. Thought he'd lose his arm, for sure."

I grimace at that. "Those things are nasty. Run-ins with them are a big problem."

I'm just about to turn away and head into the city when the guy stops me. He grabs my arm and steps in front of me. He's short, balding, and looks like he's been on the receiving end of a fist or two.

"The thing is," the soldier says with a frown, "that beastie… he was lookin' for someone." His eyes search mine as he stares hard at me.

"Yah, I heard that!" I decide to pretend like I have nothing to hide. "It sounded like the wolf was after someone—demanding to know where the person was. Called him the 'prissing' or the 'tinsling' or something. You know what that's about?"

The man nods slowly. "He was callin' for the princelin'."

I nod and say, "Ahh… that makes more sense than tinsling," but then I let confusion fill my face. I feel like I'm one step away from getting arrested or something, although I don't know what the guard thinks I've done. "But if he was after the princeling… who could that be?" I let my eyes widen in shock and ask, "Do you think he was after Prince Roran? Has he been found?"

The guard doesn't budge, and I notice the other guards begin to circle around me.

"No," the man says, "not as far as any of us guys know, but we're often the last to find out, right, boys?"

The men have us completely surrounded by this point. They don't exactly look angry, but they appear quite curious.

"Here's the thing," the guard says, stepping a little closer. "We started chattin' after you left and after we heard all about what the wolf was screamin'. We thought about how you were anxious to get out of the city while that thing was searching for the princelin'."

"Well," I say, "I think everyone wanted to leave the city when that thing was around." I add a bit of a laugh, and some of the guards join in.

"I get that." The guard steps even closer. "But we got chattin' about it. And we started to piece it together. The Talic Wolf was a lookin' for the princelin'—which means he had met the prince. I found out that you actually showed up with that beastie on your tail—a buddy of mine described someone like you comin' in the southern gate the day before. The day after you arrive, the thing gets in and is a searchin' for the princelin', and then you take off." He pauses for a moment and looks at his friends. "We think you're Prince Roran."

I hesitate for a moment and just stare at him for a bit, glancing at the other men, then back at the guy in front of me.

"And if I am Prince Roran? What then?"

The man's eyes grow large, and he steps back. "ARE YOU?"

"No," I say, "I'm not. But what if I am? What will you do?"

The man looks confused for a moment, as if that thought had never crossed his mind. "Well, I guess we'd take you to Sevord to be crowned king."

The other men nod and add their agreement. I don't think there's any deception there. They're not trying to threaten us; they're just used to pushing people around.

"Well," I say, "I'm sorry to tell you that I'm not Prince Roran."

The man leans in, and his eyes narrow. When he speaks, his voice comes out both intense and quite slow. "Are you sure?"

"Yes," I say, just as slowly as the man.

"Are you willing to swear it?" he asks.

"I swear that I am not Prince Roran."

"No, no, no," the man says as he shakes his head. I hear the others grumbling all around us. "I mean, will you swear on the Raker itself?"

I smile. Hopefully, this will satisfy them. "I swear on the Raker itself that I am not Prince Roran." Maybe now we can finally move on.

The man shakes his head again. "NO! You can't just say that. I mean, will you swear on the actual Raker?"

"I don't know what this Raker is," I say, shaking my head.

"It's somethin' Lord Hillbin has."

Lord Hillbin... I know that name. As far as I can remember, I think he might be the Lord who's over Haner.

The guard continues. "You place your hand on it, the Raker, swear whatever it is you're goin' to swear, and if you're speakin' the truth, nothin' happens."

"What happens if you lie?" I see Ellcia and Hemot shift on their feet on either side of me. They're pretty nervous.

"Well," the man says, "it's called the Raker because it... well... if you lie, it... well... imagine someone takin' a steel rake... you know... the kind you use with leaves?"

I nod and answer slowly, "Yes, I know the kind."

"Well," he says, stepping forward a little, "if you lie... it's like an invisible rake comes along and rakes your entire body, over and over. It usually takes the better part of a day, but it doesn't matter where you go, the invisible rake just keeps doin' its thing. And you die."

I shake my head. "This does not sound like something I want to see."

"No," he says, "then don't lie."

He grabs my arm and pulls me into the city. I think about resisting, but running away from this man would make me and my friends fugitives in the very city in which we were hoping to hide out.

As we move, I decide to try something else. "Hey, just thinking this through."

The man looks up at me with a look that says he's never truly thought anything through in his life. "Yeah?"

A quick look back lets me know Ellcia and Hemot are keeping pace behind us with worried looks on their faces.

Maybe I can talk our way out of this. "Well, there are two options." I find it hard to collect my thoughts as I'm dragged along, but I say, "I'm either Prince Roran, or I'm not."

"Right!" he says, still pulling me down the street. He's surprisingly strong. "That's why I'm takin' you to Lord Hillbin. We'll find out the truth."

"But I think there's something you're not considering." I would just go with the man, but I really don't want the attention of meeting the Lord of the city. I'd much rather be someone no one knows.

"What's that?" the man asks, finally coming to a halt.

I glance back at Ellcia and Hemot. Hemot looks nervous, and Ellcia looks terrified.

I explain in a whisper. "Well, if I am Prince Roran, why do you think I'd deny it?"

"Don't know."

"Well, it would likely mean I don't want anyone to know who I am."

The man nods his head, but he's clearly not getting it.

"So, if you take me there, and I turn out to be Prince Roran, you'll end up exposing your Prince, and he won't be happy with you."

The man nods his head again. I'm even more confident now that he's not getting any of this.

"So, that's a bad thing, right? Your future king might want to remain hidden for the time being. I don't think you'll want to be the one to reveal his secret."

"So…" the man says, staring intently into my eyes, "you're saying you are the Prince?"

"No, I'm not Prince Roran, but I'm saying that since you're trying to find out if I am, you might not want to do that since if I am, then I won't be happy with you. You'll have your future King as an enemy."

"But… you're not the Prince."

"No."

"Then," he says slowly, "it won't matter, because I'm okay if you're my enemy if you're not goin' to be King."

"But then, there's no point in taking me," I say, "because there's nothing to be gained. So, if I am the Prince, you'll gain an enemy. If I'm not the Prince, you'll just look like a fool before Lord Hillbin for bringing someone to him who is not the Prince."

The man looks at me for another minute, then slowly begins nodding his head. When he speaks, he says, "Right! I agree! I should definitely take you to Lord Hillbin." He then marches on, pulling me behind.

"Wait, no, that's not what I meant," but the man just ignores me. His grip is like iron on my arm.

We wander through the streets with most people stepping far out of the way. If we had wanted to go unnoticed in the city, that hope has died. Everyone stares as we move through the streets.

Shortly before we reach Lord Hillbin's residence, we come across a crowd which doesn't part. The guard pushes his way through and as he calls out, "Guard coming through. Possible Prince Roran here to see Lord Hillbin. Possible Prince Roran here."

Anyone who had not been staring before was now entirely focused on me. Some even reach out and touch my arm, and the occasional man or woman gives a little bow or curtsy.

"I'm not Prince Roran," I call out, but no one seems to hear.

When we reach the Lord's residence, two guards stand in our way. The guard pulling me simply waves. "Just someone to run through the Raker."

The guards step aside with only a nod.

"Wait, what do you mean, 'run through the Raker'?" I holler. "That sounds horrible!"

"Oh, it's just a saying," the guard says as he pulls me along.

"That's a horrible saying! Who came up with that?"

I look back and see the guards have refused entry to Hemot and Ellcia. I call back, "They're with me!"

The guards step aside, and I just barely hear one of them say, "Oh, let them through. More for the Raker."

"No," I holler back, "I'm the only one for the Raker. I mean, I don't think I need to go through the Raker, but they certainly don't." Under my breath, I add, "Oh… never mind."

I shake my head, wondering why I care what any of these people say. I feel like I'm in two different conversations—maybe two different worlds.

We continue down a fairly nice hallway. It's nothing compared to the palace, but far nicer than anything I've seen since leaving Sevord. The floors are clean, which I feel is a positive, and made of granite. The walls are wood and have some tapestries and the occasional painting, but it's clear that this is all far below the quality and value of the rooms and hallways of the castle.

We pass a window with a crooked curtain, and I hear Hemot call out to the guard, "I can help you with your curtain issue there."

I shake my head. He was convinced that he was in charge of curtains in the castle. Even if that had been true, he certainly never did much with them.

I see a stairway leading up to a second floor. As we pass it, a quick glance up lets me know that the upstairs is not for receiving guests. I see a poorly cared for wall at the top and what looks like crates that haven't even been opened yet. Just storage. This place is so different from the castle.

At the end of the hallway, we enter a large room, which appears to be a receiving room for guests. There are chairs, as well as a solid wood table, an area with a counter and stools which would likely be used for refreshments, and lots of light. On the other side of the room is a doorway. We head to that and enter.

The room on the other side of the large doors is massive. It's still small compared to some of the ballrooms in the castle, but it's quite big. I figure they could have a few hundred guests in here with room for dancing and more. On the far side, sitting at a small desk, is a man. Another man stands near him with some parchment, and it looks like he's taking notes from the man sitting down.

When we enter, the man behind the desk stands up… or… I think he stands up. He's not much taller when he stands than when he's sitting. He hurries over to us, waving the other man away.

"Ahh, what do we have here? Did they do something wrong? Do we need to have a hanging? Or did they save someone from certain peril? I have some medals around somewhere. Should we call a celebration? We haven't had one for months, and I do so love a good celebration."

His grin stretches a little too far across his face. He's short… round… and moves like he can't wait to get somewhere. As I stare at him, I realize that until that day, I had never quite understood what the word "portly" meant.

This man… is portly.

"Uh, yes," the guard says.

Lord Portly gives the guard a confused look. The guard merely stares back at him.

"What are they here for, um… your name?" Lord Portly asks.

"My name is Lumber, Lord Hillbin."

"Ahh, yes, Lumber. I remember you," portly Hillbin says, although I'm pretty sure from his expression that he has no idea who the man is. "How are you? It's been a while. How are the wife and kids?"

"Uh, never married, Lord Hillbin."

"Right," Hillbin says, the smile slowly disappearing off his face. "I must have you confused with another guard."

"Yes, Lord Hillbin."

"And what are these fine young people here for?"

"I think this one," Lumber says, pushing me forward, "might be Prince Roran."

Lord Hillbin's eyes bulge, and for a second, I wonder if he's about to keel over and die. I've never seen a portly man's eyes do such a thing. Maybe it's a portly characteristic.

"Your... Your Majesty," Lord Hillbin says, and bows before me.

The last thing I want now is to be accused of impersonating the Prince. "No, Lord Hillbin, I'm not Prince Roran. Lumber here thinks I might be the Prince, but I'm not."

"I thought maybe we could use the Raker," Lumber explains.

"Oh, right!" Hillbin says. He turns and claps twice, and the man I saw earlier runs into the room. "Clarice, please fetch me the Raker."

"Yes, Lord Hillbin," Clarice says, and scurries away.

Lord Hillbin turns back to me and asks, "And if you are not the Prince, who are you?"

I'm about to make up a name when I realize that he might ask me the same question later when I have the Raker. I don't particularly want to lie while holding that thing.

"My name's Caric, Lord Hillbin." A wave of panic comes over me. I don't know if the Raker will understand that my name is Caric, even though my actual name is Draydon. Which one should I have given?

Lord Hillbin nods. "That is too bad."

I shake my head. "What's too bad?"

"I was hoping you were actually the Prince." He pauses and adds a portly frown to his portly face.

I try to force myself to stop thinking about the word portly. It's going to slip out if I'm not careful.

"I knew the royal family quite well. You don't actually look like King Hartor at all, though. You look more like his brother, General Geran."

He remains silent and examines my face for quite some time. I see sadness there, and longing. Finally, he adds, "But alas, those days are gone."

I almost smile at the thought that I look like my father. It makes me feel close to him, even though I barely remember him. "What would you do if you found out I was the Prince?"

Portly Hillbin's eyes flick quickly to the guard standing by before he says, "Well, if you were the Prince, we would return you to the Regent, of course!"

"Here it is, Lord Hillbin!" Clarice announces as he enters the room. In his hands, he holds something that I can't quite see clearly as he rushes along.

He hands it to Lord Hillbin, who gives it to me.

"Now," Lord Hillbin says, "Are you a princeling?"

I open my mouth to answer, but then look down at the object in my hand. It looks innocent enough. It's just a bronze statue of a woman in a dress holding what appears to be a flower. If I lie, it's going to kill me… slowly. But I can't answer *that* question. I am a princeling. I'm just not *the* princeling. I end up saying, "I am not Prince Roran."

Nothing happens to me, and Lord Hillbin nods his head. He turns to the guard and smiles. "Thank you, Lumber. I will take it from here."

The guard doesn't move at first. He hesitates before asking, "But sir, we know he isn't the missin' prince, but we don't know if these three are dangerous. I can't leave them here with you when they could be a threat."

I realize I haven't seen any guards inside the residence at all. Though Lumber doesn't seem like the brightest man I've met, he's certainly loyal to Lord Hillbin.

"Oh, I don't think that'll be a problem," Hillbin says, "but just to be sure…" He turns back to me and asks, "Are you or your friends a threat to me at all?"

I shake my head. "No, port…" I catch myself and carefully say, "No, Lord Hillbin."

"There we go!" he says to the guard. "I'll be okay, Lumber. Thank you for your watchful and careful service to the city and to the people of Sevord."

The man bows, finally lets go of my arm, and marches off, back the way we came. A moment later, I hear the door close behind me.

I hand the Raker statue back to Lord Hillbin, but he doesn't take it. Instead, he waves for me to follow as he moves to his desk.

I follow him and Clarice, and a quick glance back lets me know Ellcia and Hemot are close behind. They look worried.

When Lord Hillbin reaches his desk and sits down… or… I figure there's probably a chair back there. He gets a little shorter, at least. When he does what I think might be sitting, he leans back and says, "You didn't answer my question."

I shake my head. "I'm sorry, Lord Hillbin, what question is that?"

"Are you a princeling?" He glances down at the statue in my hand, and his eyebrows quickly raise as if to remind me that I'm still holding the Raker.

"I'm not Prince Roran," I say, waving the Raker in front of him.

"I agree, young man, but that's not what I asked you."

My heart races, and I glance back at my friends. I hope my face doesn't look as worried as their's or else I'm sure I've given away the answer.

Lord Hillbin leans forward and places both hands on the desk in front of him. "I'm not asking if you are Prince Roran. I think I would recognize him. I knew King Hartor well enough that I was one of the few people who called him Harty. I remember what Prince Roran looked like, and you do not look like him."

I nod. I still don't want to answer the question.

Lord Hillbin continues, "You, however, look more like Prince Geran and Lady Tallia's son. You look a lot like little Prince Draydon, just all grown up."

I remain silent.

"So," Hillbin says, "let me ask you directly, while you're holding the Raker. Are you Prince Draydon?"

I don't feel I have a choice but to answer. I know we could probably overpower the man and his assistant and maybe even get out of here, but I can't attack him for simply asking a question. Plus, it's kind of illegal to do that kind of thing. Even if I'm a Prince, that doesn't give me the right to hurt people.

"Yes," I say quietly.

The man smiles and instantly stands up… I think. He then bows to me and says in a quiet voice, "Welcome to Haner, Your Highness."

Beside me, I hear Clarise say, "Your Highness," and he bows as well.

"Do not worry, Prince Draydon," Hillbin says, still in his quiet voice. "No one will hear us in here. I'm only speaking quietly as a precaution. I know how much danger you are in from the Regent. That usurper will pay for his crimes—one day—but for now, we must be patient." He takes a deep breath. "Are you just passing through the city, or are you planning to stay for a while?"

The relief washes over me, but I'm still a little suspicious. "We were planning on staying here for a little while." I'm hesitant, but I think we can trust the man. "We aren't really sure where to go."

He nods. "The last I had heard, you were with your uncle, General Lirnal. If you're here, you obviously either had a fallout with him, or you had to run. I don't know anything about what's going on right now in the mountain, but I'm doubtful you had a fallout with him. But either way, in the meantime, you are welcome in the city. I can't offer you protection without drawing attention to who you are. I also can't keep you here, as I would need to have a reason for three more people in my residence. With Parthun's close watch on everyone and everything, it would not go unnoticed, nor would the matter be left alone."

"We'll be fine in the city," I say.

He nods. "Then stay in the Horse and Bow on the west side of the city. The owner there is loyal to the throne, and if you need to get out of the city quickly, he will do all he can to help you." He smiles at me and says, "It is good to see you all grown up, young man." As an afterthought, he asks, "Do you need money or anything?"

"No, Lord Hillburn," I say. "Thank you for your kindness."

He nods. "You're welcome! Now, best to get moving before someone gets suspicious and reports your presence." He takes the Raker from my hand and sets it on his desk.

Ellcia speaks up for the first time since we entered Lord Hillbin's residence. She no longer seems as nervous as she had been.

"Lord Hillbin," she begins, "do you know any other friends of the Prince in this city? We are looking for some people whom we were supposed to find, but we don't know who they are."

Lord Hillbin studies her for a few moments. He is quite a short man and looks up, even to Ellcia. After a while, he finally says, "Young lady, I still don't know for sure that I can trust the three of you. I know this young man is Prince Draydon—of that, I have no doubt. I suspect you are Lord Rathar and Lady Shillin's daughter, which would make you the Lady Ellcia. You have your mother's hair, build, looks, and bearing, and your father's eyes and seriousness. Your father had a fire in his eyes which I see in yours. While I trusted your parents completely, I still do not know if I trust you." Turning to Hemot, he adds, "And you must be Hemot. I remember you. No doubt about it." With a smile, he adds, "Your nurse was so upset when she lost you." With a far off look in his eye, he says, "She used to make the most wonderful buttertarts for me when I would visit the castle." His expression turns to deep sadness as his eyes drift to the floor. "So... so very much lost."

He takes a deep breath and sits down in his chair. He seems to collect his thoughts for a moment before speaking again. "These are difficult times. It is hard to know who to trust. I am taking a risk by letting you know of the innkeeper's loyalty—but I know he would be willing to take this chance. If you have been sent by the Regent, my life is already forfeit. I will risk no one else."

"But you can trust us!" Ellcia insisted.

I put my hand on her arm. "It's true, Ellcia," I say softly. "He doesn't know if he can trust us, and he would be a fool to take that risk. We're going to have to make it with what we have." Turning to Lord Hillbin, I say in as formal a tone as I can manage, "Thank you for your time, Lord Hillbin. We are honored by your service to the kingdom."

Lord Hillbin smiles at me and says, "I wish you good travels."

Before we go, Hemot asks, "Is Marleet here?"

The man shakes his head. "Who is Marleet, Hemot?"

"She's the daughter of Lord Yune," he explains.

The man gasps. "Their little girl survived? I hadn't known that. Hmm…" He stares off to the side of the room for a moment, then turns back. "I'm sorry. I don't know anything about her."

Hemot's shoulder's slump. From the sound he makes, I think he might be deflating.

We turn and make our way back to the door. Clarice meets us there and opens the door for us. As we walk out, he whispers, "Trust no one. The guard who brought you in is loyal to a fault but is far from intelligent enough to hold his tongue. Do not tell him or anyone anything. If you are loyal to the throne, your lives are at risk. Always."

I thank him, and we move through the doorway.

7

The 'orse and Bo'

Once we're down the hall and out the door, we head west through the city. Without Rulf with us, it's hard to find our way, but judging from the sun and the time of day, we can at least figure out rough directions.

"Wow," Ellcia says. "Lord Hillbin was nice, but there was something about him…" She pauses for just a second. "I can't quite figure out what it is. He was so…"

"Portly?" Hemot suggests.

"That's it!"

I don't bother adding anything but instead just smile.

After about an hour, we catch sight of the wall around the city. We hope we've managed to end up at the west end, and we begin to ask around for the Horse and Bow Inn. At first, no one's either willing to talk to us or able to recollect where the inn might be, but finally we come across an old man, sitting by the side of the road.

"Yah," he says in his shrill and harsh voice, "I know the Horse and Bow! It's not far from here, but you're too far south. You have to head north until you pass the western gate. It's a little after that."

I thank him, and just before moving on, I notice a little bowl by his feet. I hadn't understood that he was begging. I reach into my pocket and pull out a few coins. I don't know how much we'll need, but I figure we can spare a few coppers. I drop them in his bowl, and he smiles at me.

We turn around and head to the north, but just before I leave the area, I glance back. The old man is talking to a group of boys around our age and younger. He's pointing at his pocket—the same pocket on me that I pulled my money from.

And then he points at us.

I let out a sigh, and then hiss, "We need to move!"

We break into a run. The others know by this point to run first, ask questions later.

We do our best to keep the city wall on our left, always within sight. If we do that, I know we'll likely see the gate at some point. Then we'll know we're close to our destination.

But in the meantime, I don't want to face off against those boys.

I glance back and see they're not far behind. They won't try to rob us in the open, so we have to stay on busy streets.

"Let's cut through here!" Hemot says, still unaware of the actual threat.

Before I can stop him, he heads down an alley. He's out of sight in seconds, so we follow. The alley twists to the left and right around buildings which have been built with what looks like no plans and no sense of order. We keep going until we come to a wooden barrier, blocking our path.

I haven't seen the boys behind us for a bit, but I'm sure they're back there. On the other side of the barrier, I hear people on what sounds like a busy street.

"What are we running from?" Ellcia asks.

I look back once again before answering. "Thieves. The old man sent them after us."

She makes a frustrated sound, and I draw my sword. I'm just about to cut through the wall when Ellcia warns, "No, wait. If they see that, they'll want the sword. Word will spread. Boost me up."

I sheath my blade, then give her a boost up and over the wall. She swings her body over the other side but holds at the top with her arms hanging down on my side.

"Do the same for Hemot," she says. "Then we'll pull you up."

I boost Hemot, but when he gets to the top, he swings his legs over on Ellcia's side and catches her with his foot, right in her face. She disappears over the side, and Hemot tumbles after her.

I shake my head as I slowly turn around to face the six boys coming up behind me. Though they're all about my age or younger and most of them are smaller than me, I'm well out of my league. Everyone knows a castle boy can't hold his own against a kid who's lived his life on the streets.

"Nice clothes," the one boy says. He's not the biggest, but from the way they stand, he's clearly in charge. "Nice pack too. The scabbard looks kind of beat up, so the sword's probably not much to speak of, but it'll get us a silver or two, I expect."

"Go away," I say with as much confidence as I can.

"You got it, your lordship," the boy says, and the others laugh. "However, we want everything of value. You either hand it over, or we take it." His smile grows larger. "When I say everything of value, I do mean everything. Drop the pack, the leather armor, the weapons, the clothes… it all. Then we'll take it and leave you as you are. If you resist, we'll beat you, then take it all anyway. Your choice."

My mouth drops open. My hands grow all clammy, my heart races, and I struggle to control my breathing. I have to force my shoulders to relax, as I fear if I don't, I won't be able to move tomorrow. I go through every thought from the fear of losing my sword to horror at being found naked by Ellcia and Hemot, then having to streak through the city to the Horse and Bow.

But a moment later, I smile. I'm certainly scared, but I come to grips with something.

I've been running my whole life.

I acted as though I liked my life in the castle, but truthfully, it was safe.

I ran from danger by hiding in the castle.

I ran from Rulf on the street.

I ran from Captain Tilbur.

And I've been running ever since I left Sevord.

I no longer want to run.

It's time to be a Prince. It's time to be a leader. It's time to be a soldier in the King's army.

I unbuckle my pack and drop it to the ground. The boys all laugh. I'm guessing they think I'm giving them what they want. I hear Hemot and Ellcia on the other side of the wall. They're looking around for something to climb on to get to the top. It sounds like they're trying to boost one another up, but they're arguing over how it isn't supposed to go.

"Now the rest of it," the boy says.

I stretch my shoulders in a dramatic way, make eye contact with the boy who appears to be in charge, and say, "Young man, it's time you learn to pick your fights with a little more wisdom."

I draw my sword and hold it before me. I notice in that moment that after all Rulf's training and my time in the mountain, I'm holding the sword in a different way than I did when I first left the castle.

All those weeks ago, I held the sword like I didn't know if it would turn around and attack me. Now I hold it like it's an extension of my arm. My muscles are strong, and the sword holds steady in my hand.

I take a step forward and ask casually, "Which one will die first?" I make eye contact with one of the boys just to the right and a little back from the one in charge. "You."

"Me?" he says. His voice shakes a little.

"You," I say. "You will die first."

I then point with my sword to another boy and say, "You, second." Then a third, and fourth, and fifth. Finally, I point at the boy in front. "I'll kill you last. I can see you are the leader of this band of miscreants. You'll die knowing that you led them to their deaths."

I stretch my shoulders again in that same dramatic way and start forward with my eyes on the first boy I marked for death.

Before I can take a second step, he's running for his life. In another step, the other boys are all following after him. In seconds, the only boy left is the one in charge.

He hasn't moved, but his expression has changed. The color has mostly drained from his face, and his eyes are wide.

I raise my sword up to his throat but keep it back enough so as to not cut him. My eyes bore into his own.

"Well, my friend," I say, my voice steady and calm, "I see two paths for you. One is forward, and that path will cost you your head. The other path is behind you." I pause for a moment, then say, "You'll notice your friends are still alive."

The boy stumbles back a few steps before he turns and runs for his life. I feel surprisingly relaxed. I certainly didn't want to hurt them, but I no doubt would have, had they tried to fight me.

"Caric!"

I turn around, and Hemot is hanging his arms over the wall. He turns back and hollers, "I'm trying to move fast. Why don't you try doing this?"

I faintly hear Ellcia say, "I told you I'd rather do it!"

"Too bad," Hemot says. "You can't lift him."

"I'm lifting you," Ellcia growls.

Before they can argue too much more, I run to my pack and pull it on. I grab Hemot's hand, and he slowly lifts me upward as I help by pushing off with any foothold I can find. When I reach the top of the wall, I heave myself over, and in another moment, I'm on the ground on the other side.

Ellcia comes in and grabs my arm. I can't help but remember that she would have wrapped her arms around me in times past. She's a lot more standoffish since the whole incident with the wizard.

"Are you okay? What about the thieves?"

"I'm fine. No worry about the thieves. We need to find the inn."

I turn and scan the area, and my eyes catch sight of the large west gate standing open a short distance away. The inn is close by.

We move north and search the streets. After another fifteen minutes, we come across a rundown inn with a sign that reads, "orse and bo". On the ground, below the sign, is what looks like the missing letters.

We climb the few steps to the door, and I pull it open. On the other side, we're instantly hit with the wonderful smell of cooked food mixed with an unpleasant aroma of far too much sweat.

I step in with the others right behind me and wait for my eyes to adjust to the darkness. Common rooms of inns are notoriously dark. There are always windows, but they're either mostly covered in curtains or dirt.

When I can see again, I notice there are about a dozen men and women in the room. Most are seated at tables or the bar. The man behind the counter wipes a glass, but it looks like he's not actually cleaning it; he's just keeping his hands busy.

"Welco'," he calls out to us, "to the 'orse and bo'."

I stare at him for a moment. I don't know if that's a joke due to the sign out front, or if someone knocked those letters off because that's the way he speaks, or if it's just coincidence.

"Can I ge' ya anythi' to ea' or drin'," he asks.

I'm not sure I've ever heard his accent before. Come to think of it, I'm not sure it is an accent. It just sounds like he can't be bothered to finish most of his words.

"We'd li' the bigges' mea' you can gi' us!" Hemot hollers back as he makes his way to a table.

I shake my head and wander over to the man. "Yes, we'd like a meal, but not the biggest one you can give us." I hear Hemot groan in disappointment. "We also would like a couple rooms for the night."

"Ye,' certainleh'," the man says. "We ha' mutto' and cheeeeese."

I'm a little disturbed by the way his eyes go big as he intensely stretches out the word "cheese". I'm not sure why, but I am finding the guy annoying.

I head to the table and find Ellcia trying to console Hemot. She keeps explaining that she's sure the meal will be big enough.

We sit in silence for a while. I like that. I feel like I need a bit of time to relax.

After about half an hour, a woman a couple years older than us comes out and sets down our plates. She smiles sweetly at me and asks if there is anything else she can get us. As she asks, she places her hand on my shoulder and only talks to me.

I notice Ellcia tense up. She looks like she's ready to attack the woman. I don't know what to do about it, but I gently push the woman's hand off me, trying to send a clear message. Ellcia seems to settle a little, and the woman looks amused.

The woman then says the innkeeper will be around shortly to bring us our keys. She smiles at me before she walks away.

We dive into our meals, and it turns out Hemot is far hungrier than I had thought. He finishes his meal, then eats what Ellcia doesn't eat. When he's done, he looks mournfully at my empty plate.

"Welco' to ma inn," the innkeeper says, pulling us away from our focus on hungry Hemot, and forcing us to concentrate to understand his words. He appears to miss nearly as many letters as he remembers. "I ha' two key' here fo' the roo'. They ah secon' floo', rooms three and fou'."

We work out a price with him, and he takes our money. Before he leaves, he gives a deep bow to us, and I take the opportunity to whisper, "Lord Hillbin sent us to you. He said you are loyal to the throne."

The man stands up, giving no indication that he has heard anything. Instead, he says, "I'll be dow' hee' if ya nee' anythi'," and walks back to the bar.

"Well, that leaves us kind of hanging," Ellcia says. "I wish we knew if he heard."

I nod my head in agreement. I'm not sure if the innkeeper will help us at all. But then again, there isn't much we need help with at the moment. Maybe we won't need anything at all for our entire time here. Now that I think of it, I can't imagine what he might do for us.

We stand and head past the bar at the back of the large common room to the stairs. The steps leading up are old and shockingly worn. Each step has a smooth dip in the center where countless shoes have climbed and descended. I put my weight on the first step, and I'm pleased to find it's quite solid. As I move up the steps, not a single one so much as creaks.

We reach the top and find out why we have rooms three and four. There are four rooms on that floor, and the first two are open and in terrible disarray. It looks like they might be under repair. There's another flight of stairs going up, and I assume there are more rooms on the third floor.

We head into room three and drop our packs on the floor. Ellcia is about to sit on the bed, but Hemot leaps through the air and lands on the mattress. I hear a loud snap.

Hemot rolls back and forth a couple of times. "I think the bed might be broken. We'll have to mention that to the innkeeper."

Ellcia rolls her eyes as she finds a spot on the floor. Though we just sat for a while, it feels good to spread out a bit.

She settles in a little more against the wall before asking, "So, what do we do now?"

I take a deep breath. To be honest, I hadn't thought of much past reaching Haner. For the first time, I truly understand our situation. We can't go back to the army unless we have a way to avoid Captain Frindor. We also can't go back to Sevord. The Regent will either kill us on sight or imprison us.

But… what will we do in Haner? We can't really turn to Lord Hillbin. He's being watched. We have money, but it'll run out, eventually. I don't know what kind of job we'd need or where we can live for the long term.

"Ellcia…"

She nods and waits for me to continue. I'm overwhelmed by a warm feeling inside as I see that she trusts me. If she's trusting me, somehow I feel like I can do anything.

"If we consider the cost of our meals and the cost of the inn, how long will our money last us?"

Her head tilts back, and she stares at the ceiling, her lips moving as she runs through the calculations.

A few seconds later, amid Hemot's snores, she lays it out. "If we eat one meal a day and go down to one room instead of two, we can manage to last somewhere around forty days—assuming we have no problems. If we buy our food at the market, we can likely last closer to two months."

"We have that much money?" I whisper. I don't want anyone to overhear.

"We do. Marleet's dad was quite generous. There might even be more money. Most of what he gave her was spread out in different compartments in her pack." She opens the top of her own pack and pulls out a pair of Marleet's pants. After checking a few pockets, she finds a few more golds and silvers. She makes a face and then adds, "That'll carry us another few weeks."

I feel grateful, but also a little guilty. I don't know if her dad would have given so much if he'd known what would happen to Marleet.

The next two days are entirely uneventful. We stay out of everyone's way, and no one bothers us.

The innkeeper seems not to care about us one way or another. In fact, he barely speaks to us at all. The only one who seems to notice our presence is the young woman who serves us our meals in the common room, and she only pays attention to me.

I keep my ear out for any news of anything that might give us a clue about what to do, but most people just chat about the regular stuff of life. We're just finishing up our meal on the second day, however, when I hear it.

"Shhhh," I hiss.

"Don't shhh me!" Hemot says. "As I was saying, I'm concerned about the castle curtains. I found few people cared for them like I did. I think when we get back, I'll—"

"No, shhhh!" I put my hand over his mouth, earning me an angry look. "Listen!"

I lean over just a bit to hear what the men at one of the other tables are talking about.

"… never seen anything like it, actually," a short, round man says.

"I'd like to see that myself," a taller, thin man replies.

"How many you figure?" the third man at the table asks. He wears a hat with feathers sticking up in a very distracting manner.

"Thousands!" short-man declares. By this time, most people in the inn's common room are listening. "I couldn't tell for sure, but I've never seen that many people traveling across the Talic. There had to be over a hundred Shaloomd circling above them."

My concentration's interrupted by a whisper in my ear. "That's a very distracting hat."

"Be quiet, Hemot," Ellcia scolds. "Just listen."

"Were they catching anyone?" hat-man asks.

"No," short-man replies, "I think they have archers positioned throughout the army."

"You think it's an army?" a woman at another table calls out.

"What else could it be?" short-man answers. "I think it's the Rebels!"

"They're not Rebels!" a loud voice calls out from the crowd, followed by murmurs of agreement. "I hear they found the Prince. They're returning him to his throne!"

"To the Prince!" short-man calls out, raising his glass.

We each pick up our own glasses and join in. "To the Prince!"

When the people settle down, I lean over to the man. "Where are they now? How far have they gotten?"

"Didn't you hear me, boy?" Short-man looks at me with a deep scowl on his face.

I shake my head. "I'm sorry; I missed that part. My friend here was talking about curtains."

The man's expression changes to one of confusion for a moment before he shakes his head. "They've just reached Leito. I don't know how long they'll be there, but it looks like the Lord of the city doesn't want to let them in."

"But if the Prince is with them, Leito can't refuse him." Ellcia looks at me, and I nod in agreement.

"Lot of people afraid of the Regent, girl. It's been long enough that many assume his right to the throne." The man turns back to his friends, and it's clear the conversation is finished.

Ellcia looks disappointed. I feel it too. I would have thought the cities would get behind the Prince—especially Leito. It was the one city that was rumored to support the Rebels.

"Well," Hemot whispers, "we might as well go and join them."

"What?" I look at Hemot like he's crazy. Ellcia just shakes her head. I don't think she can be bothered to try explaining it. "We can't join them," I hiss. "Just because they're no longer in the caves doesn't mean we can go back. If Frindor and his men catch us, we're done! My uncle can't be everywhere."

I hear footsteps coming up behind me and turn around. It's the innkeeper. He doesn't look or smell like he's shaved or bathed since we first met him a couple days ago.

He leans down and says, "I thin' yu' shoul' co' wi' me."

I sit there without moving for a moment, other than to glance at Ellcia and Hemot. Hemot nods his head as though he understands, but I'm confident he doesn't. I wish the guy would finish his words.

Ellcia has that look she gets when she's trying to figure something difficult out. After a few seconds, she leans over and translates, "He wants you to go with him."

I nod. My stomach turns, and my hands go all clammy. I don't know if I can trust this guy, and going somewhere alone with him seems like a bad idea. I trust Lord Hillbin, but there's been nothing about this guy that's seemed even friendly, let alone trustworthy.

Someone whispers behind Ellcia, "He wants all of you, hun."

I glance back to see the young woman who works for the innkeeper behind us, wiping an empty table. She nods her head at me and smiles.

I feel a little better about the three of us going, but then I think about how that means Ellcia and Hemot might be in danger as well. I look to the doorway and consider bolting, but strong hands grab me and yank me toward the bar.

"We ha' to ta' abou' yu' roo'. Yu' leavin' it a mess!"

I hear a few people in the common room chuckle as I stumble forward from another push. In another moment, the innkeeper's led us into a side room with a small table. We find ourselves with our backs to a solid wall and three people standing between us and the door: the innkeeper and two large soldiers I've never seen before.

"Thas' them," the innkeeper says. "The' bee' hee' fo' abou' three day'."

So much of what he says is hard for me to understand, but the final thing he says is clear enough.

"The' ar' enemehs of the Regen'."

Our swords are out, and we step far enough apart that we won't easily injure one another when the fight begins. The innkeeper pulls a knife out of… somewhere. I barely saw his hand move, but the knife is long and sharp.

He spins around toward the door, and says, "Whas' wro'? Are' we unde' atta'?"

"Hold on, hold on." A large man steps out of the shadows and puts his hand on the innkeeper's shoulder. "Settle down, Phil. You just brought them into a room, placed them up against a wall, and now three people block the door. You think maybe that has something to do with it?"

The innkeeper stares at me for a long time. I can see his brain working, but it looks like it's stalled somehow, and he has no idea how to get it moving again. Eventually, his eyes brighten, and he puts his knife away. "I see. Well, I lea' yu' to cha'."

He turns and walks out the door.

"So, you're Caric, you're Ellcia, and you're Hemot," the second person from the shadows announces.

She steps out, and I get a good look at her. She's tall and thin, has a large smile on her face, and wears leather armor with a sword on her hip. Her left leg is missing from just above the knee, and in its place, she has a wooden post, allowing her to walk.

The man beside her has an equally large smile and is dressed in a similar way, although he's much, much larger than the woman. I notice he's missing his left hand.

The man uses his left arm to wipe his forehead and then lets his smile turn into a laugh. "I guess introductions are in order, eh?"

The woman chuckles and adds, "I think that's best, Terr."

"Well," Terr says and plops down in one of the chairs by the lone table in the room, "it's time we met. We didn't get a chance to meet you when you were in the mountain, but the General sent us here to speak with you."

I relax a bit. I'm hoping these people can be trusted.

"So, I'm Terr, and this is my wife Gerr," Terr declares.

Gerr waves. "Hi!" She makes her way to the table and drops into a chair next to her husband.

I put my sword away and sit down, and so do Ellcia and Hemot, but we keep an eye on our two guests. I'm already running through a plan on how to get out of here if the need arises.

Terr leans over and growls, "Let me see that sword, boy!"

I shake my head. I'm not about to give up my weapon. Besides, I don't want him knowing what it can do.

Both of our new visitors break out in laughter. "Good!" Terr says between laughs. "The General let us know what sword you have. It's good to know you're following his orders not to let others know about it."

I still don't know what to make of them, but that makes me trust them a bit more. They seem like a cross between the most dangerous people I've ever met and the happiest people I've ever met.

"Our orders are simple," Terr says. He reaches over and puts his hand on Gerr's lap. "The missus and I were sent to find the two of you. We checked with Lord Hillbin, and he said you were staying at Phil's place."

Ellcia puts her hand on my arm and leans forward. "How do we know we can trust you?" I feel a little uncomfortable with her just throwing that out on the table like that with these two, but it's best to get the answer right away.

The man's expression turns from a happy one to a sad one. "Unfortunately, Lady Ellcia, I don't think there's any way we can prove our loyalty. We were just chatting about that, actually, before we entered the city. The General didn't give us a note because he said you might not recognize his handwriting. We don't have any secret codes, because nothing like that was set up—as far as we know. Everything I tell you could just be made up."

"We're sorry," Gerr adds. "There's just no way to prove who sent us."

I nod. I find that actually helps. I think if they were trying to trick us, they would give an elaborate answer, rather than just admit that they have no proof.

"So, we were supposed to find you, and bring you up to speed, and give you your orders." Terr scratches his chin through his thick beard. "If it's all right with you, Prince Draydon, we'll jump right in. General Lirnal wants us back with the army right away."

I nod. "Jumping right in sounds good to me."

"All right," Terr says, "here goes. Not too long after the four of you left, Lady Marleet showed up again."

Hemot jumps to his feet, and his chair goes crashing back against the wall. "Marleet's okay? She's in the caves?"

"Calm down, calm down," Gerr says. "She's fine. She's no longer in the caves, though. Just… calm down and let my hubby tell you what we know."

Hemot sits down again. Unfortunately, he doesn't bother picking up his chair first. We wait as he navigates his way through that little problem, and in another few moments, he's picked up his chair and is once again seated. But this time, he's wringing his hands in anticipation.

"So, as I mentioned, Lady Marleet arrived," Terr continues. "Of course, Lord Yune and Lady Aldora were happy to see her, but also quite upset. They weren't expecting her back so soon, and certainly not without the three of you. Frindor says he tried to have her arrested, but there was no actual evidence that she'd done anything wrong."

He leans back in his seat. "She announced that she had a special message for the Prince but insisted that she tell him in private. Frindor tells us that he wouldn't allow that, of course. He insisted that he be in there, because of, as he describes it, 'his intense love and loyalty for the throne.' Anyway, he takes her there. It ends up just being Prince Roran, Lady Marleet, Captain Frindor, and two servants in the room. The servants described the situation. They said the Lady Marleet walked up to the Prince and touched him on the face."

We wait. I can't imagine the story ends there.

"Best continue, Terrly," Gerr said. "I don't think they understand."

Terr's eyebrows shoot up. "Oh, sorry. That's a pretty clear sign that an enchantment has been placed upon someone else. Especially when you find the Prince has been acting different lately."

"Mic's enchanted?" Hemot asks.

"I don't know who this 'Mic' is," Terr says, "but Prince Roran definitely is. Those with giant blood can smell an enchantment. Once Rulfor showed up, he smelled it on the Prince right away."

I shake my head. "So, that's what it was about."

"What are you talking about, Prince Draydon?" Gerr asks.

I take a moment and talk through what happened in the mountain. I leave out the part about how I let her go and about how some of us were clinging to others, but aside from that, I let them know the rest.

Gerr frowns. "Yes, that makes a lot of sense. We have long suspected there was a Spellcaster in the mountains but could never track him down."

Terr lets out a loud sigh. "So, that fills in those details for us. We'll be sure to tell the General all about it. Unfortunately, we have no actual proof that he's enchanted."

"Well, we just told you," Ellcia says. "And you have Rulf who can smell it on him."

"Yes," Terr says. "You see… with all that's happened, we're in a tough spot with that. We can't just take the word of other people."

"Can you make him draw his sword?" I realize I haven't told the others about how drawing his sword can cancel any enchantment. Ellcia and Hemot's confused expressions let me know I should have shared that detail.

"Nope," Terr says. "Can't do it. The law applies to the King, not the Prince. We have asked him repeatedly to draw his sword, but he has declared that he will not do so until he takes the throne."

I close my eyes in frustration. All the muscles in my back have tensed up, and my stomach churns. Sometimes, things just don't work out the way they're supposed to.

"Why didn't you bring Marleet with you?" Hemot asks.

"Now, Hemot," Terr says. "I don't want to be disrespectful and all, but I'm trying to give you a lot of information. Can the three of you just let me tell you what I'm supposed to tell you? We actually have to be out of the city in the next hour or so, or we'll be stuck inside until morning. Our orders are to return to the army as soon as possible."

"I'm sorry," I say. "Please continue. We'll save our questions to the end."

I look over at Ellcia and Hemot, and they nod their agreement.

"So, I'll answer that question quickly. One of the effects of an enchantment is that sometimes, in this kind of circumstance, the one enchanted finds himself… hmm… the enchantment kind of warms the heart of the enchanted person toward the one who carried the enchantment." Terr pauses for a second as he studies Hemot's face. "What I mean is… we couldn't bring the Lady with us. Prince Roran is not only enchanted, but he's now madly in love with Lady Marleet."

I'm shocked at this, but then quickly put my hand up toward Hemot. I manage to stop him from going off on the matter. We need to hear what Terr has to say.

"So, quick rundown," Terr says. "The Prince is now enchanted, he's also fallen in love with the Lady Marleet, she can't leave because the Prince won't let her, and he has declared his intention to marry her."

I tense up at that last one and hear a whimper come from Hemot. I glance over at him. His face has drained of all color.

Terr leans forward. "So, the army has left the caves. General Lirnal is taking the Prince back to Sevord to be crowned King. We don't know what the enchantment is all about, but the only thing we can do is crown him, and then order him to draw his sword."

Terr points at me. "Now, you, Prince Draydon, cannot return to the army. General Lirnal knows you weren't part of the attack on the Prince—the Prince cleared you when he awoke—however, you are a target for the spies and traitors among us. That means if you show up, you might be killed before the General can protect you. We also don't know if the enchantment on the Prince is targeted at you."

"Why would it be targeted at me?" I ask, forgetting for a moment that I wasn't supposed to ask questions.

"You're next in line for the throne," Terr explains. "Whatever's going on, it's always been about the throne. There's no doubt this enchantment has to do with the Regent becoming King. At the moment, it's Prince Roran, you, and General Lirnal who stand between the Regent and what he's after."

"I don't want the throne," I say, my voice far quieter than I had intended.

"That's good, Prince Draydon!" Terr says, and Gerr lets out a loud laugh. "Those who aspire to the throne tend to do things that hinder the rightful heir! However, know this: if it comes to it, and you one day have to take the throne, it does not matter what you want! It's your duty as a Prince of Sevord."

The words hang heavy on my heart, but I find myself nodding. He's right. I know he's right.

"Back to the matter at hand," Terr announces. "General Lirnal is moving across the Talic Region with the army, and he's sent word for the troops who have hidden across the land in villages and cities to return. They are quickly joining him, and the army is growing." Terr takes a deep breath and then says, "Now, for your orders."

I glance over at Ellcia and Hemot. It feels strange to think we have orders. We took orders all the time at the castle, but I hadn't thought of ourselves as taking orders now that we're on the run.

However, we are in service to the Prince.

"We're ready to receive our orders," I say. "And we'll fulfill them to the best of our abilities."

Terr nods, and Gerr grunts her approval. Terr looks over to his wife, and she says, "You've been ordered to head to Nimville and remain there. It won't be easy, but you'll have to settle in until you are summoned."

I remember hearing about Nimville, but not too often. It's a small fishing village to the north of the capital city of Sevord.

"How long?" Ellcia asks.

Gerr frowns. "I'm sorry, Lady Ellcia, I don't know. It could be days, weeks, months, or even years. I would recommend that you do not wait long to find work. If you are there for a while, the sooner you start that process, the better. Perhaps the boys will find work on a fishing boat. It will be harder for you, Lady Ellcia. Women do not work on fishing boats, unless they're related to the ship's captain. There might be work you can do in the village."

"Will we be safe there?" Ellcia asks.

Gerr nods. "Absolutely. They are good people, in Nimville. Very good people." Terr grunts his approval. "They are loyal to the throne to a fault and have no love for the usurper. But they will expect you to work hard and provide for yourselves. If you do that, they will welcome you with open arms. When it's safe, someone will come find you."

"That's all we have to say," Terr announces as he stands up and his wife joins him. "Do you need anything?"

I shake my head. We have plenty of money and all we need.

"Then, with your permission, Prince Draydon, we will return to General Lirnal."

I nod, and the two turn and walk out without another word. I feel happy to have a bit more information, but somehow I feel far worse knowing what we now know.

Life was easier before.

8

⸺•⸺•⸺●⸺•⸺•⸺

The Orders

No," I say again. "Only food that can travel."

Somehow Hemot can't seem to wrap his mind around the idea of not taking sandwiches and stew. I admit, the stew smells amazing, but cheeses, dried meats, and foods like that are definitely what we need.

Truthfully, I think he's just trying to distract himself. He won't talk about the whole matter of Marleet and the Prince. We're all happy to find she's alive and safe, but the thought of the Prince having his eye on her is bothering Hemot—a lot.

After we leave the food section of the market, we buy some thin rope that Hemot says he can use for snares to catch rabbits, then a map of the region. Finally, we stop at a cobbler to have him take a look at Ellcia's boots. They haven't been feeling quite right. The cobbler resoles them while we wait, and we're back in Ellcia's room before dark.

We plan on heading out first thing the next morning. I want to talk over the journey with them before we set out, and I lay out the map on the floor. We lean over it and examine our options.

"It looks like there's a road heading west from Haner," I say as I run my fingers across the map. "If we take it, we can head south when we reach the cliffs and then meet

122

up with the main road leading through Switcher Pass. If we hurry, we might stay ahead of the army. Otherwise, we'll have to remain in the Talic Region until the entire army gets through."

We're interrupted by a knock on the door. I fold over the map, climb to my feet, and open the door. On the other side is the young woman from the inn's common room.

She smiles and pushes past me. When she reaches Ellcia and Hemot, she joins them on the floor.

"Well, this is nice," she says. "Do we just all sit around on the floor in this room?"

"We're having a private conversation," Ellcia says, not hiding her disdain for the woman.

"Lovely! I enjoy private conversations."

I don't really know what to do, but I close the door and come sit down. I notice Ellcia slides a little closer to me.

The girl smiles at us in her teasing way and says, "So, my pa suspects you three are leaving tomorrow morning."

We just stare at her. I find I rarely know what to say to people. I should probably learn how to reply with wisdom and insight in these situations, but every time I try, something dumb comes out.

She smiles sweetly at me. "I'm assuming since you're not denying it, that it must be true. We figured that Terr and Gerr probably gave you some instructions on where you're to go. My pa wants me to let you know that you should take the back stairs as they lead down to the kitchens, rather than go through the common room. Most of the guests here are loyal to the throne, but sometimes people just talk. It's better if you just slip out unnoticed. The gates won't open until nine tomorrow morning, but if you want, we can get you out of the city a bit earlier." She looks at me. "Is… that what you want?"

I nod. I figure we're just going to have to take our chances with this woman, just like with so many others.

"Good. What time?"

I hadn't thought that far ahead, but I say, "Six AM."

"Anything else you need?"

I shake my head, but Ellcia speaks up. "We need some changes of clothing for Hemot. He…" She glances at him out of the corner of her eye and adds, "He stinks."

Phil's daughter smiles and nods. "I had noticed that. I'll find him something." She then stands up and says, "Okay, I'll come knock on your doors at half-past five. Go down the back stairs, and we'll have a hot breakfast waiting for you. When you get to the west gate, ask for Gillan. Tell him that Phil sent you, and he'll let you out." She smiles sweetly at me again and says, "Goodbye, Princeling!" and winks before she turns and heads out.

When she's gone, Ellcia punches me in my arm.

"What's that for?" I demand.

"For smiling at her."

"I didn't smile at her!" I protest.

"But she smiled at you! A lot!"

"I don't control her lips," I say, feeling quite frustrated.

"Why do you keep talking about her lips?" Ellcia asks with a frown.

"Yeah," Hemot says. "It's a little odd to talk so much about her lips… if you're not interested in her."

"This is the first time I mentioned her lips!"

"There you go again… more about her lips!" Ellcia stands up and storms off to the side of the room.

I turn back to Hemot, and he has a big grin on his face. I reach over and punch him in the shoulder, but he just laughs.

When I turn back to Ellcia, she's facing me and also has a big smile on her face. I shake my head. Sometimes I'm so slow to figure out when I'm being teased.

The next morning, Hemot and I awake to the sound of a quiet knock on the door. I hear a faint, "Are you up?" coming through the door, and I whisper back, "We're getting up now." I then hear the young woman walk down the hall and knock on Ellcia's door.

I light the lamp and turn it up just enough to give us the light we need. Hemot didn't sleep much last night. He woke me up a lot as he turned in his sleep. I'm pretty sure I heard him crying a bit. I'd ask him how he's doing, but he doesn't look like he wants to talk.

We get ourselves ready as quietly as we can. From what the innkeeper's daughter said, we need to be secretive. We're not sure who's after us at the moment, but there always seems to be someone.

Once we're dressed and have our packs on, we head into the hallway. I lightly knock on Ellcia's door, and a moment later, her door opens. She looks tired but smiles at me.

We head down the hallway to the back stairs. Hemot and I went down them once the day after we arrived. They're skinny, and I find my pack scrapes the walls on either side as I descend. When we get to the bottom, the door to the kitchen is open and a tired-looking man stands next to a large grill. Seated on a stool in the corner is the innkeeper's daughter. I've never actually taken the time to ask her for her name, but I think I'd better not do that, considering the way Ellcia seems to react to her.

We head to a small table with three chairs, and a moment later, a hot breakfast is placed before us. The cook pulls up a chair and sits down between Ellcia and me, and the innkeeper's daughter sits on my other side.

The innkeeper's daughter dives into her breakfast, but now and then when I glance her way, she smiles at me. I'm beginning to think she's just trying to make me feel uncomfortable.

The cook shoves a large chunk of bread in his mouth and then points at me with his fork. When he speaks, I see far too much of his breakfast. "So, are you really Prince Draydon?"

I shake my head in frustration. I decide it's too early to try to avoid answering. "Does everyone know?"

He stares at me for a moment, then answers before he swallows. "Nope, just Phil, Laanna here, and me."

"Who told you?" I ask the cook, making a note in my head that the young woman's name is Laanna.

"Terr told me. We served together under your dad at the battle of Reber's Gate. That's where Terr lost his hand and Gerr lost her leg."

I hadn't realized that Terr and Gerr had lost their limbs in a battle under my father's leadership. I don't know how to feel about that.

He leans over and looks at my hip. "I gather that's your father's sword?"

I don't answer, but he just nods. "It looks like the scabbard your father wore. Keep it close, Your Majesty."

"Thanks," I say. "Did you know my father?"

The man's eyes drop to the table, and he slowly swallows. After a long pause, he nods. "Your father was a good man, Prince Draydon. I have heard of Generals who run at the first sign of danger, but General Geran often led the charge. When the Cobalds came over that pass, I thought we were done for, but he rallied the troops and fought harder than the rest of us."

He meets my eyes and says, "I would follow a man like that to the gates of death and back again. And I did. I would even follow your Uncle Lirnal now and you one day, but my fighting days are behind me. My knees would never last even the trip to Sevord." He takes a deep breath and then puts his large hand on my shoulder. "Serve your people well, Prince Draydon. Lead the King's armies like your father led them, and Sevord will be strong once again."

I nod at first. I can't help but think he's forgetting something. "I'll try, but General Lirnal commands the armies of Sevord."

The cook's face fills with confusion for a moment. He glances over at Laanna before asking me, "What do you mean, Your Highness?"

"I mean, General Lirnal is the leader of the armies of Sevord. I might have to lead because I'm a Prince, but I won't lead the armies. He's already doing it."

The cook stares thoughtfully at me, and then he glances again at Laanna as if to say, "You take this one."

I turn to look at her, and she smiles at me before she places her hand on my arm.

I'm shocked to hear what sounds like a growl from Ellcia, and Laanna pulls right back. I glance over at Ellcia, and she looks like she's about to climb over the table.

"Um," Laanna begins, clearly taken aback, her eyes darting everywhere except in Ellcia's direction. "Prince Draydon, you are next in line for the throne. That means if you are loyal to the King, you are the first General. General Lirnal is your second. If it came down to it, once you're eighteen years old, if you are not already, you could claim leadership of the loyal armies, and only the King, or the Prince in this case, could remove you."

I'm taken aback by this news. I had no idea it worked that way. I'm trying to make sense of it all as I remember another uncle. "What about General Corter? He's been leading the armies at Sevord for all these years."

The cook spits and shakes his head.

I can't help but notice that the cook's spit actually landed in my food. I'm sure he didn't mean to, but I'm definitely done with my breakfast… now.

"General Corter," the cook hisses, "is a traitor and a thief, not to mention the most incompetent man in all of Sevord. He's not a true General. If he had remained loyal to the throne, he could be a Captain or a politician, or even a cook, but he cannot be a General. And certainly not now that he has lived as a traitor to the throne."

As if to add effect to what he said, he slams his fist down on the table as he stands up. The entire table shakes, and Ellcia's glass tips. The cook then storms over to the sink and begins to scrub dishes as if each dish were his personal enemy.

I nod to the others. It's time to go.

We thank the cook, who growls a response to us. He's still quite upset. We then say goodbye to Laanna. I can't help but notice that she gives both me and Ellcia a lot of space. I assume the growl did it.

Before we go, the cook points over at four sacks sitting on a shelf. We pick them up and find more traveling food inside three of them, and the fourth has two changes of clothing around Hemot's size.

"Thank you for the clothing," Ellcia says, although Hemot looks annoyed. "Did you have to buy them? Do we owe you money?"

Laanna smiles at Ellcia and shakes her head. "No, they belonged to my brother. He…" She glances around and then back at us as if she doesn't want to say anymore. In a quiet voice, she adds, "You three are not the only ones to lose family on the day when Parthun murdered the King." Turning around quickly, she slips out the kitchen door into the other room.

"The road west from here is rough," the cook says pulling us back. "But if you take it and move fast, you'll reach Switcher Pass before the army or the scouts see you. Gerr told me that you'll need to avoid the army. I don't understand why, but I trust Terr and Gerr with my life, so move fast, Prince Draydon."

I thank him again, and we head out the back door.

The sun's coming up as we leave. It's barely bright enough to see clearly in the streets, but it's already warming up. It's going to be a hot one today.

We've been out a few times since arriving, and we know the way to the western gate. It's not hard to find.

Few people move around the city this early. The occasional merchant wanders by with a cart full of wares, but everyone else still seems to be inside their homes.

When we reach the gate, the guards standing on either side of the closed doors just ignore us at first. I think the one might actually be asleep. He's on his feet, but I hear a soft snoring sound coming from him.

I approach the other one. "We need to speak to Gillan."

"Who's asking?" the guard growls.

"I am," I reply. In my head, that sounded better.

I figure the guard is about to chew me out for such a response, but he turns around and bangs on the door to the guardhouse. A moment later, he has a quick exchange with a tired-looking man, and a few minutes after that we're standing before a large man who appears to be trying to hide the fact that he clearly just woke up.

I step in close and keep my voice quiet. "Phil sent us. He said you can let us out before the gate opens."

The man laughs and puts his hand on his sword. "No one gets out before the gates open at nine. Get out of here!"

I step back at the threat. I'm not sure what else to do. I guess we can head back to the inn for a few hours.

I'm about to turn away, when Gillan grabs me by the front of my armor. He pulls me in and says, "Didn't you hear me, boy? I said get out of here!"

I open my mouth to tell him that I can't leave while he's holding me when I notice his eyes aren't on me. I look back and see a man sauntering across the street a short distance away. He doesn't seem to be looking at us, but as soon as he's out of sight, the guard lets go.

"Quickly," he hisses quietly.

We follow him into the guardhouse. As soon as the doors close, he turns to me. There are no windows in the building, and the walls are thick.

"Sit!" he orders and points to three chairs.

We sit down. I notice two guards stand in front of the door we just entered and another two in front of the door we need to go through to leave the city.

He pulls up a chair of his own and drops into it. "Tell me why it is that Phil would risk his own safety and the safety of the entire lower guard of the western gate to send you to me. If we let you out and you're caught, we stand to lose a lot, so that makes me curious as to what I'm risking my neck for."

"Lord Hillbin will kill you for helping us?" I feel shocked. I didn't get the impression he'd do something like that.

The man laughs. "Lord Hillbin? No, certainly not. The Portly Lord is a true noble. But Lord Hillbin is not the only man of power in this city. If we're suspected of acting in a suspicious manner, Lord Hillbin won't have time to investigate. We're under orders from the Captain of the

Guard. He's far less patient if something arises that causes him concern."

"Is he loyal to the throne?" I ask.

The man laughs. "Everyone's loyal to the throne, young man. The question is who we think should sit on the throne."

I nod. That makes sense to me. "Who does the Captain of the Guard think should sit on the throne?"

"The Captain of the Guard thinks the Regent should, of course," Gillan says. "But I'm curious who you think should be on the throne."

I place my hand on the hilt of my sword, and the reaction is immediate. Every guard in the room readies himself, but I don't move my hand.

When I speak, I make sure my voice is confident. "It doesn't matter what I think. What matters is that the right person be seated on the throne. Prince Roran is the rightful heir to the throne, and I will give my life to see that he is crowned King!"

The man leans forward. "The Captain of the Guard would run you through with his sword for saying that." He nods and leans back in his seat. "So, young man, I understand that we have similar views on the matter of the throne, so I will assume that I can trust you. However, I still want to know why Phil would send you."

"We are under orders from General Lirnal to head west." I take a quick look at Hemot and Ellcia before adding, "I do not feel I can tell you any more. Secrecy is of importance."

The man's expression changes at hearing our orders, and he smiles. "Then, if the good General has ordered it, by all means!"

He nods at one of the guards who adjusts the lantern, and the guardhouse goes dark. I feel someone pull me, and a moment later, the dim light of the morning comes through an open door.

Gillan is beside me. When he speaks, his voice comes out in just above a whisper. "Head immediately off the road to the left and walk along the riverbed. There's not much water in there at the moment. That'll keep you out of sight for a bit. I'm not sure of the loyalties of all the men on the wall above." He pushes me out, but not before adding, "Good travels, young man. Fulfill your orders well!"

We step out and quickly scramble off to the left and down into the riverbed, of which Gillan spoke. It isn't that much lower than the actual road, but there's enough shadow that if we crouch, I'm hopeful that we'll stay out of sight.

The sun is still behind the mountains, and we're on the west side of the city. With all that, I think we'll be hard to see.

We move along in this fashion for a long time, stretching out our backs now and then. The path soon veers off to our right, but we stay in the riverbed until we can get behind another one of the many hills in the Talic Region. When we do, we make our way over to the path and set out at a proper speed.

It doesn't take long before my legs feel good, and I'm happy to be on the road again. We've done so much traveling lately that it feels like it's exactly what we're supposed to do—all the time.

We pick up our speed as we move along, and in a short while, we're nearly at a jog. The path winds back and forth a bit and is certainly not as smooth as the main road we used when we first came through the Talic Region, but it's not bad. The three of us can still move along, walking side-by-side the entire way.

We keep our eyes on the sky as much as we can. So far, there's no sight of the Shaloomd, but I doubt it'll be long. The closer we get to the cliffs, the more we'll see, and the more danger we'll be in.

The day's travels are mostly quiet. There's a point where we pass a merchant traveling toward Haner, and he mostly yells at us. He appears to be upset about something regarding horseshoes. I don't know what it was about. A short while after that, we pass another merchant, and he yells at us about broken carts.

I think everyone who travels this road must be a little on the insane side of things. When I mention that to Hemot, he quickly points out that we are traveling the same road.

At night, we find a small forest off to the north. It's big enough that Hemot figures we should find plenty of food. He sets his snares and then comes back and helps Ellcia and me as we struggle to light the fire.

I find it far harder to start the flame than Hemot. Somehow, he just manages to light it without too much trouble.

The night is coming on, but we decide to take the time to do some sword practice. I use Marleet's sword, rather than my own. I don't particularly want to chop my friend's swords in two, nor do I want to accidentally kill either of them. We do, however, want to strengthen our arms.

Marleet's sword is a little lighter than mine, but it's a solid weapon. It looks old. I actually like the grip on it more than my own. It feels like it was made for my hand, and when we start into the forms and moves, I find I'm so relaxed that I barely have to think about what I'm doing.

I start out facing Hemot. He begins to circle me, and I turn, careful to keep my footing on the uneven ground of the forest. When he comes for me, I easily step aside and use the flat of my sword to smack his butt.

He doesn't seem to appreciate it, but I hear a laugh from Ellcia. A moment later, I push his blade off to the side and have my blade at his throat.

I feel like the small amount of training I've received has made me a master with the blade. It's hard to believe, but when Hemot comes after me again, I reach out, and with a careful flick of my wrist, Hemot's sword drops to the ground.

Hemot frowns, picks up his sword, and turns to Ellcia. "Your turn."

Ellcia steps forward. I position my feet just as Rulf taught me and keep my eyes on Ellcia. She waits for me to come, and I know she won't grow impatient enough to make the first move. I step forward, and she tries to parry my attack, but I get past her defense and have my blade in the center of her stomach, point right against her armor.

When I lower my blade, she doesn't raise hers. Instead, she stares intently at me. "Where did you learn these moves?"

"Some from Rulf; some in the mountain."

"You want to teach us, rather than just show off?" Her frown is the one she pulls out when she's really not impressed.

I think of a few smart replies but decide I'm better off just agreeing. We stand side-by-side for a few minutes while I walk them through what I did. Neither seem able to master the moves right away, but they make quick improvement.

"Any other moves you want to show us?" Hemot asks with a smile. He seems happy again now that he's learned a bit more.

"Just this," I say. I turn to a log, jump up, launch myself off it with one foot, flip completely over, and land on my feet while I bring my sword down on a branch, slicing it off the tree, right at the trunk.

"Whoa," Ellcia says.

I've never seen her so impressed before. It's no wonder. I'm pretty fantastic with my blade. I likely could defeat the entire group of assassins by myself at this point. In fact, I might actually be able to fight off a large group, maybe even a small army. The big issue would be that I'd need to stop now and then for meals, but other than that, I'd likely be able to fight entire wars all by myself. Maybe even…

I drop the sword on the ground, and my head clears. "What just happened?"

Ellcia steps forward, concern all over her face. "What do you mean? You just showed us how much you've learned in the mountains. I… I will admit, Caric. I'm amazed."

"Hemot, could I borrow your sword for a moment?" I ask.

"Sure!"

He hands me his blade, and I face off against Ellcia.

"You want to show me up again?"

"No, let's just try the same moves again."

She nods. I assume she thinks I'm just checking to see if she's improved at all.

I feel awkward standing before her. I remember that feeling. It's what I've felt my entire life, except for the few minutes when I held Marleet's sword.

Ellcia steps forward, and my suspicions are confirmed. She doesn't get past my defenses all that quickly—I'm still definitely better with the sword than she is—but I can't just slide past her own defenses this time.

"You're holding back," she says, frowning at me again.

"No, I'm not." I lower my sword and shake my head.

"What's wrong?" Ellcia comes to me and puts her hand on my arm.

"Marleet's sword is enchanted."

She stares at me for a moment, then understanding crosses her face. "Really?"

"Did you notice a difference between when I was fighting with it and when I wasn't?"

Hemot grabs the sword off the ground and smiles. A moment later, he steps to the same log I used and launches himself off it, flipping through the air and tangling his legs in the branches of a tree. He hangs there, swinging back and forth. "Nope, don't think it's enchanted. I couldn't do the same move."

I move over to the fire. "Let's have a seat."

Ellcia comes over and sits across from me while Hemot untangles himself from the tree. When he's down, he comes over. The curiosity written on their faces is pretty strong.

"What were you thinking when you did the flip?" I asked.

"That I wanted to do the flip!" Hemot said with a smile.

"No, what *exactly* were you thinking?" I lean forward. "It's important—think about exactly what was going through your mind."

Hemot's face grows serious, and he proudly says, "Oh magic sword, grant me thine power to leap and do a super-move like Caric."

I look over at Ellcia to see her reaction to Hemot. The look on her face is a mix of surprise, confusion, and concern. I feel better knowing she's feeling the exact same emotions I'm feeling.

"That's really what was going through your head?"

"Well, most of it," Hemot explains. "I didn't finish because my legs got caught in the tree."

I stare into the fire for a moment. "There's an enchantment on the sword. I'm sure of it. It gave me skills I hadn't mastered yet. But it doesn't just do that in every situation, otherwise Hemot's move would have worked. And

Marleet wasn't that good with her sword, so it definitely doesn't just make someone great."

"Yeah," Ellcia says. "Marleet really was pretty bad."

Hemot nods, but then sadness crosses his face. I decide to forget the sword for the moment.

"Hemot, how are you doing with the whole thing with Marleet?"

He frowns, and he seems to shrink on the log. "Maybe I should go check the snares." He quickly stands and starts into the forest.

"No, Hemot." Ellcia jumps up, grabbing his hand. "I think you need to talk about this."

Hemot comes to a halt and drops his head. He clenches his fists but doesn't turn around.

I hate to see Hemot like this. "Tell us what's going on."

When he speaks, his voice comes out quiet and filled with sadness. "Marleet's going to marry the Prince."

"You don't know that," Ellcia says.

"Don't I?" Hemot yells and turns to her. "Don't I? I do know that! You can't turn down a Prince when he asks you to marry him. Can you? Besides, even if she could, he's going to be King! I'm just a curtain man."

Ellcia looks over at me. I'm really not sure if she *can* say no. I've never even thought of that kind of thing. Maybe a Prince can just take whomever he wants as his wife. Instead, I say, "She loves you, Hemot."

When he turns to me, his face is not sad, but angry. "What does that matter, Caric? If she has to marry Prince Roran, it doesn't matter who she loves. She can love me or you or whoever. It makes no difference. She'll one day be the Queen of Sevord. I…" He drops right down on the ground. "I'll just be a distant memory for her, and she'll have to love the Prince."

Ellcia sits down next to him and rubs his back. I'm glad she's here. I'm not really good with this kind of thing. I'd probably say something dumb like, "Well, at least she'll be rich. Maybe she can buy you nice stuff."

Best for me to keep my mouth closed for now.

I decide to turn my attention back to the sword. I think figuring that kind of thing out is a lot easier than trying to comfort Hemot.

I was feeling really confident when I used the sword, so maybe it just worked on me. Or maybe it only works on royalty.

I play around with the royalty idea for a moment. I'm not sure that makes sense. I wonder why Hob would give it to Marleet if it wouldn't work for her. I'm pretty sure, the more I think about it, as insane as I think Hob is, he definitely knew what he was doing. I doubt he'd make that kind of mistake.

The idea of being confident reminds me of something. Marleet's dad…

"Wait!" I holler. "What did Marleet's dad say to her just before we left the cave?"

Ellcia gives me a cross look, and I remember what Hemot's going through. That was pretty insensitive of me.

Hemot looks up at me for a moment, then he slowly sticks out his chin and opens his eyes wide in a fantastic impression of Marleet's dad. He then says in a slow, deep voice, "Marleeeeteeee, youuuu take good care of these threeeee. Remember where to find my friendssss. Be couraaaageous and be confidennnnt in your blade."

Ellcia and I both break out in laughter. Hemot sounds just like Lord Yune.

When I calm down, I say, "Confidence! That's what it is. Marleet's dad told her to be confident in her blade. I was confident while I used it, and the more I used the blade, the more confident I got. And the better I got. I think it's kind of like my armor. I have to believe that nothing can hurt me while I'm wearing it. With the sword, it works depending on what you're thinking. If you think you're really good with the sword, you will be."

Ellcia nods. "That explains why Marleet could never master anything. She always thought she couldn't learn how to fight with a sword."

Hemot nods and comes over to me. "Let me try again."

He picks up the sword and closes his eyes for a moment. When he opens them, he smiles and charges toward the log, leaping off it, flipping through the air, landing on a low branch, spinning around, jumping out again, and finally, landing on the ground, swiping the sword just a hair above the ground.

"Whoa," Ellcia says.

I realize my mouth is open, so I close it. "That was impressive." I shake my head in shock. "You know, when I was using it, my confidence grew the longer I held it. I began to think that I could fight off just about anyone with the sword, even to the point of winning entire wars on my own."

Ellcia's lip curls up in a sneer, and she rolls her eyes. When Hemot sees her do that, he shakes his head. "No, Ellcia, I think he's right. I really think I could defeat just about anyone. The only thing that could stop me would be arrows or spears… or maybe if too many people attacked at once, but even then…"

"Wait." I put up my hand. Something is bothering me. "Do you remember all the stories about enchanted objects? They all had some kind of trick or weakness or something bad attached to them."

"Right," Hemot says as he absently swings the sword around in an impressive manner. He looks like he's showing off, but he doesn't really even seem to notice it. "It was because all the Spellcasters were evil. Even the ones who seemed good would always put something wicked into it."

Ellcia looks at the sword with suspicion. "I had read once that there's something about the magic that corrupts the Spellcaster. That there has never been a Spellcaster who didn't go insane or all-out evil."

Hemot tosses the sword down on the ground like it's going to bite him. He steps away and walks the long way around to stand by us.

I shake my head and pick up the sword. Right away, I can feel that I can win any battle.

"Listen, I don't think we have to worry." I sit down on a log with the sword across my knees. "Remember that I've been wearing this enchanted armor for a long time, and it hasn't corrupted me. I've also been carrying an enchanted sword. Mic, or Prince Roran, was also wearing enchanted armor, and the king's sword is enchanted, and he has to carry it. There might be something bad about this sword, but it didn't affect Marleet in all the time she wore it or used it."

I can see neither of them are happy with my explanation. I think they're feeling spooked by the enchantment. I grab Marleet's scabbard and put the sword away, setting it down by our supplies.

"Let's just practice with sticks tonight," I say and go grab one. I use my knife to clean off the little branches, and in a few minutes we're battling it out. As the sun sets, we settle down for the night. We're all tired, but it'll be good to get an early start.

9

The Pass

Okay, I'm really angry, okay? You happy now? IS THAT WHAT YOU WANTED?"

I shake my head. "Hemot, no, we're not happy. This isn't about us trying to hurt you. We just thought you'd want to talk about it."

"Well, I don't!" he shouts and storms off ahead of us. A moment later, he pulls back and mumbles under his breath, "Stupid Shaloomd. Can't go walking off by myself, or I'll get eaten and won't have a chance to punch Mic in the face for marrying Marleet."

I glance up, and sure enough, three Shaloomd circle above us. They've been above us for the last two days. Sometimes there's three; sometimes there's two, but they're always there.

I try one more time to offer some comfort. "I don't think they're married, Hemot. She's only seventeen, and he's sixteen. Besides, Marleet's dad is a smart man. He won't let his daughter marry an enchanted Prince."

Hemot stops and pokes his finger into my chest. "First, what makes you think he'll have a choice? Second, what makes you think he won't jump at the opportunity to be the father of the Queen of Sevord? Third, what makes you think Marleet doesn't want to be Queen? You remember how much she liked dressing up and pretending to be royalty? This is a dream come true for her!"

I open my mouth to answer, but then I stop as the doubts flood in. He's right… she did always talk and dream about being royalty. It was something she wanted from a young age. And truthfully, I don't know her dad well enough to know he wouldn't take the opportunity to gain influence and power by marrying his daughter off.

But Ellcia catches the real issue. "Hemot," she says in a soft voice and puts her hand on his arm. "She may dream of being royalty, but I know for a fact that she does not want the Prince. She's had her eye on one guy for years—and you know it's you." She puts her other hand on his other arm and pulls him a little closer. "Listen closely. We can't do anything about what's going on right now with Prince Roran or with the army or with Marleet. All we can do right now is get to Nimville."

"What about Marleet?" Hemot asks, his voice just above a whisper.

Ellcia doesn't seem to know what to say, so I pipe in. "We'll have to just trust her. She'll do the right thing." I put my hand on Hemot's shoulder. "You know she'll do the right thing, don't you?"

He stares at me for a bit before a smile creeps up on his face. He nods and says, "Yes, she will. She always tries to do the right thing." His expression changes, and I see confidence in his eyes. "She won't marry him just to be Queen. You're right. We can't do anything about it, other than to trust that she can take care of herself."

"I think that's a good idea," Ellcia says.

The three of us continue on. Hemot seems to be happier now than he's been in days. We have to pick up our speed just to keep up with him, and more than once, either Ellcia or I have to remind him to stick close to avoid becoming a Shaloomd snack. A Shalack… a snackoomd…

a shackaloomasnad… hmm… I must be bored because right now, figuring out exactly the right way to combine Shaloomd and snack into one word seems a high priority. Snackoomd? I'll get it… I just need time…

That night, we settle down again in a forest. Hemot sets his snares, and we train for a while. Each night we've spent time in practice not only with sticks and our own swords, but also with Marleet's sword.

I've found that the more I use Marleet's sword, the better I am with my own. It's as if practicing with a sword that makes you a master while you use it, improves you even when you're not using it.

Ellcia and Hemot have found the same thing. We now practice intensely with that sword. We each practice and learn, then have some fun doing amazing stunts.

I watch Ellcia as she flips over fallen logs and slices branches off. A bee flies by her, and she growls. A moment later, two halves of the bee fall to the forest floor.

She's never liked bees.

Two days later, we find ourselves on top of another one of the countless small hills in the Talic Region, looking out over what's left of the land before us. The difference with this hill is that it's the last one before the cliffs.

The cliffs run north and south along the edge of the Talic Region, separating us from not only the ocean but also Sevord City and the villages along the coast. To get to Nimville, we're going to have to take Switcher Pass, which connects the coast to the Talic Region. That means we'll come within a short distance of the capital. We'll also have to pass near a village in Switcher Pass full of people who think we're murderers, and to add to it all, we suspect the Regent might have his soldiers patrolling the area.

"It's going to be dangerous," Hemot says for the third time this morning.

"Yup," I say. "At least we won't have assassins chasing us this time," I reply for the third time this morning.

"But we also won't have Rulf with us," Ellcia says, also for the third time this morning.

I take a deep breath. "I think we're getting ourselves down. We should focus on more positive things."

"Like that?" Hemot points up into the sky with an expression of loathing on his face.

"Not another one!" Ellcia cries.

I feel like throwing up. That's the fifth time we've seen a Shalloomd fly overhead, carrying one of their prey. The Shaloomd are predators. They feed on animals and even people, if they stray too far from others.

When a Shaloomd sees someone wander off by themselves, they swoop down, grab the person, and fly away. If you resist and fight your way out of their claws, you fall to your death. They then pick up your lifeless body. If you don't fight, they take you to their nests, high up in the cliffs, and feed you to their hatchlings.

It's horrible.

"How is it they're getting so many?" I ask.

"Even soldiers can't protect everyone," Ellcia says. "With thousands of people moving across the Talic Region, there are bound to be some who wander away from the group. The Shaloomd will get you the moment they can."

I shake my head. "That one looks like a woman."

The others, so far, have appeared to be men, although most of them are a little high up to see for sure. This one's wearing a dress.

On the one hand, I don't want to think about it because there's nothing we can do to help her, but on the other hand, that's someone's daughter or sister or mother or friend.

My mind goes to Marleet, and I feel even worse. I know she's traveling across the Talic Region, and I worry about her. Then again, I'm sure the Prince will make sure she's well protected. At least there's that. On top of it all, the woman above me is low enough to the ground that I can see she's not wearing one of Marleet's beautiful frilly dresses… assuming she gets to wear them now that she's the daughter of Nobles.

Shame washes over me. I recognize that I'm not as upset by a woman in the clutches of the Shaloomd if it's not Marleet. I force myself to remember that the woman above us is known and loved by someone.

I shake my head as we walk. I'm an emotional mess.

We follow the path down the hill and within an hour or so, we're at the base of the cliffs, and we turn south. The path is a little wider here as this road is used a bit more for travel to the northern Talacian tribes and villages, but it's still far from what we were used to on the main road.

The main road leading east and west across the Talic Region is well cared for. It's smooth and paved with stones, perfect for wagons and for walking. It makes for fast traveling. These paths are fine, but they aren't as easy to walk on as the main road.

We move south for some time. The road leading from Haner toward the cliffs not only runs to the west, but it also veers south somewhat, so we don't have too far to go until we'll get to the main road.

We walk arm and arm along here. At the moment, there are nearly a dozen Shaloomd above us. This close to their nests, they seem to be all over the place.

By evening, we find a small forest and settle in for the night. We expect to be in Switcher Pass sometime tomorrow.

"There it is," Hemot says.

Mid-way through the morning, he picked up speed and decided he wanted to lead the way. Ellcia and I have struggled a bit to keep up with him, but it's still been good. We have the endurance to push forward, so when Hemot rushes, it just means we'll get where we're going sooner.

"It took longer than I'd have thought," Ellcia points out.

I agree. The main road leading through the Talic Region lays ahead. We're almost to it, but I'd have thought we'd have reached it by yesterday at the latest. The Talic Region often surprises me as to how big it is.

When we reach the main road, we turn west. Switcher Pass is just ahead. The last time we'd been through here, we were running from angry villagers.

We do seem to anger a lot of people.

We enter Switcher Pass and relax. I noticed Ellcia's shoulders drop just a little, and Hemot slows down. A smile comes over my face, and Ellcia starts to hum.

I laugh. "Why are we all so happy? The last time we were here, we spent the entire time running for our lives!"

Ellcia hums a little louder and steps up next to me, bumping into my side while we walk. "I think it's nice to get out of the sun. And it's nice to know there's going to be loads of water. And it's nice to know the Shaloomd can't see us amongst the trees. And it's nice to know we're almost home."

She stops when she says that last part and slows down. Her smile disappears.

I take her hand. I know what's going on. "Just because we don't have a home at the moment doesn't mean we won't soon. If Sevord accepts the Prince's return, and I can't see why they won't, we'll be brought back to the castle soon enough."

"Wait," Hemot says, his eyes filling with fear. "You're a Prince, so you belong in the castle. So, when Mic—I mean Prince Roran—takes the throne, you'll be living there. You'll probably have your family's old rooms. Ellcia will probably live with her brother. And she's a Noble. But… me… Where will I live? I'm not a Prince. I'm not a soldier. All I am is the guy in charge of curtains. Will I have to be a servant again?"

I don't respond. I have no idea how it'll all work out.

Ellcia takes a stab at it. "But Hemot, you lived in the castle before. That means your parents were likely nobles. If that's the case, you'll probably inherit their wealth and land, if they have any, and maybe Prince Roran will name you a lord."

"Or a Lady," I say.

"Not helping, Caric," Hemot says with a laugh. "Or maybe I'm a Duke."

"What is a Duke, anyway?" Ellcia asks.

I shrug my shoulders and shake my head. I have no idea. I just know they're important.

"Off the road!" Ellcia hisses.

We scramble after her, moving in amongst the trees to the south. I'm not sure what we're avoiding, but it doesn't matter. If we have to run, we're used to it.

We do our best to push through the undergrowth without leaving a trail, keeping low as we move. Ellcia pulls us down behind some large ferns, and we wait.

"What did you see?" I ask.

She shakes her head. "I'm not sure, exactly. The road curves ahead, and I think I saw the shine of armor through the trees."

We don't see anything for a few minutes, so I suggest we start moving deeper into the forest. We don't want to be caught by soldiers.

We keep low to the ground and move as silently as we can. Not too far from the ferns, we find what appears to be an old riverbed, but there's no water. Along the floor of the riverbed and the sides, plants and ferns grow.

We move along for a few minutes before we hear voices. Scrambling up the bank, we peer through the trees.

Back on the road, a dozen soldiers move along slowly—quite slowly. It's no wonder it took them so long to come within sight.

I can just barely make out their words.

"That's close enough," one of the men says. "Let's head back. I don't need to see the Talic Region to know I've patrolled the entire road."

"Tilbur won't be happy," another man calls out.

"Who's gonna tell him? You?" the first man replies.

They laugh as they turn around and start back toward Sevord. They move at the same, slow pace, and we return to the dry riverbed.

I glance at Ellcia, then Hemot. The earlier excitement at being back in the forest is now completely gone. "It looks like we're going to have to stay off the road. We now know for sure that they're patrolling the area."

Hemot looks unconvinced. "But if Tilbur is your uncle, and he's loyal to the throne, we can maybe trust his men, right?"

I shake my head. "We know he sent them, but we don't know if they're loyal to him or to the Regent. It's not worth the risk."

We move off along the riverbed, careful to be as quiet as we can. We're low enough that we can't see the soldiers, so we're safe for the time being.

The riverbed is wide enough for all three of us to walk side-by-side, but we end up walking single file. I'm in the lead. I'm fine with that. However, I keep wondering if they're still behind me. I have this sneaky suspicion that they're just going to stop and set up camp, but not bother to tell me. Every few seconds, I find myself looking back to see if they're still there.

I check again. They are still there. They always are.

Although the riverbed snakes back and forth a little, it seems to head mostly west. I can see the cliff to my left, and I know that as long as it's on my left, we're moving in the right direction.

I worry a bit, though. We're on the south side of Switcher Pass. That's the same side as the village we went through. Those people think we're murderers, so I'd rather not meet up with them.

We push on through the supper hour. We're anxious to get through Switcher Pass and on to whatever's next for us, but it's still a long way.

I'm actually quite tempted to try to just live in the pass. There's a lot of land here and loads of water. We could just camp out for months, living off the land. Hemot could teach us how to set snares. We could maybe even build a shelter for ourselves.

The truth is, I don't want to live and work in a fishing village. It's not that I don't want to work. I've worked hard my whole life. It's more that I just have no idea what to do on a boat. I'm not sure I've ever even been out on one.

Unfortunately, I don't really have a choice. At the moment, I'm under orders from my uncle, General Lirnal. I guess when I'm older, I'll outrank him, but for the time being, obeying him is the same as obeying the Prince. If there's one thing I know, it's that I'm loyal to the throne.

I won't disobey.

When we finally settle down, it's actually starting to get dark. That's not a smart move as we don't want to have to start a fire after the sun has set, but at least we made good time.

We're also a long way from the main road, which I think is good. It means we shouldn't have to worry about soldiers discovering us in the night.

Hemot heads off right away to set his snares, and Ellcia and I work on the fire. Hemot, as difficult as he can be at times, is a decent teacher when it comes to this survival stuff. With his direction, we've learned to light a fire. It's still not easy, but even Rulf struggled to get a fire to light at times.

By the time he returns, we have the fire going. It's just small, and the wood is dry, so there's very little smoke. After an hour of sword practice, we chat for a bit and then quickly fall asleep.

"That way!" I hiss, pointing to my left.

The three of us rush through the trees and bushes, desperate to avoid capture. It's all so frustrating. The people we're afraid of should actually be our allies.

But for now, they're not.

Not long after we entered Switcher Pass, we caught sight of the Free Armies of Sevord. It wasn't the entire army, of course. It was the advance scouts. We couldn't take our chances that one of them might recognize us.

We suspect they might actually be searching for us. They're combing the forests and questioning every person they find. We've caught sight of Frindor a few times. He's the last one we want to meet right now.

"Down there!" Ellcia hisses, and we follow her.

We don't question anything any one of us says. If one of us says to run, we start running. If one of us says to hide under a bush, we hide under that bush.

Day and night for the last two days, we've barely had a moment to rest.

We duck out of sight again as a group of soldiers on horseback crash through the undergrowth. Rabbits and groundhogs scurry out of the way. We've even seen a lot of deer running through the area. I don't think I saw any the first time through.

"I think we're nearly out of the Pass," I say.

I think how ridiculous this all seems. First, these are supposed to be the good guys, yet we're running for our lives. Second, we thought the big danger was going to be the village people who thought we were murderers, but they turned out to be just as scared of the scouts as we are. Third, I had figured we'd be able to take it easy going through Switcher Pass, but we've had nothing but sheer terror and constant running for days.

And to make it worse, we can't even make good time because we're hiding, then running, then retreating, then running, then hiding… I feel like it's taking us forever to get out of the pass!

"There's Frindor again," Hemot whispers as we move behind a tree and rush off through the woods.

I wish we could find another dry riverbed. It would give us some cover, but also a relatively flat path.

I come around a tree and crash into four soldiers. The one I slammed into goes down, but in a moment, he's on his feet, and I'm pinned to the ground.

They twist my head to get a look at my face, and one of them says, "This is him! We caught him! It's Prince Draydon!"

"Get off him!" Ellcia cries out and runs into one of the men.

I appreciate her attempt, but Ellcia's not the biggest person in the world, and the guy she hit looks pretty solid.

"Run!" I cry out, hoping at least she and Hemot can get away.

I hear grunts behind me and swords clashing. It sounds like a group of people have come to our rescue, but I can't see much of anything until the man holding me down is knocked off to the side.

I scramble to my feet and draw my sword, but the four men are already down. To my left, Ellcia is still on the ground, looking stunned from when she slammed into the soldier holding me.

To my right, Hemot stands before us, holding Marleet's sword.

"I didn't kill them," Hemot says quickly, "just knocked them out. This sword is awesome!"

I get to my feet and pull Ellcia up after me. "Let's move!"

We race off through the forest again. Now we're really in trouble. At least before they didn't know for sure we were here, but now, when those men wake up, Frindor is going to double his efforts.

We don't have much time left.

We run as hard as we can, no longer trying to hide our presence. If they're tracking us, we won't be able to move fast if we're trying to avoid leaving a path. The only hope we have now is to cover more distance than they can.

After what feels like a month, but is likely closer to an hour, we catch sight of the road. We've been avoiding it as much as possible for the last couple days, but we reach it, and since there's no sign of soldiers, we run down it, making better time than in the forest.

It's not long after that when we see the end of the cliffs, and we exit Switcher Pass. Now we just have to make our way north to Nimville, and I think we'll be safe for the time being.

"There's a path!" I point north and rush off the road. A beaten path is perfect for what we need. Both the main road and now this path will hide our tracks.

We weave our way through the forest. The path itself runs mostly north, but also a little west. This is just about perfect. We need to head toward the ocean, but also avoid Sevord.

We slow down after a bit, but continue to make good progress. I think we're pretty much safe from Frindor's men for the time being, unless they know where we're going. I can't see how they would.

Eventually, we come across a small stream, and we stop to refresh ourselves. As soon as I sit down, I realize how tired I am. I pull off my pack and drink my fill of water. When I'm done, I pull Ellcia to her feet and wake Hemot up—somehow he's already snoring.

"We can't stop now. Fill up your waterskins and let's keep moving. When we find a safe place away from any path, then we can stop."

Although Ellcia isn't impressed with me, she nods her head. Hemot, however, looks at me with loathing.

We start up again, but I find I can't do much more than walk. I try a couple times to pick up my speed, but it's as if that little stop was enough to remind my body that it has no more to give.

"I smell smoke," Ellcia whispers.

I do too. It smells like a woodstove. I begin to imagine sitting by a fireplace, eating something hot and tasty. Anything other than rabbit.

We round a bend in the path, and I catch sight of a small cottage. The walls are stone, and it has a thatched roof. Most of the houses in Sevord are slate roofed, but I had always liked the looks of thatched roofs.

The path leads right by the front door and continues on through the forest on the other side. A man sits in a chair on the porch, just in the shade of the trees around his cottage, and I reach to pull my hood up. The fewer chances we take at being recognized, the better.

Before I get it fully pulled up, my heart jumps in my chest. I know the man. I don't say anything because he doesn't seem to recognize me, but Hemot has no such hesitation.

"Hob!" he calls out, surprising the man. "It's us! From the castle!"

"It really is him!" Ellcia whispers in surprise.

The thin, old man leans forward in his seat, a look of shock on his face. I don't know why he's out here, but it's definitely Hob, the man who oversaw the armory where we first received our armor and weapons before we set out to find the Prince—the man who gave us our own armor and weapons.

Unfortunately, as much as Hob helped us before, he's certainly not a sane man. I know one thing for sure. We have to get out of here fast.

18

The Old Man

I grab Ellcia and pull her along, hoping Hemot will follow, but he just stands there. I glance back. He doesn't have his hood up, and he's got a big smile on his face.

"Hemot!" I whisper. "We can't stay. We don't know if we can trust the guy!"

"What do you mean?" he asks in a loud voice. "It's Hob! Of course we can trust him!"

Hob just sits there with a shocked look on his face. He hasn't said anything, but after a moment, he stands up, opens the door and waves us in. He walks in ahead of us and disappears inside.

Hemot moves forward without hesitation, but I grab his arm. "Hemot, I'm serious! We *really* don't know if we can trust him. He's a little on the insane side. Sure, he seems loyal to the throne, but then again... you know... the insane thing! Besides, what's he doing out here? It's gotta be a six-hour hike to the city, at least! If he's here, how did he get here? And... did I mention he's insane?"

"I'm guessing he hiked," Hemot says. "For six hours."

"No…" I put my hands over my face for a moment and try to calm down. "That's not the point! We really don't know if we can trust him right now. A lot's at stake!"

Hemot nods slowly. He glances at me, then toward the cottage, then back at me again for a moment before he pulls away and walks through the door.

I let out a sigh of frustration and move in after him.

"Are we sure this is a good idea?" Ellcia asks.

"I'm pretty sure it's not," I say, but add, "What choice do we have now that Hemot's gone in?"

I step through the door. Inside, the house is quite warm. I'd rather it be cool after running for what feels like two days straight, but the smell is nice. Hob's been cooking something, and my mouth begins to water.

When the man speaks, his voice is gruff and sounds like he's spent a lot of time yelling. "I don't have quite enough for all of you, but I'll give you what I've made and put something else on. So, we'll have a small snack now, and in a couple of hours, we'll have a proper meal. That is, if you're staying."

"If there's food, we'll stay!" Hemot says with a large grin.

"Hemot!" I say, finally deciding not to worry about what the man thinks. "We really don't know this guy."

"What do you mean? It's Hob!" Hemot looks confused. It's as if he doesn't quite remember how unpredictable Hob can be. It's also as if he doesn't remember that even in the castle, we barely knew the guy.

The man dishes the food onto four plates and sets our meals before us. Fear passes over me that he might have poisoned the food, but he hasn't placed any of the dishes before any one of us in particular, and then he turns around and walks over to a small table near the far wall. If he were trying to poison us, I would think he'd keep an eye on where the poisoned food was and wasn't.

Maybe I'm just being paranoid.

Hemot grabs a plate and wolfs it down. A moment later, he says, "Wow! This is the best rabbit I've ever had!"

I nearly groan. I really wanted something else for a change, but when I take a plate and taste some of it, it's not like any rabbit I've ever had before.

Hob returns to the table with a jug of water and four cups. He then grabs a plate, eats the small amount of food in a few bites, and sets it down. "I'll be back in a few minutes. I have a few snares set, and I'll go get what I can." He looks directly at me and says, "You are staying for a bit, right, Prince Draydon?"

I don't know how he knows my real name, but then again, I've learned I apparently look a lot like my dad. Just about everyone outside the castle seems to recognize me. I resign myself to the situation... for the moment.

"Yes. We'll stay for a bit."

"Long enough to eat my food?" he asks. "I mean, you can leave earlier if you want, but I don't want to go collect a couple rabbits, clean them, cook them up, and try to serve them to you and find that you're long gone. It's just a practical thing, Your Highness."

I smile. I like this Hob better than the in-castle Hob. "We'll stay."

Hob heads out and closes the door behind him. The suspicion and distrust gets the better of me, and a moment later, I go check the door. It's unlocked. I feared he was going to try to keep us here.

We settle back in the chairs. They're quite comfortable, actually. The warmth of the woodstove and the quiet make it hard to stay awake—especially after all the running. And it's not long before I doze off.

I don't remember falling asleep, but I wake to the sound of someone banging on the door. I bolt to my feet, but I'm not sure where to go.

A loud voice comes through. "Open up, in the name of Prince Roran! We are Soldiers of the Free Armies of Sevord!"

Ellcia and Hemot are on their feet as well, and the three of us spin around, looking for a way out. There are a couple of small openings that might be considered windows, but the door we came through is really the only way in or out for anything larger than a cat.

"Open up, or we're coming in!"

I start looking for some way to disguise ourselves, but I can't imagine that'll work. It's not like we can cover our faces and then come up with a reason why we shouldn't be looked at.

I hear another voice. It's Hob. "Calm down; calm down. What are you after, son?"

"Do you live here?" the soldier asks.

"I don't know if you'd call what I do 'living', but if that's your choice of words to describe it, I can work with it. Yes, I live here."

"Does anyone else live here?" the soldier asks.

My heart jolts inside. If Hob is going to betray us, now's the time.

"Does anyone else live here?" Hob asks with a loud laugh. "Look at me! I'm old and cranky and shriveled up like a raisin left too long in the sun. If there's a woman who would put up with me, she'd have to have the patience of royalty, but the looks of a Reber Troll. I ain't got no wife or kids." There's a pause for a moment before I hear him add, "But, if you happen to know of a fine, available, trollish woman, I'd be up for meeting her."

The men laugh, and Hob continues. "So, tell me, what are the Free Armies of Sevord doing at my cottage? You here for a meal? I ain't got much other than rabbit."

"No," the soldier says. "We're searching for some runaways—traitors to the throne. Prince Roran has been found along with Prince Draydon. Sadly, Prince Draydon wanted the throne and tried to kill Prince Roran. Captain Frindor is trying to capture the rogue Prince to bring him to justice."

My heart races. I believe Hob is loyal to the throne. If that's the case, he won't hesitate to turn us in.

"You've found Prince Roran?" he asks in wonder.

"We have," the soldier replies.

"Then what are you doing here? You should be returning him to Sevord. He should be put on his father's throne this very minute!"

"Yes," the soldier replies, "we're doing that, but in the meantime, we have to find—"

"No, no, no!" Hob says. "Young man, do not delay! Get our Prince to the throne. Do not waste your time at my cottage. Come on! Come on!" The sounds outside make me think Hob is ushering the soldiers away. I hear the snort of a horse and then Hob says, "Good travels, my friends. I wish you the best. I'm grateful to know I've lived long enough to see Prince Roran's return! Now, GO!"

I hear the horses move off, and Hob enters the cottage. Our host waves out the door, then closes it behind him.

He smiles at me. "Ah, now that is interesting. Not only do I have Prince Draydon in my cottage, but he's accused of trying to kill my future king. If I wasn't so familiar with the ways of royalty, I would have turned you in. But…" he looks at me again and lets his smile grow, "I am. I'm quite familiar with royalty. I've spent a lot of time brushing shoulders with your family. In fact, that's how I recognized you."

I hesitate for a moment. "How do you know we aren't guilty?"

"I'm a pretty good judge of character, Your Highness. I'm also familiar with the suspicions that surround our young Captain Frindor. If he had told me that General Lirnal had ordered your arrest, I would have turned you in—even dragged you out of my cottage myself. But Frindor… that man's a cheat and a scoundrel. I won't turn you in to a man like that. I think Frindor probably has something else he's up to. But I doubt you did anything worthy of arrest."

"How do you know of Frindor?" I ask.

Hob laughs and shakes his head. "You know, Prince Draydon, you may be a Prince, and your family has my undying allegiance, and I have lived and fought for the throne, but at this time, since you are estranged from the throne and from your family, I cannot be faulted for refusing your question until I get one or two of my own answered."

I involuntarily step back. I suddenly see Hob in a new light. It's his eyes. There's skill and danger and years of training and experience there. I had not seen this before.

He's not quite the man I thought he was in the castle. He's a warrior. Oh, he's old, but he's definitely dangerous.

I find myself overwhelmed with the belief that even with my sword, and if Hemot or Ellcia takes Marleet's sword, the three of us still might not defeat the man in combat—if it came to it.

I nod my head. I'm not sure what else to do.

"First question." He tosses three rabbits, already cleaned, onto a small table. Cleaned or not, it's a bit of a gross thing to see. He then spins a chair around so it's facing us and sits down. "Why, my dear friends, do you call me Hob?"

I'm speechless. I glance at the others, but they're looking at me. "We… thought that was your name. Isn't it?"

The man examines me for a moment. His face fills with the slightest hint of anger. Somehow, a little of his anger seems like more than I ever want to see again. But, just for a second, I also see sadness. "That's not really an answer to my question, Your Majesty. You don't just assume people's names for no reason. When I ask you why you call me Hob, I'm not asking you if you thought it was my name. I'm asking you where you came up with that name to begin with, and what made you think I bore that label."

"We met a man," I say, trying to choose my words carefully—I still don't really know if I can trust this guy, "whose name is Hob. He helped us a short while ago. He… looks just like you."

At my answer, the man's face goes through a range of emotions, from strong grief to intense rage. The rage is scary enough that I'm about to try to get Ellcia and Hemot out of the cottage, but I realize that what he's really feeling is the sadness. The rage is his… cover… his shield. He's hiding behind it.

I examine his face again, but this time trying to remember what Hob looks like. After a few seconds, I blurt out, "You're Hob's twin! I didn't know he was a twin, but you're either Hob, or you two are twins!"

"Where did you see Hob?" His words come out in a growl.

Before I can say anything, Hemot blurts out, "He works in an armory in the castle. It's one of the old ones. They call it the Forgotten Armory."

The man's mouth drops open and tears stream down his face. "He's still alive?"

Hemot nods.

The man leans over and begins to weep. Not just a little cry, but great sobs. He just cries and cries and cries.

I feel awkward. I've never been good with crying people. I feel like I should say something, but I know I'll say something dumb like, "Yah, I get it. He's old enough that I would have thought he'd be dead by now, too." I don't think that's the thing to say, so I just pat him on the shoulder.

Hemot gets up and wanders over to the rabbits. He pulls them off the table and heads to the stove. To my dismay, Ellcia gets up and rushes after him.

I feel like a terrible person, but I just don't want to be stuck with the crying old man who looks like Hob, but isn't. I think I'd rather try to figure out how to cook a rabbit. I feel upset at Ellcia and Hemot for leaving me here.

I turn back to the man and find he's staring at me. He wipes his tears and explains in a quiet voice, "I haven't seen Hob in years. I lost contact with him a few months after Parthun killed the King."

"Could you not go into the city and find out?"

He shakes his head. "No, a few months after the rebellion, Parhun restricted travel through the gates. I wasn't on the list of people who could get in."

"Why did you think Hob was dead?"

He pauses for a moment, staring at his feet. A few more tears drip off his nose while I wait.

"After the King was killed, Hob…" He takes a deep breath before he continues. "Hob was one of the most loyal men in the kingdom. He loved the King. He served with him years ago and even helped to train Hartor before he was crowned. Hob was an excellent soldier and a skilled swordsman. When the King was killed, Hob blamed himself. He was sure he could have stopped the assassination. He couldn't stop talking about it, and it was starting to drive him mad."

The man shook his head. "Hob began to act more and more erratic. He was getting in trouble with the other soldiers and causing quite a stir. During those early days, anyone who caused trouble found himself with a noose around his neck. One day, I heard a rumor that they were after him. I rushed to the gates of the city, but the guards told me they were not allowed to let me in without special permission. None of them knew for sure what happened to Hob, but they told me there'd been a hanging that morning." He looks into my eyes. "I never heard from him again. I thought… I thought he was dead."

"He's alive," I say, just to add the confirmation.

The man smiles. "And he's in the Forgotten Armory?"

I nod.

"Is that who gave you your sword and your armor?"

I nod again.

His smile grows into a toothy grin, and he wipes more tears away. "Well, isn't that interesting? He told me he was trying to collect the royal family's weapons and armor to save for the day when the Prince returned. It's interesting that he managed to give this to you. He must have known who you were." He then asks, "Is he well?"

Without thinking, I say, "Oh, he's quite mad."

The man nods as though that's the most normal thing I could say. "Yes, that doesn't surprise me. I expect he continued to slip more and more into his insanity as the years went by. But if he could give you this, then he must have had enough wits about him to recognize you and give you what he should."

"What's your name?"

"Berin. And you're right. Hob and I are twins. He's actually the older one. He never let me forget it."

He turns around and sees Hemot and Ellcia in his kitchen. "No, no, no." He stands up and rushes over. "You're my guests. You go sit down. Let me cook these for you. I'm going to make you a nice stew."

The thought of stew makes my stomach growl, and it's not long before my mouth is watering. I have to force myself to calm my excitement. I know stew takes a while to cook.

While he works, he asks us to tell him anything we can about Hob. He even asks us to describe our time in the armory with him. At first, we're all a little hesitant to tell him too much. Not much that we can say about Hob is positive, but Berin seems quite pleased to hear anything at all about his brother.

He asks about the weapons Hob gave us, and we leave out a lot of details at first, but then he points out my sword and my armor again. He also points out Marleet's sword and seems to know a fair amount about it—even to the point of telling us it's called Dexterios. Finally, he asks for details about all the armor. I decide it's best to just tell the guy. He doesn't seem to be a threat, and he seems to know all about the armor and weapons, anyway.

He's just finished dropping a handful of spices into the pot when I mention that Mic's armor made us ignore him. At that, he stops and turns around. "The armor did what?"

I don't want to reveal Prince Roran's identity. I don't know if I should—even though he's on his way to the castle—so I just continue to refer to him as Mic. "Hob gave one of our number, a guy named Mic, a suit of armor that made it hard for us to see him."

"It made it hard for you to see him or impossible to see him?"

The man can be quite intense at times, so the way he asks makes me nervous, but I tell him anyway. "It didn't make him invisible or anything. We could still see him, but it took effort. We had to concentrate to make sure we remembered him."

Berin turns slowly back to his stew and throws in a few vegetables before taking a seat near us. His eyes are on the ceiling, and he appears lost in thought.

Finally, he looks back at me and says, "That really is interesting, Your Majesty. You'll notice that he gave you the sword which actually belongs to the second in line for the throne. The armor, also, belonged to your dad, and therefore it's yours now. This young Lady Marleet, Lord Yune's daughter, was given Dexterios. From what you described to me of her, she doesn't sound like the most confident young woman. I suspect that Hob's gift of that particular sword to her was likely intentional."

I nod. Sometimes that's all I can think of to do.

He continues. "If that's true, then perhaps Hob gave each of you exactly the enchanted armor or weapons that he thought you needed."

Ellcia shakes her head. "No, the rest of us didn't get anything enchanted."

"Why do you say that?"

"Because..." Ellcia begins, but then stops.

I catch her eye. "We don't actually know who has enchanted stuff. We only learned about Marleet's sword a few days ago." I notice a hopeful look in Ellcia's eye, and I add, "Maybe what you have has an enchantment too."

Berin continues. "It's all quite interesting. First, I hadn't realized Hob had all of this. I suspect he's spent these years identifying the enchanted armor and weapons and collecting them. He would not just give them to anyone. He obviously knew exactly who you all were."

"Well, we were servants in the castle. I think most people knew of us," Hemot adds.

"True," Berin replies, still appearing to be deep in thought. "But I suspect he not only knew of you, but knew who you were. Who you... really were."

"What's second?" I ask. When he looks up at me in confusion, I say, "You said 'first', so I assume there's a second."

Berin smiles. "Yes, Prince Draydon. There is a second. Second, I'm guessing that he actually gave each of you something." He turns to Hemot and says, "Open your cloak, and let me see your armor."

Hemot does, and the man comes close and examines it. He nods again and then asks to see Hemot's sword. Hemot draws it but doesn't let it go. The man then asks Ellcia to show him her armor. She does, but doesn't look as confident. He then asks to see her sword.

He tells Ellcia to put her sword away again and then stares at her for a moment. Finally, he says, "Can I see your mail shirt? Can you take it off so I can see it?"

She doesn't look like she wants to, but before I can say anything, she pulls it off and hands it over. I can see she wants it back right away in one sense, but from the way she moves, she seems happy just to have her regular shirt on for a while. Mail shirts are heavy.

"Ah, yes," Berin says and hands her mail shirt back. "I think I not only understand the enchantments, but I understand each of you a bit better."

Ellcia takes her mail shirt back but doesn't put it on. "What do you mean?"

Berin takes a deep breath and smiles. "Prince Draydon received his family's armor and sword, which Hob obviously rescued from wherever it had been. The sword's name is Astamatiti, and the armor is named Prostasia."

It had never occurred to me that my sword and armor might have names. I like the names, but then again, I'm not sure what I'm supposed to do with that information. I wonder if I'm supposed to use the names or if I should even bother trying to remember them.

"Lady Marleet received the Sword of Dexterios, likely to give her the skill she needed. Hob, I suspect, knew enough of her to know that was exactly what she needed. He was always a good judge of character. Hemot here has the Anoixe."

"The what?" Hemot asks.

"Come here, young man."

Hemot moves over near the man, and Berin reaches up to Hemot's shoulder. He pulls back a small piece of the leather that I had always assumed was nothing more than decoration and slides his fingers into a small hole. A moment later, a tiny key is in his hand, and he drops it in Hemot's hand.

"Wow! I had no idea that was there!" Hemot turns it over in his hands. "What does it open?"

"Anything."

Hemot stares at the man, clearly not comprehending what the man could be suggesting. "Anything?"

"Anoixe will open any door or lock you can find—assuming there isn't a stronger enchantment on the lock than on the key."

"Quick!" Hemot screams. "Find me a lock!"

The man shakes his head and laughs. "I don't have any locks here. I don't know why exactly you were given this, but I can tell you one thing: this key has often been strongly connected to the Milterite family. Are you related to them?"

Hemot shakes his head. "I don't know."

"Didn't your nanny tell you anything about your family?" I ask.

Hemot shakes his head again. "Nope. She wouldn't talk about them. She said it was too painful. I think I heard someone mention my mom's name once. They called her Hetterine or Hemaline." Hemot turns to Berin. "Do you know who my parents were?"

"Hetterine?" Berin stares at Hemot for a moment before he asks, "Could it have been Hettaline?"

"Maybe. I have no way of knowing."

"This may be a strange question," Berin asks slowly, "but you mentioned a nanny. What was her name?"

"I don't know that either. She made me call her Nanna. She was really stubborn. She wouldn't even make me buttertarts." At the last comment, his face falls, and he looks like he's about to cry.

The man nods with a look of confusion on his face. "Okay, no buttertarts. So, Lady Ellcia, your armor is… wait…" He turns back to Hemot. "What do you mean about buttertarts?"

"She used to make me buttertarts when I was a kid and then swore she would never make them again when she thought I was dead. But now that I'm alive, she still won't make them. It's quite annoying."

Under his breath, Berin says, "Borlynne…"

"Who?" Hemot asks.

"I don't know for sure, but there was a nanny named Borlynne who was well known for her buttertarts. She escaped to the mountain with the Free Armies of Sevord. I didn't know she'd sworn never to make her buttertarts again. That, in itself, is a tragedy. They were quite good."

"So, you think that might be her?" Hemot asks.

The man stares at the ceiling again for a moment, then back at Hemot with a large smile. "Absolutely! She was a nanny for the Milterite family. She cared for Duke Berav and Duchess Hettaline's son—so you were close in remembering your mother's name. Borlynne was always quite stubborn. When she set her mind to something, nothing could change it."

"So, I'm a Duke?" Hemot asks.

"Well," Berin replies, "the son of a Duke. You don't inherit that title in Sevord. You're definitely nobility, but you have to earn or be awarded a Dukedom. Your title would typically be Lord Hemot, but it's not formally given until you come of age, and sometimes not even then. The Dukedom nobility is a complicated matter."

"And this key belongs to my family?" Hemot asks.

"No, it's often been connected with the Milterite family. It's not really yours, it was just often held or controlled by the Milterites. Anoixe was never something specifically owned by a family—not like Astamatiti. That sword belongs to the Royal line and has been given specifically to the one second in line to the throne."

"What were you saying about me?" Ellcia asks.

"As for you, Lady Ellcia, you are nobility, of course, the daughter of Lord Rather and Lady Shillin. You look like your mother, but I can see your father in you as well. You have a living brother named Granel. The last I heard, he was a Lieutenant in General Lirnal's army."

"He's a Captain now," Ellcia says.

"Ah, that's good. He is an honorable young man. He takes after your father. But as for you and what Hob gave you… it's not that your armor is enchanted, but something has been added in." He points at the armor in her hands and asks, "Do you see that line of scarlet running through your mail shirt?"

Ellcia nods as I lean over to see. In the dim light, I can make it out, but just barely. I remember seeing it in days past. I had thought it was decoration.

"That is," Hob explains, "what is called The Heart of the People. It's an enchanted thread that's woven into your armor. It's a difficult enchantment to put your finger on as it's not clear-cut what it does. It's understood that it gives the wearer the ability to know another's heart and either strengthen it or destroy it."

Ellcia just stares at the armor with horror. "If I wear this, I can destroy someone's heart?"

"You can," Berin says, "but you can also strengthen it. The choice is yours."

"Why did Hob give it to me?"

"I don't know, Lady Ellcia, but I can guess. I suspect he knew there was someone in your group who needed an extra… push. Someone who might not have believed they were up to the task ahead. I suspect Hob believed you could strengthen that person to do their task." He then smiled at her. "Or maybe he just gave it randomly."

"Do you think that's the case?" she asks.

His gaze seems to bore into her, and he leans forward. "Everyone else received armor or weapons specific to them."

"So, you don't think it was random?"

He smiles again, and this time ignores her question. "Now, of course, Rulf, the big guy. Is he Rulfor, the son of Traltor?"

"Yes," I say.

"Then he has giant blood in him, so Hob likely wouldn't have given him enchanted armor. Magical creatures can't use enchanted items without the enchantments eventually turning on them. So that leaves the young guy, Mic."

He looks at me with that piercing gaze of his. "Now, if he gave Mic armor that made him hard to pay attention to, then that's likely the Armor of Agno. It… hmm… how do I say this. It makes people think you're not important. It makes them think you're so unimportant that they forget about you. Does that sound right?"

I nod. "That's exactly what it was like."

"Then, if Hob was giving armor and weapons specific to each person, and he gave armor to this young man which would cause him to be ignored, then I suspect Hob knew the boy was actually quite important but needed to go unnoticed. Does that sound right?"

I nod yet again. I don't want to say anything about the Prince. I don't know what I should say or shouldn't say. But I think the guy has it figured out.

"Would it be safe to assume that you were traveling with Prince Roran?"

"We were!" Hemot announces, jumping to his feet with his hands in the air. He looks like he's cheering for the winner of a tournament. "Wow! You really have this all figured out!"

I nearly groan out loud. "Hemot! You really shouldn't give any information about the Prince to anyone!"

Berin laughs. "He's right, Hemot. Although I'm loyal to the Prince, it's hard for you to know that for sure. But I figured it out, so you're really not responsible."

"Why didn't Hob tell us all this?" I ask.

"I don't know," Berin replies. "But when I last saw him, his guilt and grief were getting the better of him. He was already going mad. I wonder if giving it to you was all he could manage." The man leans back in his chair. "Now, Prince Roran…" he says slowly. "Did Hob give him a sword?"

I shake my head. "No, Mic took his father's sword from the throne room."

Berin's smile looks like it might split his face in two. "That's great news! I'm so glad! It can cancel any enchantment upon the holder, if he only draws it from its scabbard. It's also quite powerful. In fact, I believe it can do as much damage as your sword, Prince Draydon, if the owner knows how."

"But Mic was never able to chop through anything," Ellcia says. "At least not like Caric's sword."

"Caric?" Berin asks.

"Oh, sorry," I say, "Caric is the name I use. I don't go by Prince Draydon. I've used Caric since I was a little kid."

"All right," Berin says, accepting the name without question, "then I believe the sword can do nearly as much damage as Caric's sword—that is, if it's used right." He puts his hands up as we all open our mouths to ask about that. "I don't know how. I only say this because I have seen the King use his sword to chop through a tree, a few chains, and even kill a giant once."

He turns to me and asks, "Caric, what do you know about your sword?"

"Well, I know that it was the king's sword, then it was my father's sword, and I now know it's tied to my family. I also know it can cut through just about anything."

Berin nods his head. "That's a good start. It's more than that. It's actually tied to your family through the enchantment. The farther someone is from the throne, the more dangerous the sword is for them. You, being second in line, can use the sword your entire life without worry. When you die, it should go to the next person who is second in line to the throne. If it goes to the third person… they might be okay, but the sword might turn on them. If it goes to someone far from the throne, they will not likely be able to carry it past a day or maybe even a few hours."

I try to take all that in. Neither Hemot nor Ellcia are able to use the sword for much more than a few minutes, or hours at most. I'll have to be careful.

"Anyway," Berin says, standing up, "that's enough for now. I need to finish making the stew."

He pulls himself away and returns to the stove. He appears deep in thought, so I don't say anything else to him. Instead, we just chat among ourselves.

I find the chair comfortable, and the cottage warm. The smell of stew relaxes me, and I'm sound asleep again before I know it.

"Time to eat!"

I bolt awake. I don't know how much time has passed, but less light shines through the tiny windows than when I fell asleep.

We gather around the small table. There really isn't enough room for four chairs, but we squeeze together.

The stew is fantastic. I don't know if it's the best food I've ever tasted, or if I'm just really, really hungry. I gobble it down and, without even having to ask, I find my bowl filled again.

A wave of suspicion passes over me, and I wonder again if we're being poisoned, but I tell myself to knock it off. I can't go through life suspecting everyone is my enemy. Besides, he's eating the same stew as us.

When we finish, we head back to the more comfortable chairs and have a seat. I feel like my stomach is going to burst open, but I don't regret a thing.

Berin lets out a contented sigh and looks at each of us in turn. "Here's what I suggest. Stay here for the night. I don't know where you're going, but you're obviously trying to stay away from the Free Armies. And I suspect you wouldn't be here if you wanted to get to Sevord. I'm a little out of the way for that, so I expect you're heading north. By now, Frindor's soldiers are going to be all through the area. I could probably get you through without being caught, but that's 'probably', not 'definitely'. So, stay here for at least tonight, if not a couple days. Wait till things settle down, and then carry on."

From how tired and sore my body is, I want to agree right away, but I know I need to check with the others. I glance over at Hemot and Ellcia to find them vigorously nodding their heads.

I let out a little laugh. "Okay, Berin, thank you. We'll take you up on your offer. Is there a place we can sleep?" For the first time, I notice that there's not even a bed in the small cottage.

"You're sitting in it!" Pointing to his own chair, he adds, "I sleep in this very chair every night. Since you were all able to sleep quite soundly in those chairs before, perhaps they'll continue to be all you need."

I think we'll manage. I expect it'll leave us sore in different ways, but at least we won't be sleeping on the hard ground of the forest.

"Well, since I have some guests, I'm going to go do some hunting and check my snares."

We watch Berin walk out the door. He seems quite happy at the idea of us staying with him. I get the impression he's been alone for a long time.

11

The Loss

Over the next few days, we settle in nicely. It's hard, in a way, to stay inside the cabin so much of the day. We can go out a bit at night, but Berin tells us the forest is filled with soldiers, so we stay hidden as much as we can. While it's nice to be indoors after so much time outside, I feel imprisoned within the walls of this cottage.

Berin keeps an eye out for us. Whenever soldiers come by, he warns us to keep quiet. He has a small storage area under the floor, and we're prepared to climb down there if we need to, but the need never arises.

Berin is great to talk to, and he's a genuinely nice guy. Late on the fourth day, he came in and gathered food and bandages. Apparently, he found a vagrant or someone in need out in the forest, trying to make their way through. He zipped out quickly and returned after a while, happy he could help.

It's also been a long time since we've eaten this well. Berin cooks like no one else—maybe even better than Tereese in the castle. He caught a deer for us early on, and we've also had pheasant. He can even make squirrel taste great.

However, we're starting to get a little frustrated. We know Berin isn't lying to us about the need to stay inside. While he definitely loves the company, we see soldiers through the tiny windows often enough, and they come knocking on the door at least once a day.

At lunch on the fifth day, Berin finally lets us know that things are changing.

"I have good news!" he begins just as he's dishing out food. "The Prince and General Lirnal made it through Switcher Pass yesterday. They should be at the city by tomorrow."

"Will we be able to leave by then?" Ellcia asks.

"Actually, I think we can leave this afternoon, if you want."

I'm a little confused. I still see soldiers regularly through the windows. "Won't we be caught?"

Berin leans back in his chair. "I don't think so. Word has gotten out along the coast that the Prince has returned. People are coming from all directions to witness his approach to Sevord. Most of the soldiers have pulled back, and I think they've mostly stopped questioning people. I think we could head to the city."

That won't work for us. Sevord is not too far away, but it is still to the southwest. That's not the direction we've been ordered to go. "We're heading north," I say. We haven't told him our plans yet, but I have grown to trust him.

"Interesting. Is that your choice?"

I shake my head. "General Lirnal's orders."

"Ah," he says. "I admit, that still doesn't make sense to me, but I expect the good General knows a lot of stuff that I don't. It also fits with why you showed up at my door when I'm a little out of the way of Sevord City. This all complicates matters somewhat, but not terribly so."

Ellcia's eyebrows shoot up, and she glances at me. "How?"

"Well, I think you can make your way to Sevord with little trouble right now without being noticed. However, if you're traveling in the opposite direction, I think you'll be caught right away, as so many are moving toward the city—not away from it." He closes his eyes for a moment as if he's deep in thought. "Here's what I suggest, my friends. Come with me to see the Prince's return. That'll get you out of the cottage. We'll stay out of sight, but you'll be able to see him return and be welcomed into the city. Then, when everyone else is returning to their homes, it won't seem out of place for you to head up the coast. What do you think?"

The others nod at me, and I tell Berin we'll go with his plan. The thought of getting out of the cottage is quite appealing to me. I'd also really like to see the Prince approach the city.

That afternoon, we set out. We keep our hoods up, Berin too, just in case we're noticed, but it's not long before we're walking among others, also heading to Sevord. We pass dozens of soldiers, but none pay much attention to us. They're here to keep order—that's it.

At night, we camp amongst the trees. It's actually a strange feeling. In the past, we've camped under the trees countless times, but we've always done it in hiding. This time, I can count at least six other campfires that I can see from our campsite, and at least a dozen people have stopped by to chat.

Berin turns out to be a bit of a popular fellow. Most people recognize him as soon as they see his face. He knows them all by name and chats with them, but steers them away from asking us any questions.

Berin's a good guy. I can see the loyalty he speaks of in just about everything he does.

The next morning, we sit on a rise overlooking the city, well above the road. The hill we're on offers a great view of the front gate leading into the city, along with the road leading away from Sevord.

Countless others stand or sit across the same hill and along the side of the main road leading to the city gates. There isn't anyone within hearing distance of us—if we whisper—but closer to the road and to the city, the thicker the crowd grows.

People are excited. Some wave banners, some cheer, and everyone smiles.

I don't know what to expect from the Regent, but at present, the front gates stand open. Not only that, but soldiers line the side of the road, all dressed in formal armor with sashes across their chests and plumes on their helmets.

To add to this, trumpeters stand on the tops of the walls. I gather they're going to play soon. Large banners hang from the walls, and even from this distance, I think I hear a roar of a very happy crowd inside the city.

I can't see Prince Roran at first, but I know he's arrived. The cheers in the crowd have turned to shouts of joy.

I notice I'm grinning like a fool. Ellcia comes up beside me and takes my arm. I glance down and see tears stream down her face. Her grin matches my own. Hemot is bouncing, and Berin is weeping harder than Ellcia, mumbling, "Return, my Prince," over and over.

When I catch sight of the Prince on the road, I shout with joy without thinking. Ellcia laughs, and Hemot actually twirls around a few times.

The crowd, by this point, is barely holding themselves back. The road is covered in flowers tossed there by the people, and many are jumping up and down along the side of the road.

When the trumpets start, it catches me by surprise. In my excitement, I'd already forgotten about them.

I can't help myself—I start to laugh. I don't know if I've ever been so excited—certainly never been so caught up in a moment. A desire to run down there with the crowds and see Mic—see Prince Roran—as he goes by overwhelms me, and I start forward, but Berin pulls me back.

Mic, or Prince Roran—I have to get used to that— moves along the road on horseback. We're quite far away, but he's dressed like a king should be. He stands out. The honor guard around him pales in comparison.

I scan the crowd for Marleet. I think I can make out her parents. They're walking near a man whom I assume is General Lirnal, but there's no sign of a young woman who walks alone—and certainly no one who is centered out as betrothed to the future king.

However, what we see is only a small part of Prince Roran's army. There would have been thousands upon thousands with him traveling across Sevord, but I gather this is just an honor guard.

"What's going to happen?" Hemot asks Berin.

I'm about to tell him to wait and find out, but I'm struggling with anticipation as well. The approach to the castle is slow—no one appears to be in a rush.

Berin laughs. "I'm not sure. I'm guessing that if all goes well, he'll approach the front gate and be welcomed in. He'll then ride straight to the Castle and remove the Regent." He pauses for a moment. "Which is strange, because if the

Regent wanted to resist, he wouldn't have opened the gates… I'm not really sure what's going on."

A commotion at the gate catches my eye. A dozen or so men and women step out of the city and move a few paces past the wall. I can't recognize any of the people from this distance, but from the way they stand, the man in front is clearly in charge. There's no doubt the Regent has shown his face.

As if to confirm this, boos, jeers, and catcalls echo up from the people down below. I add my own, and so do Ellcia and Hemot, but Berin remains still.

It's a strange sight. On one hand, thousands of people cheer Prince Roran, but hundreds, those standing near the gate and many others, continue to shout out their disapproval of the Regent. I preferred it before when we all simply cheered.

Prince Roran, on horseback, finally reaches the gate. I'm hoping the Regent will fall to his knees and beg for mercy. As much as I now despise the man, I don't want him killed.

But… I do want him to pay.

I feel so conflicted.

"This is odd," Berin says. "The Regent just walked out of the gate… I can't imagine Parthun is going to try to talk his way out of…"

Berin gasps, and I try to make sense of what I'm seeing. I don't understand what's wrong, just that everyone's shocked. Roran… Prince Roran… climbs out of the saddle and turns to the Regent.

"No! No, no, no, no, no! This isn't right!" Berin hisses. "He's the returning Prince. He should not dismount before the Regent!"

I look back at General Lirnal and at Marleet's parents. A moment before, they had stood straight and tall. Marleet's mother had held her husband's arm with one of her own. Now she's gripping his arm with both her hands. General Lirnal's hand is on his sword.

Prince Roran walks toward the gate. Two soldiers follow—two men from his honor guard. The crowd has gone silent. I don't know if it's because they agree with Berin that approaching on foot is inappropriate, or if they're straining to hear what Prince Roran says.

I see the Regent's arms moving. He's someone who talks with his hands. The gestures are certainly grand. After saying a few things, he bends forward and bows to the Prince.

I frown. I would think he would bow properly and with deep respect, but what I see is something he might offer to a visiting dignitary before inviting him in for a light lunch.

The sound of murmurs flow up from the crowds below. I'm tense, and my heart races, but I still don't understand.

Until… it happens. My mouth drops open, and my heart turns to ice.

Prince Roran, in all his royal splendor, drops to his knees before the Regent, and bows until his forehead touches the ground.

I look back at General Lirnal and Marleet's parents again. Their shoulders are slumped, and their arms hang limply down at their sides. The soldiers all around stand in a similar fashion—one even drops his spear and doesn't bother to pick it up.

I hear a scream from below. It's a woman's voice. She's screaming one word: "NOOOO!"

There's more movement by the Regent. I can't make out exactly what's causing the stir, but one of the men standing behind the Regent has something in his hands.

Prince Roran climbs back to his feet and walks to the man holding the object that has everyone's attention. A moment later, from the way Prince Roran picks it up, it's clearly the crown.

He turns back to Regent Parthun, and with very little ceremony, places the crown on the Regent's head. He then unbuckles his sword, hands it to the Regent, and then takes his place with the other men and women, standing behind Parthun.

A shout rises from among the crowds—not everyone, just a few. It's like one man over here, and another man over there… shouting. They cry out, "All hail King Parthun, Ruler of Sevord and the Talic!"

No one else joins in.

I can't move. I just stand there in shock. I can't understand how this all could have happened.

The Regent—or should I call him the King—I don't know… he raises his arm. Soldiers rush out of the castle gate and surround General Lirnal. They bind his hands behind his back and bring him to the Regent.

The soldiers drive him to his knees, and the Regent appears to speak to him for a moment before the soldiers drag him through the gate and out of sight.

People scream, and many turn and rush away. They're running in just about every direction but toward the city.

It's time to flee.

Someone grabs my arm and spins me around. "Caric!" Berin hisses. "Run!"

I stare at him. I can't make sense of all that's happened. My head is spinning, and I think I want to try doing this day over again.

"Caric," he says again as he shakes me. "Listen to me! If you and your friends want to live, you have to take them and run for your lives! Prince Roran has abdicated the throne. Lirnal has been arrested. Parthun may have seized the throne, but you are still a threat. You're the only one who stands between him and an unquestioned rule. You must remain alive if the people are ever to be free!"

When I don't move, he spins me around, facing away from the castle and to the north. I hear him whisper, "Forgive me, my Prince," and he shoves me as hard as he can. I stumble forward, barely able to keep myself on my feet.

Behind me, Berin hisses, "Go with your Prince! Get him to safety!"

I feel Ellcia's hands on one arm, and Hemot's on my other arm. They pull me along.

Away from Sevord.

Away from my home.

Away from the man who has taken the kingdom.

Away from the man who has taken *my* kingdom.

Away from the man who now wants me dead.

12

The Wedding

We run.

Running is something I'm used to these days, so it doesn't take any thought at all. It's a good thing, too, because all I can focus on is keeping pace with the others and avoiding roots and ruts on the path.

Now and then, someone faster passes us—we're not the only ones running—but for the most part, no one else gets in our way. I hear crowds behind me. A lot of people are trying to get away.

I don't know why. I don't know why they're running.

I thought we were the only ones in the entire world who had to run from every danger. I thought we were the only ones who lived under constant threat.

I feel someone pull me to a stop. I can't be bothered to even care who it is. If it's Captain Frindor, he's likely to kill me on the spot.

That's okay. I've had enough.

I find myself facing Ellcia. She's staring up at me. I can see uncertainty in her eyes, and it reminds me that I'm not alone.

She glances down at her armor for a moment, and I follow her gaze. My eyes land on the scarlet thread moving through her mail shirt. She returns her gaze to my eyes, and a look of hope comes over her.

"Caric," she says, "we need you! This isn't the end. We don't know what happened, but we've survived everything so far. We can survive this too."

I feel myself overwhelmed with a sense of strength. I'm about to nod, but then I find myself saying, "But we haven't all survived. We lost Marleet."

I hear Hemot beside us. It's a true sound of despair.

"No, Caric," she says, "we haven't. We lost her for a bit, but we'll get her back." She places her hands on each of my arms and grips tightly. "We can do this, because this is how it happens for all the heroes."

I shake my head. "What do you mean?"

"I mean," Ellcia says in a whisper, "none of them had it easy. None of what they did was solved in a matter of weeks. Sometimes not even months. The heroes suffered and struggled and had to fight hard, sometimes for years. We can do this too! We'll be the next heroes."

I smile. She's right, absolutely right. We can do this, and we will do this. "I'm sorry. I... don't know what came over me, Ellcia. I know we can do this."

I take off with the other two following behind me. I think we've traveled about a mile before I realize she used the enchanted armor on me. I don't mind, though. I think it would have worked even without the armor. Ellcia's always had that effect on me.

We don't know our way to Nimville, but we know it's a fishing village. I'm not sure if it's ten miles or a hundred miles. The map we have shows villages along the coast, but none of the villages are marked with names. I think no one believes the fishing villages are even important enough to remember what they're called.

We rush on as fast as we can. To our left, the ground slopes off down toward the water, but at present, there's a good path ahead of us. I glance down the hill as we run, and there's another, larger path below us, closer to the beach. Some people on horseback ride along that path, some moving quite quickly. I think if we want to stay out of sight, we're better off up here.

When the sun is nearly set, we move back east off the path, away from the beach and toward the cliffs. The land moves up somewhat for a short distance before it levels out, and we push our way through the undergrowth. The ferns grow thickly here.

Unfortunately, that means we're leaving a nasty trail, but I'm hopeful that no one is specifically after us right now. Once the sun sets, our path will be difficult to follow regardless of how much of a mess we make.

We find a lower area of ground that should give us a decent amount of cover and set up camp. When Hemot heads out to set his snares, Ellcia goes with him. She had told me at one point that she wanted to get better at setting the snares.

I'd like to learn more about it too, but for the moment, I want to be alone with my thoughts.

I set about to build a fire. Once everything's in place, I pull out my flint and steel and try to get the flame to catch. It's slow work, and I let my mind drift.

Just a matter of weeks ago, I had lived in terror that I was actually Prince Roran. It had bothered me—a lot. I really don't want to be King. Now that the Prince has abdicated the throne, I'm actually in a position to claim it. In fact, I'm now the rightful heir to the throne.

My uncle Parthun is the King at present, but that's only because he stands unchallenged. I wonder for a moment about General Lirnal but discard the thought. If he's been arrested, he's likely considered a traitor, and he will not be able to put forward a claim.

It looks like I'm it. I'm the one who must rise up and challenge Parthun.

I don't know what that means, actually, or how to go about it. I assume if I come forward, I'll need to have some proof that I'm Prince Draydon. Then the nobles, I think, will have to recognize my claim.

I shake my head and blow lightly on the flame that's starting to catch in the dry grass I've collected. The fire will take.

I have no doubt that it will be relatively easy to convince the nobles. I look enough like my father that they would affirm me. On top of that, I have my family's armor and sword. From what I've learned, a lot of the nobles are loyal to the throne, so they will only support the Regent if they are too afraid to take a stand against him.

The fire takes. It licks its way up the small, dry sticks laid across the grass. Once they light, it won't be long before the large, dry pieces of wood catch.

My concern is, of course, that the nobles might actually be scared enough of the Regent that they won't stand against him. They could argue that he's older, more experienced in leadership and ruling, and that the transition to me would be difficult.

They would be right. The Regent does have more experience, but at the same time, it would be the wrong choice. The Regent is wicked.

The logs catch, and I lean back. In a few moments, we have a roaring fire, ready to cook something if Hemot and Ellcia happen upon a catch quickly, but also perfect to give us light and heat as the sun goes down.

I know what I will do.

I will go back to Sevord. Not right away, but I will go back. General Lirnal's orders are for me to stay in Nimville for the time being. I must obey his orders, but I also must return and claim the throne—whether I want to or not.

I make my decision as the fire burns brightly before my eyes. I will live and work in Nimville until I'm eighteen. At that point, I will return to Sevord and claim the throne that I do not want. It is my duty. I think this is what Gerr and Terr were talking about.

Ellcia and Hemot step into our little clearing. They have a rabbit they caught almost right away in a snare set by Ellcia.

We take a look inside our packs and find that Berin has added a bit of food for each of us. Once the rabbit is cooked, Hemot pulls out a jar of spices which Berin had given him. It doesn't take much, but when we dig into our meal, the spices make all the difference.

"How are you doing?" Ellcia asks.

I smile. She looks so pretty in the firelight. I stare at her for a moment, and her beauty overwhelms me. I can't imagine life without her. I make another decision. If she'll have me, when I take the throne, I'll make her my queen.

"Why are you looking at me like that?" Ellcia asks with an awkward grin on her face.

I laugh. "I'm sorry, Ellcia. I've just had some time to do some serious thinking." I decide to tell them some of what I've decided. I'll leave out the part about Ellcia for now. That's probably not a conversation to have when Hemot's around. I get a lump in my throat. That conversation is going to be awkward.

"If Prince Roran has abdicated the throne, then I am next in line. General Lirnal cannot take the throne while he sits in prison, so it means I have to. If I don't, then the Regent has no challengers."

"So, we need to go back to Sevord?" Hemot asks with his mouth still full of the last of the rabbit.

I shake my head. "Not yet. I know it seems strange, but I think we need to follow our orders."

Ellcia leans forward, a confused look fills her face. "Then how are you going to claim the throne?"

"My uncle, General Lirnal, ordered us to go to Nimville. We have to remain there as long as necessary."

"How long will that be, do you think?" Ellcia asks.

"About six months." I stare into the fire for a moment while they wait for more information. When I speak again, I speak quietly, but with confidence. "I think we need to act with integrity. I think we need to do everything properly. We need to follow General Lirnal's orders as long as I remain under his authority. When I turn eighteen, I'll be an adult, and I will legally be in the position of First General. At that point, I won't be under General Lirnal's orders."

I look up at Ellcia and Hemot. "We will then return. I'll be an adult and have a full claim to the throne. I'll also have full authority over the armies, as long as I'm not declared a traitor in the meantime. Parthun won't be able to dismiss me on any legal grounds, and no one will be able to accuse me of disobeying orders. In six months, I will be eighteen years old. That will be the time to move."

When I finish, Ellcia remains silent for a moment while Hemot licks his fingers far too loudly. She looks sad.

"So, I guess you're going to be King after all."

I nod. I know it is what I must do. I hope she will still have me. She doesn't want to be Queen—that I know for sure—but I have to do this for Sevord. If I lose her, it will be the greatest loss of my life, but a King must serve his people.

She surprises me by nodding and standing to her feet, adding an air of formality to the conversation. She glances over at Hemot, who rises uncertainly. "Then if that is what you must do, we will stand by you, Caric. We will do all we can to return you to Sevord at the appropriate time. I wish we had Rulf to help get us through the gates, but it doesn't matter. We'll find a way, and in six months, we'll remove that crown from the traitor's head."

I find myself overcome with gratefulness, and the tears just flow down my face. I don't want to do any of this alone, but knowing they are there with me makes all the difference.

And I have six months to convince Ellcia that being the Queen won't be the worst thing in the world.

We make our way slowly up the coast.

On the third day of traveling, we stop a guy wandering along our path, heading to Sevord. We ask him what village comes next. He simply yells, "PORT!"

I pull back a bit. He's only a step away. There's no need to yell. "I'm sorry, what Port is coming next?"

"PORT!" the man yells a second time.

I am about to try again when Ellcia pipes up. "You mean, it's called Port?"

"Yup!" the man says and continues on his way.

"Wait," I say. "What's after Port?"

The man turns around, clears his throat, and spits on my foot. I look down at it, then back at him in disgust, but I realize he's not trying to be rude, he just seems to have no concept of proper interaction, no idea that others may not appreciate that kind of thing on their foot.

"After Port comes Grimmer. After Grimmer comes Deliver. After Deliver comes Nimville. After Nimville comes Shizzer."

Ellcia thanks the spitter, and he continues on his way. "So," she says, "Port, then Grimmer, then Deliver, then

Nimville, then Shizzer. I think we have quite the walk ahead of us."

I can't see any towns yet along the coast. We're still up on the ridge above the ocean, so we can see for quite a distance, but the coast juts in and out. Maybe a town or village is hiding in the next cove.

We settle down that night a short distance off the road. The hunting is good in this area, but we see a few skunks, so we're careful not to go far from our fire.

"There it is!" Hemot says.

It's the sixth day since we left Sevord City. We passed Port mid-morning on the fourth day, then Grimmer later that day. We walked past Deliver on the fifth day, and ahead we see another fishing village. According to the spitter, the village ahead should be Nimville.

We find a path down from the ridge and step out onto the main road, moving along the coast. It's easier traveling along here. It's smoother, straighter, and we don't have to watch out for ruts or roots or dips or holes.

It's nearing the supper hour when we enter the village. We pass a sign that declares the place to indeed be Nimville. At first, I'm thrilled by this, but then my stomach twists.

We don't know anyone here. We don't know anything about surviving on our own in a fishing village. We somehow have to settle in, find jobs, and live. We're here for at least six months.

I wander down the main street of town. I assume it's the main one. There aren't too many streets, and this one seems the busiest. Shops and more line the one side of the road, and the other side slopes down toward the beach.

On the beach, fishermen sit doing something with their nets. I figure in time I'll actually know what it is they're doing, but for the moment, what they're up to makes no sense to me.

Despite the churning in my stomach, I hear a growl. It's time for something to eat, and we have plenty of money. I don't know how far our money will take us in this town, but I expect it'll get us through a few days.

Our orders are to settle here. The General wanted us to get jobs, so that's something we'll have to do. We'll figure it out. I hope.

"There's an inn," Hemot says, pointing up the street.

We move in that direction, and the closer we get to the inn, the more I smell what's cooking. There's a strong fishy aroma to it, but it smells good. With every step, my stomach growls even more. I guess I got used to eating well at Berin's cottage and want that kind of thing again.

We climb up the steps and enter the common room, taking in the sights and sounds.

I haven't been to all that many inns. There wasn't much need to visit an inn while living in Sevord. I entered a few now and then to take a message or to grab a bite to eat, but that's it. Since we left Sevord, I've been in two common rooms in Haner, but I still haven't had much experience with this kind of atmosphere.

But every common room of an inn I've seen or heard of has all been the same. They're dark, smelly, and a threat of danger hangs in the air.

This common room, however, is nothing like those others. The windows sit open, letting in the sea air. The walls and floor are clean. The people seem happy and good natured. And the smell… it's making me want to run into the kitchen and start eating everything I see.

Ellcia grabs my arm and pulls me to a table. I see she has Hemot's arm as well. He appears to be doing worse than I am, and he struggles a bit against her pull.

A moment later, an older woman with a sweet smile comes to our table. She stares at us for a moment, but her look doesn't seem to be one of threat or even scrutiny, but more affection. When she speaks, she sounds like a woman talking to her grandchildren. "Hello, dears. I don't believe I've seen the three of you around here. You look tired, though. What I can I get you to eat?"

I don't really know what to ask for, but Hemot blurts out, "We'll take it all! We're so hungry!"

"Oh, sweetie," she says and puts her hand on his shoulder. "You're so kind. We try our best to make sure the food is just what people need. Can I suggest the fried fish?"

"Yes!" Hemot growls. He looks like he'll eat her hand if she doesn't bring food quickly.

"I'll be right back." She turns and wanders away. As she moves, she stops now and then to smile at someone else or encourage them. She calls each person by name, and I begin to think that she genuinely loves each one of them.

Ellcia leans toward me. "Wow! In those few seconds she was here, I think she convinced me that she's the sweetest, nicest person on the planet."

I laugh. I can't disagree.

We don't really chat much as we wait for our food. We're pretty tired. I think if we were still in the forest, we'd feel fine, but being at the end of our journey makes me want to lie down and sleep for a week.

When the food comes, the woman sets down a huge plate in front of each of us. When she said "fried fish" I was thinking she meant she was going to bring us some fried fish—and only fried fish. On our plates are potatoes, green beans, some kind of sauce—I assume for dipping—other vegetables that I don't recognize, and more fish than I think

I can eat. She wanders slowly away for a moment and then comes back with two drinks for each of us. A large glass of water and a hot drink. I don't know what the hot drink is, but it smells great.

"There you go, my dears. If you need anything else, you just holler. My name's Hella, and my husband is Nordin. He'll likely be around in a bit to get to know you. He won't want to miss chatting with you all."

She then smiles sweetly at us again and wanders off.

We dig in, and I quickly learn that while Berin was a good cook, he was nothing compared to this woman. I've always hated green beans, so I eat them first to get them off my plate, but I find they're really good. I've eaten half my food before I even look up again at my friends.

I hear a chair scrape across the floor, and a large man sits down across from me. He has a nasty scar across his face that pulls down his left eye, twists across his nose, and pulls up the right side of his mouth into a sneer. He looks angry, like he's about to throw us through a window. From the size and build of him, I think he could do it.

"Welcome!" he says in a loud growl. "I'm Nordin. Ya met my wife." The other side of his mouth comes up, forming what appears to be a smile.

I'm struggling a bit with the guy. He looks mean and angry, but his voice, as scratchy and rough as it is, is nothing but friendly.

"Thanks, Nordin," I say. "We did meet your wife. She was really nice. And the food is amazing!"

"Thanks!" Nordin says, and I see in his eyes that there's no malice there. I think it's the scar that makes him look so dangerous. Hella walks up behind him as he speaks, and he glances her way before continuing. "Hella is a great cook, and she's taught her staff well. Although she can be a little grumpy at times."

At that remark, others in the room laugh, and Hella playfully swats Nordin on the shoulder. "Oh, don't you be spreading stories about me."

Hella grabs a chair and pulls it up to the table alongside her husband. Around the room, the dozen or so people all get up and bring their chairs around. In a matter of seconds, we're surrounded.

At first, I think we're in danger, and I start sizing people up. None of them are armed, and none of them look like soldiers.

I glance around again. None of them are armed… that's so strange. In Haner, few people wore swords, but most had a knife on them at least. I can't tell for sure, but it looks like no one carries any kind of weapon.

"Where ya from?" Nordin asks.

"South of here." I'm not sure what information to give.

Everyone laughs, and Nordin's chair creaks as he leans back. "We know that, young man! Ya walked into town from the south! I mean, ya're not from Deliver or Grimmer or Port. None of them wear armor or carry swords. I'm guessing ya're from Sevord. But I don't know what ya'd be doing in these parts. There's no battle to be fought here. Unless… ya want to fight Britha."

Everyone laughs again, but their laughs are different from what I've seen in other inns. I don't think they're making fun of us. I think they're just genuinely laughing.

In response to my look of confusion, Nordin explains, "Ah, I expect ya haven't heard of Britha. It's just an old legend about a giant fish that no one's been able to catch. But enough about that. What's yar names?"

Before I can answer, Hemot blurts out, "I'm Hemot, this is Ellcia, and that's Caric."

I can't help but think that we've explained to Hemot before not to give out our real names in a situation like this, but it's Hemot. Hemot does what Hemot does.

"Those are noble names," Nordin says. "We don't have any names like that. Although, there was a Caric a few years ago who passed through here. It's not a common name, but I've heard it a few times. But Ellcia and Hemot, those are names for castle livin'."

The men and women in the room nod their heads. It's not with disrespect or fear or anything negative. They just nod like it's information everyone's aware of, and they've accepted it as fact.

"We are from Sevord." I figure maybe I can give enough information to settle their questions, but not enough to give away who we are or why we're here.

But before I can say anymore, Nordin continues. "Good!" Everyone else nods. "We've been hearing strange rumors from down that way. Bits and pieces floating up the shore, as they say. But none of it makes sense."

"What have you heard?"

"Ah, strange stuff, for sure! Some say the Prince has returned. Some say he threw the Regent out the tallest window of the castle. Some say the Regent killed the Prince and has laid claim to the throne. And some just say the Prince handed the throne to the Regent and even crowned the Regent himself." He looks around at a lot of worried faces. "If you're from Sevord, we're hopin' ya can bring us up to speed."

I relax a bit. They're just after the latest news.

"Some of what you've heard is true, not other parts." The people shift in their seats, and their eyes fill with worry.

I take a deep breath and decide I'll trust what Gerr and Terr told us. These people are good people, loyal to the throne.

"We were there when the Prince returned. He reached the gates of Sevord along with General Lirnal." Smiles break out on the faces of the people, but I can see concern as well. They know something's not right. "The Regent came out of the city and met the Prince at the gate. When the Prince reached him, he got off his horse—"

"Wait!" Nordin says. "I don't know much about royalty, but why would our Prince step down in the presence of a traitor?"

I feel a wave of emotion wash over me, and I know my eyes have turned red. When I speak, I do my best to keep my voice steady, but it still shakes a bit. "The Prince is… it's suspected that the Prince is under an enchantment. He bowed to the Regent and then crowned him King right in front of us all. Then the Regent ordered General Lirnal's arrest."

The people stare at me in shock for a moment, and I see their faces just fall. Nordin puts his arm around a defeated-looking Hella, but I don't think it's for her. He looks like his world has ended.

Nordin's mouth moves, but nothing comes out at first. When he manages to find his voice, he sounds on the verge of tears. "Parthun… is now… King?"

I nod.

The people around the room react in different ways. Some cry. Some hang their heads in defeat. Some just stare at me like they're expecting me to tell them something different.

"What are ya doing here?" one of the men asks. "Are ya just bringing the message to the cities on the coast?"

I shake my head. I figure since they called Parthun a traitor, I can be a little more open. "When we saw the Prince crown the Regent, and the General arrested, we ran. We got out of there quick. We don't know what's going to happen now."

Nordin's face turns serious, and he grabs me roughly by the front of my armor. He pulls me in, and at first, I'm afraid he's about to blame me for what happened. "Listen Caric, I don't know who ya are or why ya're here, but if ya're against that scoundrel, that murderer, that traitor on the throne, ya're a friend of mine. Ya're welcome here in this town as long as ya want!"

The others in the room all give their agreement, and Hella speaks up for the first time in a while. "What do you need? Do you need a place to stay? We have rooms, and you're welcome to them."

"Thanks." I glance at the others before adding, "We're looking to settle here, actually. We expect to be here a while, if you'll have us."

The people around the room nod, and Nordin says, "We will, young Caric! Ya have a home here. Ya'll be welcome among the people of Nimville! I expect ya'll need work, then. Ya boys can work on my boats. The young lady can work here in the inn, if she'd like. There are other jobs around she could work, but I think Hella will take good care of her."

I thank Nordin, and he raises his glass to me. "To Caric and his friends!"

I take a sip of the hot drink. It's the first I've tasted it. It's quite good, whatever it is.

Hella leans forward and puts her hand on my arm. "You and this young lady, Ellcia. Are you married? I see the way she looks at you—like you've been married for years, though you're so young."

Unfortunately, I'm halfway through another big gulp of the delicious drink. I cough and sputter and find the hot drink is now all down my front. Hella hands me a handkerchief, and I begin to wipe away the mess. I don't want my armor smelling like food gone bad.

"Well," Nordin says. "I'll take that as an affirmation that you're not married. We can fix that problem." He turns his head slightly and yells, "Warner! We're having a wedding!"

Hella laughs and claps her hands, jumping to her feet and hollering out orders to make food for a wedding feast. The men in the room pull tables out of the way and set up chairs in rows. A moment later, two of the women come up to Ellcia, and one starts on about how her old dress from when she was married should fit just fine. I feel myself pulled to my feet, and some guy—I assume Warner—begins to coach me through the upcoming service.

Hemot comes up beside Warner and asks what his job will be, if he should find a nice suit to wear, or if what he's wearing will do. He pats me on my shoulder and says, "I'm proud of you, Caric. You're finally marrying that girl!"

"Wait!" I call out, but no one listens.

"STOP!" Ellcia screams. "We're not married! But… we're not getting married today!"

Everyone stares at her for what feels like an hour. I pull myself out of Warner's grasp and move over to stand beside Ellcia. "Thank you, but I think this is something we'll leave for now."

They stare at the two of us for another moment. I feel awkward. Perhaps more awkward than I've ever felt in my life—which is saying a lot.

After a painfully long time, Nordin steps forward. I can't quite make out what his expression means. The scar really complicates that kind of thing. He opens his mouth, and the loudest laugh I've ever heard comes out.

As soon as he laughs, the others in the room join in. Warner even starts pulling tables back out to where they were before the wedding talk began.

Nordin comes over to me and puts his hand roughly around my shoulders. "It's been a long time since someone came through Nimville who hadn't heard that one. I feared we were too rusty to pull it off, but ya fell for it just fine." He smiles at me and then wraps his arms around me, squeezing me so tight I fear I'll pass out.

When he lets go, the room has settled down and the tables are back in place. I glance back at Ellcia, and her face is bright red.

"Well, young Caric," he says, "I think ya'll fit in fine here. But I'm guessing ya can't go by your names. So, I'll call you Ric, the girl, Cia, and the other boy, I'll call Mot. Right now, I have to go check on the boys down at the beach, but ya settle in here at the inn for the night. The girl will stay next door with Hella and me. Our daughters are married and moved out. Hella will enjoy having another woman in the house. Meet me at the docks an hour before first light."

"How will we get up at that time?" Hemot asks. "We never wake up that early."

The man laughs. "I don't think ya'll be able to sleep in. The entire town wakes up. When ya hear everyone going about their business, get up, get down here and eat, then meet me at the docks. Easy!" He looks me up and down and adds, "And best to leave all that fancy getup in yar room. Ya won't need a sword on the boat." He then leans in and whispers, "Unless we meet Britha," and chuckles as he wanders out the door.

The rest of the people have returned to their seats and conversations. Everyone looks happy, except for one. He's an older guy, sitting in a corner by himself. He has at least a week's stubble along his chin and looks like he hasn't bathed in a while. The frown on his face is unnerving.

He shifts slightly, and I catch sight of the first weapon I've seen since entering Nimville. It's just a knife, but it's a soldier's weapon.

"Do you guys see that man over there staring at us?" I ask the other two.

Ellcia shakes her head. "He's not watching us, Caric. He's watching you."

"Yeah," Hemot adds. "And he looks like he hates you more than anything in the world."

I roll my eyes. "Thanks, Hemot. That's really helpful."

I'll need to keep an eye out for that guy. I don't think I want to have a run-in with him.

That night, Hemot and I settle into our new room. Actually, I'm not sure I'd call it night. The sun hasn't really set, but just about everyone in town is in bed. I look out the window and see two people walking along the street. They both whisper like they don't want to disturb anyone, and they're yawning every few steps. A moment later, they part ways, and I'm pretty confident they're heading to bed.

Ellcia is already over at Hella and Nordin's house. I feel nervous for her, but I think they're safe people.

What a whirlwind of a day!

13

—·—·—●—·—·—

The Fishermen

I awake to the sound of people laughing in the streets and loud voices in the common room beneath us. At first, I can't make sense of what's going on. It's dark—really dark—and the people just won't stop laughing and stomping.

"Uuuuugggggghhhhh," groans Hemot and rolls over on top of me.

"Get off me!" I growl and push him away. I'm irritated that they gave us a room with just one bed, and a small one at that, but at this point, I don't think they're charging us for staying here. I just wish Hemot didn't roll so much. Or steal the covers. Or cough on my face. Or snore so loudly. Or insist that I pass the ketchup to him in his sleep.

He rolls back the other way, and I hear him hit the floor. Below, the voice of one of the men carries through, "Sounds like our new neighbors are awake!" and everyone laughs.

I crawl out of bed and get myself dressed. There's a jar of water and I use it to clean up a bit, and then I stash my

202

pack, sword, and armor off to the side of the room. Hemot shoves his things next to mine once he's ready.

We climb down the stairs, doing our best to walk straight. At the bottom, Hemot stops and leans against the wall. I punch him quickly to wake him before his snores catch everyone's attention.

When we enter the common room, the men cheer and welcome the "city folk" to the start of a "real" workday. We do our best to pretend we're awake and excited about the new job.

When we take our seats, Ellcia comes up to the table. She doesn't make eye contact with me, but she takes our order. Hemot lists off what he wants, and she growls at him. He doesn't seem to notice.

"Is everything okay?" I whisper.

Her eyes bore into me, and I think she's going to climb across the table and attack me, but she closes her eyes instead. I think she's counting to ten. It's something I've seen her do when she's really frustrated.

I wait and guess she might be counting to twenty. Not a good start to a day.

When she opens her eyes, she says in a quiet voice, "I'm sure it must be hard to get up so early, but I think I've been awake for over two hours. The men sleep till five. The women sleep till about three."

I frown. "I'm sorry, Ellcia." I don't know what else to say, so I add, "It's only for a short time."

She nods and heads back into the kitchen. I can't help but notice she didn't take my order, but I decide I'm better off just eating whatever she gives me.

When she returns, she's a little more relaxed, but she doesn't speak to either of us. Hemot doesn't notice, but it bothers me a lot. I don't know what she wants. Maybe she wants to be on the fishing boat, not in the kitchen.

Two hours later, I'm confident Ellcia would much rather get up at three in the morning and work in a kitchen than work on this boat. It's not so much the smell that's the problem. It stinks, for sure, but I'm getting used to that part.

I think the problem with the fishing boat comes down to five things. First, the moment we left the docks, the seasickness started. I held on for a lot longer than Hemot, but we were barely past what I learned are called the breaker waves, when I lost every bit of food I've eaten over the last six years. Even Nordin, who now calls me Ric, was impressed at how much I had in me… and no longer do.

You'd think once I'd emptied my stomach, the seasickness would go away. Not so. It's not as bad, but I still feel like dying.

Second, I'm absolutely frozen. I can't stop shaking. The others don't seem to be bothered by it, other than Hemot, or Mot, as they call him. The water splashes up constantly and soaks me over and over. It's still only early fall. I don't know how they manage when it gets colder and winter sets in.

Sometimes, I can avoid the splashing waves. Then, we pull up the nets, and the water pours off, soaking my feet and drenching my chest and back. The cold is unbearable.

Third, there is constant danger on this boat. Nordin told me shortly after we left the dock how he got his scar. It wasn't in battle. It was from the crane we use to pull up the net. Something or other snapped and split his face wide open. I figured he wouldn't want to run the crane after that, but sure enough, he's the one that's front and center with it every single time.

Some of the men are missing the odd finger here and there. Most have nasty scars. One of them is missing a leg.

He says he lost it to a shark, but when he says that, the others laugh.

I don't know what that means. I'm not sure I know what anything means anymore.

Fourth, I fear I'm going to fall over the railing. I used to swim a lot in the ocean with Ellcia, Hemot, and Marleet while living in the castle, so I can handle myself in the water, but these waves are wild. I don't know if I could get back to the boat.

Finally, the fifth problem with working on Nordin's boat is the heavy work. I don't mind heavy work, but this is not like anything I've ever done before. Pulling on soaking nets full of fish is frustrating because no matter how hard I pull, I don't feel like I'm actually doing anything. On top of that, the ropes from the nets dig into my hands, and I think I'll be bleeding by the end of the day.

The only nice thing about the heavy work is it helps keep me somewhat warm. Not actually warm. It's just when I have to strain and pull, I feel a bit of warmth flood through my body.

On top of all that danger, the old guy from the inn is on Nordin's boat. Nordin has three boats in total, but this guy, named Relin, always works with Nordin. The two go way back, apparently.

Relin growls at me any chance he gets. I hear him mumbling under his breath if I go anywhere near him. At one point, I'm sure he mumbles something about a thief dying for his crimes. I'm pretty sure he's talking about me.

When the day finally comes to an end, Hemot and I stumble along the dock toward the inn. I'm not sure what time it is. I think a year has passed… maybe two. I might actually be an old man now. I'm not sure. I feel like it. I just know that I never want one of those days again.

"Good work, Ric and Mot!" Nordin hollers after us. "That was a good first day! Same time tomorrow!"

I hear Hemot, or Mot… I have to get used to that. The nicknames are a good idea. I hear Mot groan beside me, and I want to do the same.

We reach the inn but walk around the back. There's a set of stairs, and I just want to change before I go see Ellcia—or Cia.

I don't like the idea of calling her Cia. I always loved the name "Ellcia". To call her something else seems wrong.

At the sound of quick footsteps, I turn just in time to see a shape rush toward me. My whole body slams up against the wall. Relin's face is only inches from my own, and I feel his fist gripping my shirt and digging into my chest. I also feel the cold steel of his knife against my throat.

Mot steps forward but then stops. "Come on, Relin, put the knife down," he says. "We don't want any trouble. Nordin's not going to be happy with you picking a fight. We were told we're welcome here."

I want to nod my agreement, but I don't dare move my head.

"Who are ya?" Relin demands, digging the knife into my skin. I feel the sting of the dried saltwater mixing with the cut. Louder, he growls, "Who are ya? REALLY!"

"I told you," I hiss, barely moving. "My name's Caric."

"Ya're a thief!"

"No, Relin. I'm not. Aside from a bit of food now and then from the castle kitchens, I've never stolen anything."

"Ya are a thief!" Relin growls. "And ya'll die for it!"

I see the look in his eye, and I know he's going to drive the blade into my throat. I don't have any way to protect myself. If I fight back, the slightest move will end my life. If I don't, he just has to act on the desire I see in his eyes.

"Relin!" The commanding voice of Nordin booms out. "What are ya up to?"

Relin turns his head but doesn't move the knife. I don't dare turn to look. "He's a thief, Nordin! Ya know that. I know that!"

Nordin steps forward. I can now see him without turning my head. "What did he steal, Relin?"

"Ya know what he stole!" Relin shouts. "Ya saw it too!"

"I saw it, but I don't think he stole it, Relin."

I try to make eye contact with Nordin, but my new boss won't take his eyes off the old guy with the knife. "What are you talking about?" I ask. "I don't have anything that's not my own. Other than some things from a friend, but we're holding all that until we see her again."

"I don't care about what ya're holdin' for a friend!" Relin hisses. "I care about what ya stole from a man who didn't deserve the death he was given! A man worth more than this entire kingdom, ten times over!"

I open my mouth, but nothing comes out. I don't know what response to give. Relin seems insane—but not Hob-insane… more… Talic Wolf-insane.

Nordin steps closer and puts a large hand on Relin's small, bony shoulder. "Relin. We've been friends for a long time. We've been through a lot together. Ya don't think I feel the same things you do? I saw it. I'm just taking a slower approach."

Relin twists around enough to face Nordin, but the blade doesn't move from my neck. "And how long will yar slower approach take, Nordin? What if they only stay a day or two? Or a month? You think ya'll catch them sneakin' away?"

Nordin steps just a little closer and slowly shifts his hand over to Relin's, pulling the blade back from my throat. "Why don't we have a sit-down in my office? We'll talk about it." He turns and looks at me. "Promise me ya won't run?"

I nod. I'm still terrified, but I feel so much better now that the blade is away from my throat.

Nordin pulls Relin a little farther away from me, then waves for us to follow. We continue around the back of the inn, but then off through a copse of trees. The farther we walk from the rest of the town, the more nervous I get. I see a house not too far away, but that's not where we're going.

Ahead, sits a small building. It's made of logs, and it appears to be one of the most solid-looking buildings in town.

We reach the door, and Nordin pulls out a key. A moment later, he unlocks the door, and we enter. "Sit over there," he says, pointing to chairs along the far wall. I can't help but notice there are no doors or windows on that side of the building.

He turns to Relin. "Can I trust ya not to do anything Relin-like while I'm gone?"

Relin frowns at him, but says, "I'll behave."

Without another word, Nordin steps out, and Relin closes the door behind him.

There isn't much light inside this Nordin's "office", but from what I can see, he uses the single-roomed building to store old stuff. It's dry in here, and everything seems well kept. I just don't know what it all is at first.

Hemot, or Mot, elbows me and points over to something stacked on his side of the room. It's tall and obviously a group of items wrapped together in what appear to be leathers. I see oil-soaked cloths.

"Swords," I say under my breath. In a voice just barely loud enough for Mot to hear, I add, "What do fishermen need with swords? And a lot of them?"

I look around the room with this in mind, and I begin to see what everything else is. Some piles appear to be the right shape and size for shields. Strangely shaped objects hang on the wall, covered in sheets… just the right size and shape for crossbows. And in the corner of the room, what I had thought were old sticks, now look like unstrung bows.

Mot leans over and whispers, "There's enough in here to arm about thirty men."

"Closer to fifty!" Relin declares. "But no worries for us. I don't think ya'll live long enough to tell yar traitorous friends about what we have here."

I consider charging Relin. I figure we can get out of here, grab Ellcia, or Cia… no… if we're running away, she's Ellcia again. We can grab Ellcia and get out. We've escaped assassins. Certainly, we can escape a group of fishermen.

Before I can move, the door opens, and Nordin's large shape fills the doorway. He comes in, and two other men come in after him. They're both older, like Nordin and Relin, but four men is too much for the two of us.

Nordin tosses something down at our feet. It doesn't take long for me to see it's my armor. On that, lands my sword. He then sets a lantern down on a shelf and brings the wick up enough to give plenty of light.

Nordin frowns and shakes his head. "I was going to wait a bit, but we all recognized ya armor and ya sword, Ric. Out of hope that ya aren't a thief, we're covering for ya here in this village. That's why we've given nicknames to the three of ya. But Relin here wants to know right now. I don't blame him, actually. He's not alone. Phimon and Gran here are also pretty curious."

Nordin pulls out a chair and sits slowly into it, facing us. The chair looks solid, but it still creaks under his weight.

He puts his hands on his knees and leans forward. I think we're in a lot of trouble, whatever's going on.

"I'll level with ya; then ya'll level with me. We may be simple fishermen, but we're also soldiers. All four of us fought in the battle of Reber's gate." He pauses for a moment and takes a deep breath. "We know this armor and this sword. We know what they're capable of. Not everyone does, but, ya see, I was one of Geran's Lieutenants. He trusted me, and I saw that armor on him and that sword on his hip plenty of times."

He closes his eyes for a moment, and when he speaks again, I think he's trying to keep his voice steady. "All four of us served under Geran. And now all four of us see ya wearing his armor and carrying his sword. Ya may not understand what we're struggling with, but to think that this might be stolen is a little much for us to bear, ya see?"

I glance down at the pile again before I answer. Something about my armor catches my eye. I lean forward just a bit and stare at it. "It's… it doesn't look the same."

Nordin nods his head. "Hella would have cleaned it today while we were out on the boat—cleaned and oiled. She might even have sharpened your blades—although not Geran's blade. I warned her not to touch it. She doesn't know how it's enchanted." He takes his hands off his knees and makes two giant fists, squeezing tight enough that I see his knuckles turn white. "Tell me, Ric, did ya steal this armor and this sword? If not, how did ya come by it?"

I open my mouth to tell him we didn't steal it, but stop. I decide to take a different approach, based on what Berin has told us about how the sword is tied to me. "You say you know of the enchantment, true?"

"We do," Nordin says.

"Then you know that only the rightful owner of this sword can use it for a long time. Otherwise, the sword will turn on the user. True?"

"True," Nordin says, "although that part of the enchantment was not known to many. I'm surprised ya know of it."

I nod. "This sword has been in my possession for many weeks, and I've used it not only to train, but also in battle. I've slept beside it just about every night."

I let this sit for a moment. None of their expressions have changed at all.

Finally, one of the men behind Nordin ask, "How long exactly have ya been carrying the sword?"

A wave of panic comes over me. "I'm not sure! I… I think it's about six or seven weeks… or so. We crossed the Talic from Sevord, then back again, then all the way here."

"Have you killed anyone with the sword?" he asks.

The panic turns to a sick feeling. I swallow but can't get rid of the lump in my throat. "I didn't mean to, but I killed two men. I was just trying to injure them. I didn't know at that time what the sword did."

"Don't forget the giant," Mot whispers.

"I didn't!" I say with far too much anger. "I also killed a female giant. She attacked one of our friends."

Nordin glances up at the man who asked the questions. He nods, and his expression has changed. He looks shocked. "Who are ya? Really. Do not lie to me."

"Are you loyal to Parthun?"

Nordin jumps to his feet. "Parthun is a traitor and a fool! If he thinks he can get away with what he's done to King Hartor and Queen Shalsee along with General Geran and Lady Tallia and others, he doesn't know the reckoning that will one day come for him! And to think that swine took the throne! I don't know why Prince Roran would abdicate, but Parthun should not be King. General Lirnal is next in line."

I have the answer I need. I don't doubt Nordin for a moment.

I shake my head. "General Lirnal is not next in line for the throne. He is third in line." I take a deep breath. "I am the son of General Geran and Lady Tallia. I am the true owner of this sword and this armor. And I stand second in line to Prince Roran. Now, next in line to the throne of Sevord."

Relin comes forward and grabs me by the chin. He pulls up my face and examines it for a moment before he steps back in shock. When he finds his words, they come out in a whisper. "It's him! It's Geran's son. Prince Draydon."

All four men drop to their knees. I don't really know how to respond to this kind of thing, so I just remain seated.

"Forgive us for doubting ya," Nordin says, his eyes on the floor, "but we could not stand by while we thought the royal inheritance was in the hands of a thief. I only waited to observe ya for a while before I questioned ya." He raises his head and looks directly at me. "Prince Draydon, I offer ya my loyalty, my love, and my fealty. I await yar command."

The other men follow suit. Word for word, they each swear allegiance to me. When they're finished, they all come, take my hand, and kiss it.

I learn, in that moment, that I'm not particularly fond of people kissing my hand. In fact, it seems like a pretty disgusting tradition. I have to fight the urge not to wipe the back of my hand on my trousers. Especially after Relin kisses me. There was a lot of wet there. And his stubble feels weird and gross on my hand.

I stand up and decide to take charge. We can't just ignore the threat and the reason we're here. If these men are loyal to the throne… no… not just the throne… if these men are loyal to me, then I must have their support.

"I must remain in Nimville for a time. I'm not yet eighteen years of age, so I remain under General Lirnal's orders. He has ordered me to remain here until he sends for me, and I plan on remaining at least until I come of age. My identity, and the identity of the Lady Ellcia and the Nobleman Hemot, must remain hidden."

"Then ya will continue to live and work here?" Nordin asks.

"Yes, Nordin."

He gives a big nod and so do the others. He rises to his feet and proclaims, "Then ya will continue to live at the inn. Ya will work for me and receive your due wage, minus the cost of your room and board. I will treat ya as a normal hired hand, working ya just as hard as anyone else I hire. I won't treat ya with any more respect than anyone else for fear that word will spread. We will continue to call ya Ric, and your friend, Mot, and the young lady, Cia. Your identity will remain a secret in every way!"

I sense Mot shifting beside me. I know what he's thinking. I wouldn't mind it if Nordin didn't work us quite as hard as everyone else. However, I know I shouldn't really ask for special privileges, and if he does treat me differently, that might give our identity away.

"Thank you, Nordin." I glance over at Hemot and decide I will ask for at least something. "Now, we aren't used to working on a fishing boat. So, we're cold, tired, and very sore. We'd like to head in and change. We'd really like to warm up."

"Hella's already drawn you a bath!" Nordin says with a laugh. "All my new hired hands get a free warm bath after their first day on the boat. I know it's hard work out there and takes a lot of getting used to. Go in and get yourselves cleaned up. After, head down for a warm meal." He smiles and then says, "Then we'll get a hold of that pretty girl of yars and have a royal wedding."

I start to stammer, but he laughs and slaps me on my back. "Oh, Ric, if you're a Prince, ya're going to have to learn not to fall for the same joke twice!"

I gather up my armor and sword, and the six of us head out. When we reach the inn, Hemot and I climb the outside stairs. We enter through a door into a hallway, then find our room. It's unlocked. Aside from Nordin's "office", I haven't seen a single lock in Nimville.

When we head inside, I immediately see Mot's pack, my own, and Marleet's pack hanging on the wall.

Despite how sore I am, I rush over to my pack as Mot runs to his. I pull it down and examine the insides. Sure enough, it's been entirely emptied.

It's also quite clean.

I spin around, and my eyes land on a cabinet with drawers. I move over to it and find, stacked neatly in a pile, all the money that I had in my pack. There's also a note that explains my clothing is in the top drawer of the cabinet, and Mot's clothing is in the bottom drawer. I check and, sure enough, my clothing has been cleaned, mended, and folded. It smells great. I don't have a lot of clothing, so the rest of my possessions, such as my flint and steel and my knife and a few other things, are in the drawer as well.

I grab my stack of coins and put them in a side pocket of my pack. I'd rather have it in my pack than lying on a cabinet in an unlocked room.

We gather up a set of clean clothes for each of us, and wander downstairs, looking for the baths. We meet Ellcia, or Cia, at the bottom of the stairs. She's smiling, which is a relief after how upset she was this morning. She nearly gives me a hug but pulls back as she wrinkles her nose. Without a word, she points down a hallway I haven't used before, and we wander that way.

We find the room with the bath. Unfortunately, there's only one tub, so neither of us can sit and soak in it after a long day, but we manage to get clean and changed. On our way out, we meet Cia again. She takes our dirty clothes and tosses them into a bin outside the door before taking me by the hand and leading me into the common room.

When we enter, the men in the room cheer and come over.

I'm not sure what it's about at first, but they all congratulate Mot and me on surviving our first day out on the sea. It turns out it's a tradition for the men of the town to buy new workers a meal after their first day.

The most excited of the bunch turns out to be Relin. He hugs me a few times—which I immediately regret since I had a bath, and he didn't. He sticks close to me—and again… I notice that he didn't have a bath—and talks nonstop about anything that comes to mind.

Once things settle down, we sit with Cia, and I spill out everything that happened with Nordin and Relin.

When I finish, she smiles. She tells me that she actually loves it in the inn. Hella had her laughing most of the day and insists that everyone have a nap mid-morning to make up for the early rise. It turns out that getting up earlier than the men is the only negative as far as Cia is concerned—especially once Hella described what life on the fishing boat was like.

She then looks guilty. "I only have to work about four hours a day. And most of that is far easier work than even cleaning the castle."

I smile at her. I feel jealous in one way, but then I'm happy for her. I also think that in a month or so, Mot and I will have the muscle and endurance we need to survive out on the boat, so it won't always be so bad.

We'll make it here. These are good people. Loyal to the throne, and kind-hearted.

Only six months to go.

14

The Captain

"Not good," Relin says as we walk down to the beach for the morning's work.

Winter is setting in, and during the cold months, we only work a partial day until spring. The fishing's not good when the weather gets this cold, but we have to have some food. What's preserved from the harvest and throughout the warmer months won't quite get us through till spring.

But fishing is not what's on my mind.

"What did you hear?"

He stops and grabs my arm. "Ric! They're comin'. The false King Parthun is sending soldiers throughout the kingdom, demandin' an oath of loyalty be given by every man, woman, and child above the age of ten. I hear they'll reach Nimville by tomorrow."

It's been two months since we arrived. I've grown to love it here, but I can't stay if there's a chance we might be caught. It could be Granel, Cia's brother, who shows up, but it could be Frindor. Or it could be just about any soldier—perhaps loyal to me or perhaps loyal to Parthun.

I can't take the chance.

"Do you want us to fight, Ric?" Relin asks, pulling me away from my thoughts.

"Fight? No! They'll kill every last one of you!"

"It's no matter, Ric," he says with confidence. "We'll all gladly die for you."

I shake my head. There has to be a better way. And even if there isn't, fighting is still a terrible idea. There are only a few hundred in this small village. If they rebel, they won't survive against whatever Parthun will send. I know if I take the throne, there will come a day when I have to order people to war to protect the kingdom, but this is not the day.

On top of that, I've grown to adore Relin. When we first met, he despised me, but now that he trusts me, he's kind, funny, and a great teacher. In two months, he's taught us more about fighting and strategy and battle than every other teacher combined.

"We need to find a better way. Cia, Mot, and I will leave. If we're not here, they won't be able to take us back."

He stares at me for a moment. I know I'm ignoring one of his big concerns. He waits.

"But that's not the only problem, is it, Relin?"

He shakes his head.

One of the great things about this little village is the people are far from simple. They're incredibly intelligent, driven, and kind. While I've learned a lot about battle from Relin—a man who learned directly from my father—I've learned a lot about leadership from Nordin.

I know for sure what Nordin would do in a situation like this. "Call a meeting for when we return from today's work."

"Yes, Ric," Relin says and rushes off to find Nordin.

Every week, we call a meeting with a few of us. It's mainly to discuss where we're at and for me to function as a Prince, rather than a fisherman. Nordin had meant for it to be five people. He would be there; the two men whom we had met in Nordin's office would be there; Relin would be there, and me. The meeting was intended to function as a Council of Lords. We were going to meet in Nordin's office and discuss matters of state and the retaking of the kingdom.

At the first meeting, Mot had shown up. He couldn't understand not being a part of it. And Cia had come. I was happy about that. I didn't want to leave her out for a bunch of reasons.

Then, five minutes into our meeting, the door swung open and Hella came in. She has never left the village before, so her perspective on the kingdom is somewhat limited, but that day, and every day since, she brought freshly baked cookies with her. Once that first meeting got fully underway, she turned out to be quite insightful on matters of people— even people she'd never met.

So, our Council of Lords and Ladies takes place once a week, our next meeting not for another three days. But considering the threat, we can't wait.

When Relin returns, Nordin comes with him. I'm already up on the deck of the boat, preparing for the day's work, but he waves me back down to the dock. In a hushed tone, he explains, "No time to wait, Ric. We can't put this off."

I know he's right; I had just struggled with the idea of canceling Nordin's workday. His fishing provides for much of the village's food. I'm relieved to see that he still sends out all three of his boats, just with the remaining crew members spread evenly across them.

When we assemble in Nordin's office, I take my seat. They had insisted that we follow a certain amount of court protocol. As such, I lead the meeting, and they only sit on my invitation. I feel awkward with it each time, but I know I have to get used to this kind of thing.

"Please sit."

Once they are seated, I pause for a moment. Nordin explained that it was necessary for me to present an image of one who is in control. "We have received word that soldiers from Sevord will arrive as early as tomorrow. They will require each man, woman, and child over the age of ten to swear allegiance to Parthun."

I let that sit for a moment. Cia looks sick to her stomach, while Mot closes his eyes. He's grown comfortable here. I know he doesn't want to leave.

I make eye contact with each person in the room, just as Nordin taught me, and announce, "I need counsel from my Lords and Ladies."

There's a pause for a moment. Nordin taught me to anticipate responses from each person. At first, I thought that was a bad idea, but he explained that it allows me to notice when counsel is unusual or unexpected. When that happens, I have to ask myself "What's different?".

I expect Cia to remain silent as well as Mot. Neither one will make a suggestion, since the obvious answer is for us to run. While I know that's the right answer—best for everyone involved—it feels wrong. I expect Nordin and Hella to suggest they hide us, Relin will want to fight, and Phimon and Gran will want to negotiate. They might even want to try to buy off the soldiers.

As expected, Cia and Mot remained silent. However, Nordin and Hella don't suggest we hide.

Hella stands. "It's time for the three of you to move on. You cannot remain here any longer. You will have to live in the forest for a time. I recommend you hide for a few months and then come visit us to see if it's safe to return."

Nordin nods. "Hella's right. We will provide as much as we can. We have plenty of dried meats and fruits for ya to take. Hunting is terrible this time of year, but ya'll hopefully catch enough to survive. There are caves up on the cliff face to the northeast. I suspect ya could settle in one of those and survive until late winter."

I don't like the idea of trying to survive the winter in a cave, but I'm not sure I see a better option. We might even get some help from some of the villagers to carry food and supplies into the hill country.

"What about the village?" I look at each of the five Nimville residents. "The soldiers are still coming. And they won't let you refuse to swear allegiance to Parthun."

Nordin laughs. "That's the easy part."

"What do you mean?" I can't understand how they might manage with this.

Nordin laughs again. "The great thing about city folk is that they think we villagers are simple. And we are. We live simple lives, enjoy simple things, and don't stray too far from home, for the most part. But city folk think that means we're simple in mind and simple in tradition. They think we don't do anything that we haven't done for generations."

Hella and the three other men nod their heads and smile.

Nordin continues. "So, this is what we'll do. We will explain to the soldiers that we are simple folk, which is what they already believe, and that we cannot stray from our tradition. In our simple tradition, we can only swear allegiance to the throne and the royal line—not to Parthun himself. They will not kill us for that small deviation from their demand. We provide enough fish to the surrounding areas that our deaths would hinder Parthun's control over the people."

"Is that your tradition?" Cia asks.

Nordin rises. "As the leading man in this village, I declare that the new tradition of Nimville is that we will only swear allegiance to the throne and the royal line." Turning to Hella, he asks, "Will the leading woman of the village agree?"

"I agree," Hella says with her sweet smile.

"Then it is passed. Our tradition is set and cannot be changed without similar effort." Nordin sits down with a satisfied look on his face.

"Here, here!" Relin, Phimon, and Gran call out.

Phimon then speaks up. "I recommend, Yar Highness, that we end this meeting and get on with preparing ya to leave. If they are to arrive tomorrow, we do not have a moment to spare."

I nod, and we all rise. He's right. I don't look forward to the hike up the mountain, but it's time to move.

We step out of the office, and Cia—no, it's time to start calling each other by our names again—Ellcia heads to Hella's house, where she's stayed for the last two months. Hemot and I head back to the inn. Nordin and the others head straight past the inn toward the main street. I assume Nordin's calling everyone together, so he can explain what's going on.

Hemot and I get back into our traveling clothes. While in Nimville, we've adopted the traditional outfits of the people of the fishing villages and even their footwear, but none of it is good for traveling. I pull on my boots, which have been repaired by the village cobbler, who is also the village butcher, who is also the village tanner. He does fine work, and the boots fit well.

My traveling clothes, however, are a little tighter than they had been. Working on a fishing boat changes a guy. I was already quite thin from running for my life across the Talic Region—twice—but after working with Nordin, my shoulders are broad, and I have more muscle across my chest and arms.

Once packed, I pull on my armor, strap on my sword, and throw on my pack. It feels a little light, but we'll weigh it down with food shortly.

We head downstairs into the inn. I'm surprised that no one's in there, but I expect Nordin has them in the square. It's cold outside, but the wind isn't bad today. It's probably a great day to have a village meeting on the beach.

We wander to the door, but before I can open it, it swings open, and a large man grabs me. He twists me around and pushes me up against the wall. Hemot crashes up next to me, and I hear Ellcia struggle as they bring her in.

When they spin me around, I'm facing a dozen soldiers, chuckling to themselves.

"You were right, Captain!" one of the men calls through the open door. "We found the stray princeling!"

In through the door walks a man I did not expect. A man I thought hated me for years, only to find out that he was only pretending to hate me out of a desire to protect me. But now, it sounds like he's tracked me down to arrest me.

Captain Tilbur comes in. His smug look suits his face well, and he walks right up to me.

"Well, Caric, or I assume you know who you are now—Draydon, next in line to the throne. I've been searching for you for a long time. If I hadn't managed to drag it out of your Uncle Lirnal, I'm not sure I'd ever have found you."

I growl and struggle against the two men. They're finding it hard to hold me back. I think with the new muscle I've gained over the last while, I might be able to fight them off.

However, even if I did, Hemot and Ellcia are still here. And there are another ten or more soldiers to face after that, plus Tilbur.

"General Lirnal would never have told you where I was!" I say as defiantly as I can. My uncle had trusted Tilbur. I had even grown to think of him as a good guy.

Tilbur laughs. "Well, Draydon, that's where you're wrong. All it takes is the right… motivation. I can actually be quite persuasive when someone is restrained in a chair. He did, I admit, hold out for much longer than I had thought. I expected to break him within weeks, but it took closer to eight." He pulls off his gloves and says, "And I blame you for his stubbornness. I think he was trying to protect you. So, to thank you for wasting my time..."

Tilbur pulls back his arm and slams his fist into my gut.

Ellcia cries out and Hemot gasps. The two men holding me let me go, and I collapse to the ground. I concentrate on remembering that I can't be injured with the armor I wear, and the pain and sick feeling goes away quickly. When I can breathe freely again, I pretend to still be hurt.

Tilbur crouches down next to me and pulls my face up by my chin. As he examines my expression, he says, "Ah, I'm sorry, Prince Draydon, did that hurt?"

The soldiers laugh as Tilbur stands up. He approaches Hemot and draws his knife. The Captain waves the soldiers to step back, and he grabs Hemot's armor, pulling it down and out just enough that he can get his knife in behind it, pushing it up against Hemot's chest.

"Now, Hemot," he says. "You were always an annoying one."

Despite the circumstances, Hemot smiles. "Yes. I perfected that skill over many years with hard work and discipline."

Tilbur returns the smile. "Well, my boy, it's a good thing we're not after you. I have made a habit in my time as a soldier not to kill anyone I wasn't ordered to. And you, my boy, didn't even register in the King's thoughts. King Parthun never even mentioned your name."

"I don't mind killing him," one of the soldiers adds, filling the room with laughter.

"No!" Tilbur said. "We follow our orders!"

He lets Hemot go and moves over to Ellcia. I jump up, but the two soldiers behind me grab my arms and hold me back.

The Captain stops and smiles at me. "Don't fight them, Draydon. Each of these men were specifically chosen by King Parthun for their loyalty to him. They won't fail him.

I think that's an odd thing to say. I have a brief moment when I wonder if he is trying to tell me something, but discard it as Tilbur grabs Ellcia and tosses her roughly back against the wall. She hits hard, and I see she's dazed, but I don't dare say anything. If Tilbur knows I'm worried for her safety, I fear he'll be extra cruel.

"Now you, Ellcia, he did mention," Tilbur says with a large grin. The others laugh again.

My heart races. I imagine Parthun ordering Tilbur to bring her back to the castle or ordering her death or any number of things. I quickly evaluate the men holding me. I think I can toss them off me and get to her, but I'll only have one shot at it. If she's in danger, I'll risk it and do all I can to get her out. If she can make it through the door, she might get away. She's not fast, but she knows the town and may be able to hide.

"He mentioned that he regretted losing you," Tilbur continues. "He had wanted to transfer you to serve in the banquet halls. That's where he sends all the pretty ones. You and that Marleet girl were both going there soon enough."

"I'll never serve Parthun in his banquet halls or anywhere else," Ellcia says with a snarl.

Tilbur laughs and says quietly. "No, I don't suppose you would. But no worries. I have other plans for you." He steps back, takes her hand in his, bends over and kisses her on the back of her hand in a most respectful way. Once he's finished, he sarcastically offers her a respectful bow as he says, "My Lady Ellcia."

She looks stunned for a moment, but when he lets go, she steps back and remains still.

"Wait!" one of the men hollers. He's short and has no hair, except for a thin line around his ears and the back of his head.

Tilbur rolls his eyes and turns around. "What now, Baldy?"

My mouth drops open. In my head, I'm thinking, "Baldy? I can't imagine anyone naming their child Baldy. How would they know that was in his future? But then again, a lot of babies start out bald…" I shake my head and focus. Now's not the time for figuring out why a parent would curse their child to a life of follicle absence.

"Well, Captain, it's been a while, but I think I recognize that sword."

I do my best to keep a straight face. I don't want to confirm for them what the man suspects.

Tilbur growls at the man but speaks quickly. "What sword?"

"That one. The one Prince Draydon carries. It's General Geran's sword. He has his father's blade!"

Tilbur turns around with a look of keen interest on his face. I try to pull away from the two men, but they grip me tightly as the Captain grabs the hilt of my sword and slowly pulls it out.

I hear some of the men whistle, and one of them whispers, "Would ya look at that!"

Tilbur carefully holds it, examining the blade and avoiding the edges. I don't want to lose that sword, but there's nothing I can do at the moment.

Tilbur stares intently at it for a full minute before shaking his head. "It's a beautiful blade, but it's not Astamatiti."

"Astama—what?" Baldy asks.

Tilbur lets out a loud sigh of frustration. "Astamatiti! It's the name of General Geran's sword! But it doesn't matter. This isn't it!"

A wave of hope passes over me, but I'm still tense. All he has to do is drop it, and it'll slice right into the floor. It'll be hard to miss that.

"Are you sure?" Baldy asks.

"AM I SURE?" Tilbur screams as he steps toward his soldier. "Do you think I just became a Prince yesterday? I grew up with Geran! Do you know how many times I touched that sword? Examined it? Even trained with it? I know what the sword looks like. This isn't it!"

Baldy looks unconvinced. He opens his mouth to say something else, but then closes it. Finally, he says, "Well, if it's just a forgery, Draydon's not going to need it anymore. Can I have it?"

Tilbur shakes his head. "No one takes spoils of war while I'm in command!" He pauses for a moment, then says, "Unless we're at war!"

Everyone laughs. I'm not entirely sure what's going on. I hope he just gives it back. The whole comment about me not needing it anymore kind of bothers me.

"But this is not a time of war," Tilbur says, and everyone stops laughing.

I'm so confused.

"We'll leave this here for young Draydon."

Baldy shifts on his feet, and Tilbur shakes his head. "Out with it!"

"Are... sir... are you... sure? It really, really looks like it!"

Tilbur shakes his head. "What do you know of that sword, Baldy?"

"It'll cut through anything, Captain."

"Right!" He grips the sword and raises it up near Baldy's face, getting a clear reaction from the man. "So, if it'll cut through anything, will it cut through that beam over there?"

Baldy nods quickly, but doesn't say anything. He looks terrified to have the blade so close to his face.

"All right, then a demonstration! If the blade slices through the beam, it's yours, Baldy! If it does not, it stays here."

Baldy smiles. The man truly does recognize my sword.

I almost groan out loud as Tilbur steps up to the beam and swings the sword at it. I'm afraid the entire building might come down as it's one of the main support beams, but as with everything else, I can't do anything to stop it.

The blade swings through the air and hits the beam with a loud THUD, lodging itself in the thick, old, dry wood.

My mouth drops open, but I close it quickly. I… I don't know how that happened. Maybe the blade knows, somehow, that it needs to disguise itself? Or maybe Tilbur is too far from the throne to use it properly. No, wait, that can't be. Rulf used it.

I decide to ignore my questions and turn back to Tilbur.

"Satisfied, Baldy?" the Captain asks.

Baldy nods. He looks quite disappointed.

"Now," Tilbur says, "about our three friends here…"

"Shouldn't we take those two back?" a large soldier with a flat nose asks.

I'm not sure which two he's talking about. I have a sick feeling growing inside me that they have no intention of leaving me alive. That means the "two" are Ellcia and Hemot.

"Absolutely not!" Tilbur says. "Do you think I, as a Prince, am so uneducated that I would make such a foolish mistake?"

"No, Captain," flatnose replies.

"Good!" Tilbur says and faces the men. Tilbur is a huge man and can be quite intimidating when he wants to. "Pay attention. See if you can figure it out. The girl is Granel's sister."

The men pause for a moment, considering that, before Flatnose declares, "I'm not afraid of Granel."

Tilbur breaks out in a loud laugh. "You should be! Three quarters of the army would follow him in an instant if he called them to take over the kingdom!"

"Why doesn't the King kill him then?" a shorter soldier asks.

"Same reason he won't kill Lirnal. The armies love their General. If the King kills Lirnal, it'll look like he's just removing someone who could possibly challenge him for the throne. If he keeps Lirnal in prison, Lirnal is merely a prisoner—not truly a threat to the throne."

"And Granel?" Flatnose asks.

"Granel…" Tilbur begins, "if he's a Captain serving in the army, people merely follow his orders when he gives them. If he's arrested or killed, he becomes a martyr. If the King removes either man, their memory becomes more dangerous than their present station."

I feel relieved. It's good to know those two are alive and will continue to be so. The only one I worry about now is Marleet.

"Besides," Tilbur continues. "There's another reason the girl should remain."

"What's that?" Flatnose asks.

Tilbur gives me a wicked grin. "Because of what's coming next."

"And the boy?" the short soldier asks. "Why don't we take the boy back to Sevord?"

"Because," Tilbur says, "there's a greater way to hurt him. If we take him back, the King will probably kill him. But if we leave him here, he suffers more."

The men remain silent. I can see they're just as confused as I am. I'm not sure what could be worse than being executed by the King.

Tilbur growls and then shouts, "How can you all not see the obvious?"

No one moves. Tilbur has always been a scary man. He's tall, well built, and has a face that looks like he hates everyone.

He shakes his head. "Hemot here is incapable of hiding his feelings. He's had a powerful interest in Lord Yune's daughter since the two of them were little. Everyone in the castle knows that. But Lord Yune's daughter is set to marry the Prince. Despite Yune's attempts at stopping it, Roran and Marleet will be wed within the month. The King has ordered it. If we leave Hemot here, he gets to suffer with the knowledge that the woman he's loved since he was a child has married another man."

The men nod, looking unconvinced. I think they really want to kill someone. I'm getting the impression that I'm already expected to die, but that's not enough.

"And leaving Ellcia here has the same effect," Tilbur explains.

Their faces fill with even more confusion.

Tilbur growls and mumbles something under his breath about the men's intelligence, followed by asking, "Didn't the King say he wanted Ellcia to suffer?"

The men nod.

"Then consider this," Tilbur says. He walks up to me, draws his knife, and puts it at my throat. I feel the tip of the blade cut into my skin, but I can't pull any farther back due to the men holding me.

Tilbur turns to Ellcia and says, "Tell these men how you feel about Draydon. If you don't tell them, at the count of five, I'll drive my blade into his neck."

Ellcia's face fills with panic, and her eyes meet my own, but only for a second. She turns to the soldiers and cries out, "I love him with all my heart. I'd follow him anywhere. He's the reason I'm here now, and I don't regret it for a second."

I feel sick to my stomach. I'm thrilled at what I've heard, but I know she didn't want to tell me this way. I also know what this means. Tilbur wants her to suffer, and she'll suffer by seeing me die. Answering Tilbur's question only prolongs the inevitable.

Ellcia knows it too. She turns back to me, and I watch the tears stream down her face. I mouth the words, "I love you too" back to her, and she only cries harder.

The men begin to nod. They're finally getting it.

"I think the best way to make these two suffer is to leave Hemot with the knowledge that the woman he loves has gone to another and let Ellcia know the man she loves won't live to see tomorrow." Tilbur points his blade at me and growls, "Both of them can watch Draydon die!"

As Tilbur drives the blade into my chest, Ellcia's screams and Hemot's shouts are the last thing I hear before I hit the ground.

15

The Orders

Pain shoots through my chest. I try to take a breath but can't because I feel the blade in my left lung. Every move feels like it's shredding my insides.

I concentrate. Try to convince myself that my armor has stopped it. I'm okay. I'm not injured. Tilbur just doesn't know that my armor can stop anything.

I still can't catch my breath. Something's wrong. Could it be that my armor didn't work this time?

I slowly twist my neck and get a look at Tilbur standing above me. The men behind him laugh, but Tilbur's face is filled with hatred.

Lirnal was wrong about Tilbur all along.

I focus my thoughts. It can't hurt me. I have to believe that. I feel the pain lessen and think I might be catching my breath as I catch sight of Tilbur's blade. It's a nasty looking one with jagged edges. It's curved and looks like it was made for nothing but cruelty.

But what really shocks me is not the shape of the blade, but the red that drips to the floor.

I'm on my back. I try to move my head to see my chest. My head moves slowly. I hear Hemot scream at Tilbur, and Ellcia crying. Their voices sound far away.

When I can finally see my chest, I pull back my hands.

Blood. Far too much blood.

"Let's go."

The words are faint. I think it's Tilbur, but it could be anyone. Pain shoots through to my back, and I twist onto my side. My ear and my cheek are on the inn's common room floor. I hear footsteps leaving the building, but I think I also feel them.

Two people are nearby. I see Hemot, but someone else holds my shoulder. I wonder if it's Ellcia. Somehow, I think if I'm going to die, I'd like to die with her by my side.

They roll me onto my back, and I choke. I can't breathe. I try to roll back, but they won't let me. I can barely hear them. They're so quiet.

"Caric!"

That's Ellcia. I reach out for her, but I hold back. I see the blood on my hand. I don't want to soil her clothes.

"Caric!" she says again. "You haven't been hurt! Concentrate!"

I smile at her. She'll be okay without me.

"Caric!" she hisses. "You have to concentrate. You aren't injured. Tilbur faked it!"

"But…" I begin. It's hard to speak. "The blood…"

"It's not blood," Hemot says with a smile. He takes his finger and wipes up some of my blood, sticking it in his mouth. "It's cherry sauce."

The smell of the cherries wafts up into my nose. I feel the pain lessen, and I can breathe again. When my heart has calmed, I ask, "How did I get cherry sauce on me?" The pain slides away. I can still feel it a little, but it's mostly gone now.

"I don't know," Ellcia explains, "but Tilbur's obviously working against Parthun."

I try to make sense of that, but can't. "But don't you remember that he threw you up against the wall? He threatened to stab Hemot. He punched me in the gut. He kissed your hand!"

"Yeah," she says, "about that." She opens her hand, and inside is a tightly folded piece of paper. She unfolds it and examines it for a moment. A look of confusion and horror flashes across her face for a moment before she breaks out in a grin. "Tilbur put this paper in my hand. It was all an act. Don't you remember how he told us all the men are loyal to Parthun? They weren't his men. They couldn't be trusted."

Hemot reaches over and takes a bit more of my cherry blood. I don't know how Tilbur managed to pretend to stab me while putting enough cherry sauce there to make it look like it was real.

"I'm sorry about Marleet," I say to Hemot.

Hemot's face sours. "I don't understand why she would marry that guy. I thought..." His eyes drop to the floor. "I guess I never told her how I feel."

"I'm sorry," I say again.

Hemot's eyes wander, but he absentmindedly reaches over and takes a bit more of the cherry sauce and eats it.

For some reason, it really irritates me that Hemot would eat it right off my chest. When he comes in again, I slap his hand away. "Hemot! Stop eating my fake blood!"

He shakes his head as if coming out of a trance. His eyes are sad for a second, but I see him cover it up with his mischievous look. "But I can't help it! You're rather tasty, Caric."

I'm about to tell him that it doesn't matter when Ellcia reaches over and tastes a bit. "Oh, wow, Caric. Hemot's right. You are tasty."

Against my better judgment, I dip my finger in the red stuff. When I put it in my mouth, I smile. It's some kind of sweet cherry sauce. I've tasted it before. It's like what Tereese in the castle kitchens used to make—or likely still does.

I try to make a mental note about that. Tereese is in on it. She's loyal to the throne.

I pull myself up and remember the people of the village. We scramble over to a window, careful to keep low.

Outside, there has to be close to a hundred soldiers, and the people of the village are lined up. They're all declaring their allegiance to the throne and the royal line. When they're finished, Tilbur nods to Nordin, and the soldiers move off to the south.

Running over to the beam, I grab my sword. As soon as I touch the hilt, the sword slides right out. It's as if the enchantment works for me, but doesn't for Tilbur.

I turn back to Ellcia. She has a big smile on her face, mixed with an expression of total relief. Somehow, with Tilbur's help, we managed to get through this.

"What's in the note?" I ask.

Her smile grows. She looks back down at the note, then at each of us before answering.

"Our new orders."

Continued in The Lost Warrior
Book Three of the Sevordine Chronicles.

Pronunciation Guide

Now, you might think that I have tried to create a proper pronunciation guide, but I don't know how to do that. I could look it up, but not only do I not understand diacritical markings, but I think most people don't. So… I made a pronunciation guide that makes sense to me with the capital letters pointing out the emphasis.
And here it is.

Berin	BARE-rinn
Caric	CARE-ick
Corter	CORE-ter
Draydon	DRAY-dunn
Ellcia	ell-CEE-ah
Farnum	FAR-num
Frindor	FRIN-door
Frippolee	FRIPP-oh-lee
Granel	GRA-nell
Gratter	GRA-terr
Haner	HAY-ner
Hartor	HAR-terr
Hella	HELL-ah
Hemot	HEM-mot
Hillbin	HILL-binn
Leito	LAY-toh
Lirnal	LIR-nall
Marleet	mar-LEET
Morgin	MOR-ginn
Nordin	NOR-dinn
Parthun	PAR-thunn

Rainer	RAY-nerr
Reber	REE-berr
Relin	RELL-linn
Shaloomd	sha-LOOM-d
Shalsee	SHALL-see
Shawn	AWE-some
Talic	TAL-ick
Tallia	TAL-lee-ah
Tilbur	TILL-burr
Trevolay	TREV-oh-lay

CHECK OUT THESE BOOKS BY
Shawn P. B. Robinson

Adult Fiction (Sci-fi & Fantasy)

The Ridge Series (3 books)
ADA: An Anthology of Short Stories

YA Fiction (Fantasy)

The Sevordine Chronicles (5 Books)

Books for Younger Readers

Annalynn the Canadian Spy Series (6 Books)
Jerry the Squirrel (4 Books)
Arestana Series (3 Books)
Activity Books (2 Books)

www.shawnpbrobinson.com/books